THE BRIDE TOURNAMENT

WARS OF THE ROSES BRIDES BOOK 3

RUTH KAUFMAN

THE BRIDE TOURNAMENT

Cover Art by The Killion Group, Inc.
Interior Formatting by Author E.M.S.

Contact: www.ruthkaufman.com

Published in the United States of America.

England 1462: Can the woman who wins his hand in marriage win his love?

Lady Eleanor de la Tour's life turns upside down on her wedding day. Instead of her betrothed, she must wed the new earl, to whom the king has given his title and lands. Though Richard Courtenay is handsome and intriguing, she wants the man she loves and chose. And Richard pursues alchemy, anathema to her because the obsession to turn base metals into gold is destroying her father.

Richard needs and wants to stay wed to Eleanor to uncover her father's alchemy secrets. He vows to win her even as she arranges a bride tournament to find him a better and willing wife.

The happier he seems with the potential brides, the more Eleanor regrets her choices. Which man is best for her? When Eleanor rescues him after his life is threatened, Richard is stunned to realize he loves her. How can he accept the tournament winner and lose the best bride of all?

For everyone who loves historical romance.

Praise for Ruth Kaufman's *At His Command*
Wars of the Roses Brides Book 1

Lady Amice Winfield doesn't know how she can fulfill her duty to marry the king's choice because she's falling for the knight sent to protect her until she weds. But serving opposing factions that want to govern England threatens to pull them apart. Can she defy her king for love?

A wonderful debut sure to please lovers of romance!
   – *NYT* & *USA Today* bestselling author Madeline Hunter

With a bold knight and a strong-willed lady, Kaufman's story is positively medieval.
   – *NYT* & *USA Today* bestselling author Tracy Anne Warren

If a book lingers in my mind for more than two weeks, then I say the author has certainly deserved to be put on my keeper shelf.
   – Bookworm2bookworm

Praise for Ruth Kaufman's *Follow Your Heart*
Wars of the Roses Brides Book 2

She's a glass-painter making her way in a man's world. He's on a quest to redeem his family name and estate. When unforeseen passion makes their marriage of convenience inconvenient, will his dangerous secrets keep them from following their hearts?

Must-read romance: "Kaufman can certainly write an entertaining suspenseful romance and brings us a happy sigh-worthy story in Follow Your Heart."
   – USATODAY.com

"Kaufman's strong second romance…appealing protagonists…maintaining suspense and building the reader's hope that Joanna and Adrian's mutual respect will grow into love."
   – Publishers Weekly BookLife

"As the story unfolds, it will suck you in…fantastic!!!"
   – 5 Star Amazon Review

CHAPTER 1

Northumberland, England
June 1462

Lady Eleanor de la Tour clutched her blue brocade skirts as she hurried down Middleworth Castle's winding stone stairs, happiness bubbling inside her.

"Hurry!" she called to her younger sister, Alyce, and closest friend, Maud Fitzalan.

They joined her at the arched entrance to the great hall, breathing hard from their swift descent.

"If only my father had let me wed the man I wanted," Maud, a sweet-faced brunette, said.

"Yours will be a marriage of love," Eleanor's ethereal sister added.

"A marriage of love," Maud repeated wistfully. "And to a wealthy, handsome earl."

Eleanor couldn't stop smiling while her sister straightened her garnet and pearl necklace and smoothed her waist-length hair.

In the hall, colorful banners dangled from the high, wood-beamed ceiling. Ladies in fine gowns mingled with men in jewel-studded short tunics as minstrels played a jaunty tune on the dais beneath tall stained glass windows. The tempting aroma of roast duckling made her mouth water.

Eleanor moved through the crowd, absently greeting those who offered good wishes. Her father stood with several friends, imposing in his midnight blue velvet robe and beaver hat. Their conversation came to a halt when she approached.

"My pardon. Father, where is Arthur?"

Lord Edmund de la Tour turned, a grim expression on his narrow face. His companions stared as if they'd never seen her before.

What did they know that she didn't? Foreboding trickled through her.

"You'll see him anon." He raised his voice over the guests' conversations.

Only twice had her father looked this serious. Once when he told her that her older brother had been killed in battle, and last week when he caught her in his alchemy workshop.

Eleanor could barely suck in enough air to speak. Music blared, no longer festive.

"What's wrong?" Tears welled in her eyes. "Is he ill? Injured?"

"Arthur is well."

Several guests inched closer, clearly sensing something was amiss. No doubt they wondered what juicy tidbit of gossip they'd be first to hear.

Her father directed her into an alcove removed from avid listeners. Alyce and Maud crowded the small space. The air was so still the gauze veils on their tall headdresses didn't dare flutter.

"Leave us," her father ordered with a wave of his beringed hand.

Her sister and friend turned in a swish of trailing skirts and hurried away.

"You're scaring me." Eleanor couldn't keep her voice from trembling.

"You'll think me the bearer of bad tidings, daughter," he said. "But 'tis for the best. You cannot marry Arthur. Not now. Not ever."

The room tilted. Her empty stomach threatened to rebel. "Why? We've pledged our troth, which is akin to marriage."

Lack of sympathy in her father's light brown eyes brought tears to her own. "Arthur staunchly supported the old king, Henry. He has been attainted by the new king, Edward. That means—"

"It means he has lost his title." Eleanor dropped onto a bench, glad for the stone wall to support her back. "His lands are forfeit. There'll be nothing for any children to inherit." She jumped to her feet in horror. "He could be executed."

"His life will be spared. But King Edward has given Arthur's titles and estates to another," her father said. "There's a new earl of Glasmere."

"This changes nothing." Eleanor swallowed against the bitter taste in her mouth. Hope filled her. "Edward himself was attainted several years ago. If God's anointed can rise so high from such a fall, surely Arthur can be made an earl again. We shall get the bill reversed."

Her father pressed his lips together, as if biting back more bad news. "What will be is for the best."

"I must go to him."

He caught her arm. "Eleanor, stay. You'll not marry Arthur today."

"If not today, then soon." No matter what her father said. Eleanor closed her eyes and imagined all was as she'd planned. She would make it so.

She lifted her chin, determined to behave as the lady she was raised to be. No one would see how the news of Arthur's attainder or delay of their wedding affected her. "We must tell the guests the wedding has been postponed and send them away."

"No. They shall remain," her father replied. "Because you will marry today. You are bound by contract to wed the Earl of Glasmere. So you shall."

She sucked in a breath. "I am betrothed to Arthur."

"You were. King Edward asked the archbishop to annul your betrothal and procured a dispensation for the banns. You must wed the new earl instead."

"How can you ask this of me?" She grasped her fur-trimmed sleeves to warm her fingers, but nothing could warm her heart. Her dream was slipping from her grasp.

"For once I'm demanding. What woman weds at four-and-twenty?"

"You're glad of this. You want me gone." Her throat constricted, hurt and anger rushing through her fast as a river after a storm. "Because I'm determined to stop you from pursuing alchemy. What of your deathbed promise to Mother to cease? You've betrayed her."

Red mottled his cheeks. "Arthur's fall from grace is the reason. He should have wed you years ago if he wanted you."

That hurt. Eleanor had believed Arthur kept delaying their wedding because of duty to his liege. What if he'd lied to her, too?

"Your marriage to Glasmere was arranged long ago to merge estates. To make us all more powerful. Not to satisfy womanly wishes," her father repeated. "The time has come for you to live up to your name."

"An annulled betrothal. A dispensation. A different husband. It's too much. Too sudden." Eleanor's stomach roiled anew.

But her father pressed on, offering no comfort or even understanding. "The new earl is Richard Courtenay."

The name hit her with the force of a slap. "The son of your former alchemy partner? I won't."

"You will. Right now." Her father held out his arm.

Eleanor struggled to find an argument to sway him. None came.

"And yes, I'm glad of it," he said. "Now you can search for his father's notes before Richard locates them and gives them to the king." The eerie gleam in his eyes sent chills down her spine.

"Father, please don't make me do this. I won't have anything to do with alchemy. It's heresy. There must be another way."

"You will marry Richard, and find out what he knows. Or lose me and your inheritance." His gaze revealed no mercy. Nor a hint of compassion. "You will do your duty."

"No!" she cried.

The music stopped.

Alyce peered into the alcove. "Is aught amiss?"

Gowns rustled and jewels sparkled as guests gaped. In the distance, the musicians waited, bows and instruments poised to resume play.

Eleanor stood. Her father's hold felt like a hawk's talons, squeezing her very bones.

"Who knows how the king will react if you disobey?" he whispered.

'Twas as if she heard the key turn, locking her in a cell. He'd found the one argument to sway *her*. How could she put Middleworth and its people at risk? *Officium quod veneratio supremus totus*...duty and honor above all. She couldn't betray her family's creed.

Eleanor stretched her lips into a smile and followed him into the hall. A few steps later, she froze in her tracks.

This was how a deer must feel before the arrow hit.

Before her stood Arthur Stafford, his familiar face expressionless. Her heart melted with sympathy for all he had lost.

"My friends, I have news. There has been a change in plans," her father said, raising his voice. "Eleanor, meet the man you will wed this day, Richard Courtenay, Earl of Glasmere."

As her guests buzzed louder than a swarm of bees, Eleanor forced her gaze from the man she longed to marry to the man she must marry.

The new earl stood taller than Arthur. She had to tilt her head back to see his high cheekbones, straight nose and square chin. A face more chiseled than the one she loved. Wild waves of dark brown hair fell to his shoulders. Richard's eyes were an unusual mixture of gray and green, not light blue. He was handsome in the way of a rugged warrior, not elegant like the man she'd hoped to marry.

Would marry.

He bowed with grace. "'Tis a pleasure to meet you, Lady Eleanor."

His voice was sonorous, rich and smooth like his fine velvet garments. He crossed his arms, one brow slightly raised. A challenging gleam sparked in his eyes, as if he expected her to do something rash. To test him.

Edmund de la Tour beamed, arms resting on his slight paunch. He patted her on the back then left her to face the earl alone.

"Perchance I'd feel the same, my lord, had we met under different circumstances," Eleanor said. "And if you didn't carry on our fathers' heinous pursuit."

"I'm at Edward's command. He believes transmuting base metals into gold can help resolve the kingdom's problems. Who are we to deny him?" He held out his arm. "Let us see what we can do to make the circumstances more to our liking."

Eleanor felt scores of eyes on her, watching, waiting to see whether she'd accept this new earl. Arthur had disappeared. She just couldn't bring herself to make the best of the situation as he was doing. "I am needed elsewhere, my lord." She gathered her heavy skirts and turned.

Richard whispered in her ear, "Consider this. Whatever you do this day shall be returned ten-fold." His warm breath sent a tingle up her neck.

She whirled with a huff.

"How dare you?" Lifting her chin, she met Richard's intense gray-green gaze.

"I dare because I can," he cut in, his low tone emphasizing his deep voice. "I need to wed with you. So I shall."

"Other women may submit to a man's commands, but no man controls me," she hissed.

"Until now." His eyes narrowed and he put his hands on his hips. With his broad shoulders back, his square jaw set, he looked powerful and forbidding. A man accustomed to getting his own way. "'Tis up to you how we fare. Remember that."

With his broad shoulders back, his square jaw set, he looked powerful and forbidding. Like a man accustomed to getting his own way.

She wouldn't let him incite her further. "You're an earl. Surely you could find a more willing bride. One who'd support your quest."

"No doubt I could. But the king gave me you." He paused. "My men know defiance leads to hardship."

Worse and worse. What was she to make of his warnings? This earl already proved a formidable opponent. She would best him, somehow, and remain true to her goals.

All around her guests whispered, clearly craving a scandal.

"Will she wed with Courtenay?" a woman behind her asked.

"How can she not?" a man answered. "A daughter is obligated to obey her father and a wife her husband."

"I'll bet a groat she runs off with Stafford!"

They'd turned her life's upheaval into a wager. Had her face flushed from discomfiture she could barely contain? She bit her lip.

A muscle twitched in the earl's cheek. He had heard. What did he know of her?

The music started up again. They stared at each other, two soldiers trying to hold a bridge, neither willing to give an inch.

"Let us be off," her father called. "To the church!"

The guests cheered as he led them from the hall. Alyce and Maud hovered a short distance away.

The earl again held out his purple velvet-clad arm.

Her father and Richard Courtenay might have won the battle, but not the war. She would marry the man she chose and thwart her father's attempts at alchemy before it ravaged his finances. And his soul.

The shock coiled inside her threatened to explode. "In my haste, I forgot…something. I must fetch my mother's scarf to carry in remembrance."

The slight tilt of his head and raised brows told her that he didn't trust her.

Forcing the sweet smile that once worked so well on her father, she asked, "Perhaps you'll tell my father where I went?"

A moment of silence. Her heart fluttered like a dizzy butterfly.

"Very well," he agreed with a nod.

She walked toward the stairs. Eleanor glanced over her shoulder to see him doing the same as he followed the guests. She waved, waiting until he had gone out the door.

Then she ran as fast as her feet would carry her.

Time was running out.

❧❧ ❧❧

Two obviously flustered and out of breath young women stood before Richard and Eleanor's father in Middleworth Castle's bailey. The cheery sun and fresh breeze contrasted with Richard's dark mood.

"Eleanor has locked herself in her chamber." The shorter one, a fair-skinned blonde, wrung her hands.

Richard bit back an oath. His ire increased each minute he waited. How dare she defy him? He'd not come this far and risen so high to be thwarted by any woman ever again, much less his bride. He held up a hand against the sun. The guests had mounted and fortunately were too far away to hear this news.

Edmund de la Tour looked skyward, lifting his hands as if asking God for assistance. "Richard, meet my younger and more biddable daughter, Alyce, and Eleanor's friend, Lady Maud Fitzalan. Alyce, tell her she must come out. Immediately."

"We tried, Father," said Alyce, the blonde. She bore only a faint resemblance to his reluctant bride.

Maud, a pleasantly plump brunette, twisted the end of her veil. "Eleanor said she needed her mother's favorite scarf. We went with her. But she ran ahead and bolted her door."

"She seemed resigned, not upset. We didn't suspect a thing," Alyce added.

"I shall fetch her." Edmund heaved a heavy sigh.

"No. I will." Eleanor's father hadn't been able to handle her, but Richard couldn't allow her to best him. He needed this marriage.

He marched into the castle with Edmund, Alyce and Maud at his heels like eager pups. The trio barked directions until they reached her chamber. "Eleanor, open this door. Now," Richard ordered.

"No!" The wood portal muffled her voice. "I need to think."

So she could work on a way to evade marrying him? "Do you remember what we spoke of earlier?"

Silence. More silence.

"Eleanor, my lovely bride to be, if you don't open this door, I'm going to break it down," he said. "Then I shall fling you over my shoulder and carry you thusly to the church."

Edmund, Alyce and Maud gasped in unison.

Each second stretched as they stared at the still-closed door. Eleanor had made her own bed. And lie in it she would, with him.

"Move aside," Richard said.

He hurled himself at the door, pain blasting his shoulder as it met sturdy wood. The latch gave. He flew into the room and collided with Eleanor. They tumbled to the floor, but he managed to turn so she landed atop him.

"Ooooph."

Her golden hair formed a lemon-scented curtain around them. Lemons. His new favorite scent. Her full lips parted, violet eyes widened in shock.

Richard enjoyed the softness of her breasts against his chest and the way her legs straddled his. Her hips thrust toward his tightening groin, making him wish they were alone. He'd remember their exact position for after the wedding feast.

Eleanor was most beautiful, with a spirit as vibrant as her looks. Once he wore down her resistance, he'd thank King Edward for making marriage to her a condition of becoming Earl of Glasmere. Thus granting him easy access to Middleworth Castle, where his investigation into his father's mysterious death had led him.

"Let me up this instant," she demanded, pushing at his chest.

Richard loosed his grip. Eleanor clambered to her feet. Her tousled hair made her seem sweet and vulnerable. He stood, then moved forward as she stepped back. A large coffer prevented her retreat.

"Neither you nor my father can force me. My consent is required." Her face had paled to purest alabaster, her gaze revealed fear of retribution, but she continued, "I will not wed with you, Richard Courtenay."

On the one hand, he admired her bravery. On the other, the last thing he needed was another woman who preferred another man. Though he wished he didn't have to, Richard stepped forward to follow through on his promise. He picked Eleanor up and draped her over his shoulder. Her golden hair dangled past his knees. The freshness of lemon washed over him again. He doubted he'd ever tire of it.

Desire surged, making him hard. He wanted to be done with the wedding, mass and feast and get to the bedding.

"Put me down this instant!" She wriggled and kicked, but he locked an arm across the back of her legs before she inflicted an injury. He felt and heard her breathe heavily. "Put. Me. Down."

Alyce and Maud clapped their hands over their mouths as he marched toward them.

"You choose, Eleanor," he said. "Shall I carry you? Or will you walk beside me?"

"I will walk," she snapped.

Gently, he lowered her to the ground. She adjusted her hair and skirts, chin high.

Richard took her arm and led her out of the castle as her father, Alyce and Maud trailed behind.

CHAPTER 2

"What a beautiful day for a wedding," Richard said.

"Some would surely think so." Eleanor managed to sound calm as they rode to the church, but every muscle itched to snap the reins and flee. Where would she go that he wouldn't find her?

She couldn't appreciate the blue skies dusted with clouds or the sun's warmth. She admired yet wanted to spurn the man who rode beside her.

He sat his horse like a chivalrous knight from one of her treasured romances: straight, proud, shoulders back. A breeze teased his overly long hair, revealing high cheekbones. Despite his appearance, faultless enough to make women swoon, inside prowled yet another controlling man. He was intelligent, confident, powerful, and wealthy. And handsome. She could admire him, but she couldn't allow herself to care for him. Not if she wanted to be free.

"I'm sorry your father waited to tell you about my becoming earl and having to marry me," he said.

"What? He knew?" She twisted so quickly she almost fell off her horse as shock sank its teeth into her afresh. "He spoke to me every day, looked me in the eye, while concealing such news? How long has he known?"

"For several months," he confessed.

Eleanor struggled to keep her voice low, though churning fury urged her to yell. "How could he watch me prepare for my wedding knowing I'd not wed the man I expected to wed? How could he betray his own daughter?"

"I advised against it. He said no one knows your cleverness better than he. And feared if he told you sooner, you'd have found a way to prevent the change in grooms."

That her father thought her clever, that Richard didn't agree with his approach were no consolation. She had to think of a way out of this nightmare. Resolve replaced the sheer desperation that had led her to lock her door.

Somehow Richard's calm acceptance of her rebellion, his taking her side while preserving his interests, made him more imposing. He hadn't yelled or hit her, as many men would have. Being flung over his shoulder, and in front of her sister, father and friend, had stung her pride.

This wedding day could only be farther removed from her dreams if she'd somehow changed into a hunchbacked hag. Her fingers burned from gripping the reins. She closed her eyes briefly, seeking numbness.

Richard helped her dismount, strong arms lifting her easily. The intimacy of his hands on her waist, being close enough to feel his breath on her cheek, made her heart flutter. Why?

They passed Arthur, who stood among the guests, not by her side.

She stumbled on an uneven stone. Richard caught her before she fell, his muscled arm around her waist again. She'd shake off him and the sense of security he gave her as she would a nagging fly.

The elderly priest awaited them at the church steps. Raising his hands for silence, he cleared his throat. "Does anyone know a reason why this couple should not be wed?"

She held her breath, hoping her father had a change of heart. Or that Arthur would stand up for her.

The priest's answers were the whispering of silks, satins and velvets and a bird singing a merry melody.

Richard repeated his vows, his deep voice rumbling through her. Standing tall beside her, radiating power, he took her hands in his.

Suddenly Eleanor knew how she could avoid this unwanted

marriage. She could take control by withholding her consent. Consent was vital to a valid marriage. All she had to do was say....

She took a deep breath.

"Do not even think it," the earl hissed into her ear. "'Twill not bode well for you."

Her haze of shock and disbelief dissipated like fog beneath sunshine. The sun burned the back of her head. Her veil tickled her cheek. Her new shoes pinched. But she couldn't help but stare at the man she'd never seen before this day but must wed.

His shoulders, surely padded as was the custom, filled a fashionably short tunic of purple velvet. A wide chain of the new king's symbols, gold suns and white enamel roses, graced his chest. Purple hose disappeared into thigh-high, pointed boots. Though not ostentatious like most courtiers, Richard's dress confirmed his wealth and position.

If looks and presence alone mattered, he'd make a most excellent husband. For someone else.

Her turn to speak. Eleanor drew a breath, but no words came out. She felt squeezed tight as a sponge, stuck between the crowd and the church. Between the man she couldn't have and the one she could.

Richard's gaze bored into her as her vows poured out in a rush. The ceremony continued with the blessing and giving of the rings. Richard slid a sapphire encrusted band on her finger, gems winking in the sunlight. Eleanor focused on the uncustomary heaviness of the ring and what it meant.

She belonged to Richard now.

Not for long. There had to be a way to end this marriage without offending the king. For now, she needed to survive her wedding day. And her wedding night.

Slowly he leaned forward. She had to kiss him even as Arthur looked on. Eyes open, she met his gaze.

"I greet thee, Countess of Glasmere," he said.

Becoming a countess had been another benefit she'd awaited, but she found no joy in her new title.

Richard grinned, making him look flirtatious. Dangerous. He bent closer until their lips met. His were warm and smooth.

She expected a brief kiss of peace, but he slid a hand around her waist and drew her close, bringing her full against him. A kiss of possession, showing all present she was his.

Surely it was surprise that sent a delicious shiver through her, not the feel of his hard, well-muscled body. Not the intriguing sensation of his mouth on hers or the heated pressure of his hand on her back.

At last he released her. His left hand clasped hers, joining the wide band he had given her with the silver signet ring of Glasmere.

The ring that until recently had been on Arthur's hand.

Guilt washed over her. How could she have accepted Richard's kiss, the man who had stolen everything from her and Arthur? Who worked toward an unattainable dream that mayhap already consumed him as it did her father?

She tried to pull her hand away. He drew her near as they walked inside to celebrate Mass. Pressed tightly to his side, she had no choice but to follow him down the aisle or make a scene. That her pride would not allow.

Eleanor ignored the music and the crowd's cheers. She didn't acknowledge the smiling faces or the glory of the ornately carved, high-ceilinged nave.

She only saw Arthur.

🙞🙜

"'Tis time for the feast," Eleanor's father called in a jovial tone. His smile widened. "Glasmere. Eleanor. Or should I say, Lady Glasmere."

Richard liked the sound of that more than he'd expected.

Not once had his new wife's father looked him in the eye. Did Edmund keep some secret close or have lingering guilt over his long-ago quarrels with Richard's father?

"Your guests await," Eleanor's father said.

A circle of smiling, unfamiliar faces surrounded them in the great hall. Eleanor stood beside him, stiffer than a pair of wet boots that had dried in the sun.

He sighed, wishing he knew how to help her accept what must be. Wishing she preferred to wed with him.

"This marriage wasn't my choice, either," he admitted. At seven and twenty, he hadn't planned to take a bride for years, and then only to sire an army of heirs.

"Thank you. That makes me feel so much better." She nodded but didn't smile after a couple bid them well.

"Whether God's plan is what we think we want doesn't matter." He'd learned to rely on that after the only woman who'd worked her way into his heart betrayed him as his mother had betrayed his father…by sleeping with another man, and a higher-ranked one at that.

Being made an earl marked the zenith of his career. And Eleanor's hand was the honey on a fig tourtelete. Marriage to her enabled him to explore her family's estates freely and uncover how much her family knew about his father's alchemy formula.

Despite an exhaustive search of his holdings, Richard hadn't learned whether his father had found the formula for turning base metals into gold. His father's scrolls had to be in Eleanor's father's possession. If they existed at all. If they didn't, he and King Edward would be most disappointed, for none of the scientists hard at work had yielded fruit.

"Good tidings," a short, fat man said. "I hope you'll be very happy."

"How is that poss—"

Richard took Eleanor's hand and squeezed it, silently advising her to keep her true thoughts to herself. She tugged, but he maintained a firm grip until she relaxed. He liked the feel of her slim fingers in his.

"Where will you live?" an elderly woman asked with a wave of her beringed hand.

"We'll reside at Glasmere Manor when we're not at court or visiting Eleanor's lands," he replied.

"You'll be too busy with the king's business. I'd hate to encumber you," Eleanor said with such a sweet, shy smile he was almost convinced it was real. As he'd feared, she had feminine wiles like his former betrothed. "I'll not travel to court but remain at the only home I've known."

"Let it not be said I'd neglect my new wife. I will have you by my side."

Where he could keep an eye on her. And get to know her.

He drew her close to illustrate, earning a gust of sighs from the guests and an unexpected rush of desire for himself. The feel of her enticed him as it had earlier in her room. Suddenly he wanted more than a marriage of merged assets. Could he have that with Eleanor?

Their gazes met and held. Eleanor raised her chin, promising future challenges.

Richard bent his head and kissed her.

⁂ ⁂

Eleanor ground her teeth as Richard escorted her to the high table. Knowing all eyes were on her, she allowed her hand to remain in his. That didn't mean she had to like it.

But she did. Thrice she'd been flush against his hard body, twice he'd kissed her. Both times she'd experienced an unsettling rush of...what? Not aversion or repugnance as assumed, but something surprisingly pleasant and tempting. Something that made her want more.

Did he feel the same, or had he held her close to prove he could? To show the guests she was his, and he had control?

Eleanor couldn't wait to be alone with the earl. She shook her head. Not so he could touch her, so they could talk. She would end this marriage, even if doing so cost her her father and inheritance.

After she and Richard settled in their chairs, the guests seated themselves on benches at trestle tables arranged before her in a U shape. Musicians struck up an estampie. Her head pounded along with the drums.

How could she sit between a husband she didn't want and a father who had all but stabbed her in the back while the man she did want looked on?

Her father leaned close and patted her on the shoulder. "You've done well thus far, Eleanor. I knew I could count on you."

"You have played me for a fool." Though spots of fury danced before her eyes, she didn't dare say much more in front of so many avid listeners. His hand was a stone, weighing her down.

"Arthur could control you no more easily than I. Richard will make you a better husband."

The arrival of water and cloths for hand washing interrupted their conversation. After all said grace, servers brought her favorite soup of ground capon thickened with almond milk. She waved the bowl away.

Who could she turn to for aid? Not the king who had taken Arthur's title, not her father. Her only hope was the Church, for her betrothal had been annulled without her consent.

The only person she could trust was Arthur, the other victim of this day's events. But the king and her father had usurped any power he might have had to help.

She clenched her spoon. "If you knew I'd be bound to another, why is Arthur here?" she asked. "How could you force him to stand before these nobles with nothing left to him?"

"Arthur is—"

"Never mind. How would I know you spoke the truth?" She shook her head.

"He wished to say farewell. After the meal, you may have a few moments to speak with him."

"May have? You don't have authority over me anymore. I'll do as I please."

Her father picked up his cup and drank. "Arthur is a friend of Richard's. They were knighted together."

Eleanor flinched. Richard smiled at something the person next to him said. Thankfully he hadn't been listening to her.

Heaping platters of roast heron, the first dish in the next course, had been served. Richard offered her the platter. For a long moment, the noise and smells faded, leaving only him.

"Ah, already the newlyweds have eyes for each other," her father crowed.

She felt her cheeks flush. She'd been handed from a father eager to use her as a spy to a husband who had to take her to remain an earl. Neither valued her or her concerns.

All around, guests feasted upon her father's largesse, laughing and drinking, ignorant of his nearly drained coffers. The music and merriment made her long to scream or run from the room. Or both. She felt powerless to stop the events turning her life into a churning mess.

Dancing began as Eleanor escaped to the alcove where mere hours ago she'd learned her future had changed.

She rubbed her ice cold hands together to no avail. The next few moments would likely be the last she'd spend alone with Arthur. She'd be forced to live with a stranger and let the knight of her heart ride away.

Arthur appeared beneath the arch, tall, slim and endearingly familiar.

Her smile returned as he sat beside her. "Arthur, how are you? I've missed you."

Eleanor took a deep breath, enjoying the scent of his soap. Never would she smell the herbal pine mixture without thinking of him.

"As well as can be, considering."

"Father kept everything from me until this morning. Had he told me sooner I could have done…something." At last she could speak her thoughts. "Why didn't you send word? Why didn't you help me find a solution?"

"I wrote you, but received no response," he said. "What was I to do?"

Eleanor bit back a scream. Worse and worse. Her father had stolen Arthur's letters. Later she'd say a prayer of mourning. For she'd lost her other parent this day. His scheming and renewed obsession with alchemy had turned him into a man she didn't care to know.

"Look at me," she insisted.

His gaze was that of a stranger's. Had circumstances changed him?

"I thank God for Richard," Arthur said. "He petitioned King Edward for lenience and received permission to give me Woodbury Manor. Without his kindness, I'd have nothing."

"How thoughtful of him to give back your own manor," she said with a sneer. "While he steals your bride. If your friend is so reasonable, he'll agree our marriage is a mistake. I'll obtain an annulment, and be free to wed you."

"No, Eleanor," Arthur said. "You have to accept what must be."

Eleanor's jaw dropped. "What? You sound like Richard." And Edmund.

"If you don't commit to him, you'll fail your father and your king," Arthur said. "Don't make yourself miserable by hoping for what can no longer be."

She took his hands, but he pulled away. "Don't you love me anymore?" The pleading tone in her voice appalled her.

"That matters not," he said with a sigh. "Yorkists rule where Lancasters once prevailed. The loser must accept his lot."

Her heart filled with tenderness. "You're denying your love for me to spare me more suffering. If you declare yourself, you know I won't rest until we're together." No matter the cost. "Arthur, spare me more lies."

"I too am to wed," he continued as if he hadn't heard a word she'd said. "Richard has betrothed me to his ward, Margaret."

How many more unwelcome surprises must she endure?

Arthur would be beholden to Richard for hearth, home and wife. Unless she moved faster than a fox fleeing hunters, there'd be two marriages to dissolve.

"Is that what you truly desire?"

"Margaret could have looked higher than an attainted former earl. Richard shows the world that in his eyes at least, I'm not a traitor," Arthur said.

"Nor in mine." She and her new husband had one thing in common: their support of Arthur. "Does Richard's friendship mean more to you than I do?"

"I do what I must."

Duty again. If Arthur wasn't strong enough to defy Richard, she'd be strong for him.

"We can find a way to be together," she insisted.

She wanted to feel his arms around her, to know that he needed her and their future, no matter how long it took to achieve. But she couldn't betray the vows she'd spoken. She'd have them annulled first.

Arthur slid down the bench. He crossed his arms over his

dark green tunic. "We grew up close as brother and sister. I thought of you as mine. But everything changed."

"My feelings for you haven't." How could they, in less than a day? "Have yours?"

"What we feel is of no import. You are wed. Promise me you won't dwell on what could have been." He leaned forward. "Life isn't like the romances you read, replete with swoons and happy endings." Arthur lifted her hand to his lips for a formal, chivalrous kiss. "I must go. I hope we can remain friends."

"Friends, Arthur? I'd have more of you."

Eleanor turned her palm up and clasped his hand. The few, brief kisses they'd stolen over the years had satisfied a young girl's amorous wishes. But she was a woman now. For what she planned to do, the risks she was about to take, she needed proof that Arthur still wanted her. That their love could triumph over all obstacles.

"Arthur, tell me true. Tell me you want me."

For an endless heartbeat, they stood together, hands clinging.

"Eleanor, I—"

"Here you are, my lady wife." Richard's deep voice held a hint of mockery. His gray-green eyes were unreadable.

Arthur backed away as though he'd been burned.

She didn't wish to be caught displaying her feelings for another man, nor did she want to insult Richard. He too had been told whom to wed.

Or had he? She caught her breath. Perhaps he was so powerful he could maneuver people like a chess player. What if he could envision what would happen several moves ahead and had encouraged Parliament to attaint Arthur?

"Let us return to the feast." Richard held out his hand, the Glasmere signet ring glinting in the glow of the brazier.

Eleanor took it. Leaving Arthur was almost as hard as going through with the wedding. She nurtured a fragile spark of hope that could become a fire. Once she and Richard were alone in the chamber she'd helped array only this morning for herself and Arthur, Eleanor would end this farce of a marriage.

Before it couldn't be ended.

CHAPTER 3

At last all he had worked for was within reach.

Not fond of large gatherings, Richard stood apart from the crowd enjoying his wedding feast. Richly dressed nobles jabbered, servers scurried to and fro. His bride danced with one of her cousins. He knew her happy smile was an act.

"She surpasses the miniature portrait Edward sent you, does she not?"

Richard tensed at the high-pitched voice. Lady Blanche Latimer. The fly in his pudding.

"What of it?" He couldn't be polite to her. Blanche, his erstwhile love, deceived him when he was most vulnerable, like an enemy attacking a knight while he slept. In times of war, Richard kept his sword within reach. In matters of the heart, armor forged by disloyalty now kept him just as well protected. "Did you attend my wedding because you hoped I might change my mind at the last minute?"

"We were good together, and you know it. I regret the mistake I made," Blanche said. "But no. I was invited with Lady Elizabeth FitzWalter, cousin to Eleanor's father, and her son Hugh."

She hadn't changed, still slender and lovely in a tight-sleeved green gown. Her cone-shaped headdress hid hair he knew to be dark red.

"My wedding is over. Yet you remain."

"How could I leave without witnessing the bedding?" she

asked. "You've been handed a beauty, and a wealthy one, too. What more could you ask?"

He would prefer that his bride didn't prefer his friend.

"They say she's as willful as I. But I know you're up to the task of handling her." Blanche ran her hand down his arm. He stepped away.

She tossed her head, sending her veils afloat. Her sultry smile disappeared. "Henry and the House of Lancaster will rule again. Remember to whom you owe your loyalties, who your friends are. Those who have risen highest have farthest to fall."

Richard couldn't stop the frisson of alarm whisking through him. She could be right. King Edward yet faced uprisings from those who supported Henry, the previous king. In these uncertain times, another switch in power could bring Richard down as easily as a weakened wall succumbed to a siege. He had to help Edward remain king.

One way was to find his father's missing alchemy scrolls. Then, if he'd discovered a formula that worked, Edward could produce the coin he sorely needed to protect and support his realm.

With an abrupt nod, Richard rejoined his countess, who'd returned to the table.

Arthur's extolling of Eleanor's beauty hadn't prepared him for his first sight of her earlier today rushing down the winding staircase, blue skirts in both hands. She'd halted at the bottom, wavy golden hair tumbling over her shoulders to her hips.

Her lips had been full and smiling, eyes he now knew to be violet shining. Her whole being radiated joy. She'd not yet been told of the change in grooms and so knew nothing of him. Still, it had pained him that her enthusiasm was for Arthur.

Someday she'll look at me that way.

What a fool notion. What difference did it make if she cared for him? He was more than fortunate to have risen so high and to be gifted with a bride of her beauty and holdings. He looked forward to searching his new estates and learning more about their fathers' partnership.

Eleanor's exquisite form and kissable lips awakened a different type of anticipation. He imagined her beneath him, awaiting his touch, hair spread over the pillows. A gossamer nightgown would hint at treasures beneath, her sweet scent....

Soon, Richard thought. Soon.

One didn't need to love his wife to enjoy her. Or to give her pleasure.

As they left the table, he smiled. Since joining Edward's household fifteen years ago, his steadfast support and superior fighting skills had earned him a title far above any he'd hoped for as the oldest son of an alchemist.

What could possibly go wrong now?

❧ ☙

Eleanor took Richard's hand, the jaws of the trap squashing her. She was his, and to prove it he would parade her about like a cow on market day. Yet his skin was warm, somehow soothing. She'd appreciate that comfort, just for a moment.

Several couples graciously stepped back to clear space. Another song began, suitable for a basse dance. The rhythmic beat almost lulled her into enjoying it. She couldn't deny Richard cut a fine figure as he completed the slow steps.

"This day has been one surprise after another for you. I'm sorry for that," he said.

"I blame my father." Bitterness rankled.

"You deserved to know when we did."

His sympathy, his support, startled her. Softened the sharp edge of pain. "My lord," she began.

"Richard."

"Richard, then. I—"

His fingers tightened on hers as the dance continued. "You wanted to marry Arthur."

"Yes." Though true, his bluntness stung. She wouldn't lie, even to spare his feelings or pride. "Arthur told me all you've done for him. Perhaps you'll do one thing more—agree that you and I aren't truly wed. I argue thusly: my betrothal to Arthur was annulled without my knowledge or consent, so said annulment isn't valid. 'Tis of course no reflection on you."

Why did she care how her words affected him?

He didn't speak.

"Can you know what it is to have hoped for something all of your life, then have it snatched from your grasp?"

"Yes." Pain flashed in his gaze, sparking sympathy in her. "And I regret it happened to you. But what we want matters not." He sounded just like Arthur. "Many, including your father and the king, wish our union. It is done. So let's make the best of our marriage. Can you, will you, do that?"

The heat of his gaze made her skin prickle. Eleanor looked down, only to see his muscled thighs flexing as he moved, brushing intimately against her skirts. Their faces were inches apart. His skin was flushed from their exertions, with a thin beading of sweat on his brow. She felt his rapid breathing. His heat burned through her gown. Would this dance never end?

"I need to sit," she whispered.

They returned to their seats. Eleanor's face ached from forced smiling, her feet throbbed, her stomach threatened to rebel. She rose, prompting a cheer from the men and squeals from the women. Without meaning to, she'd made it time for the bedding.

What difference did a few minutes make? There was no way to avoid the inevitable procession to the bridal chamber. Eleanor had no need to fear what came after, for she'd ensure there'd be no consummation.

Women chattered like a nest of hungry birds as they climbed the twisting stairs. In her large chamber, some scattered fresh rose petals on the curtained bed, others helped her undress. She clenched her teeth as they helped her climb into bed and smoothed the covers over her.

For ages brides had withstood this public display to prove they came to their grooms unblemished. So could she. But there'd be no endless stream of lewd comments and even lewder gestures. Alyce had been instructed to forcibly shoo the crowd out like a herd of swine, if need be.

Her sister leaned close, arranging Eleanor's hair over rose scented pillows.

"Alyce, what am I to do?"

"What all women do. Accept their fate," she answered.

"What choice do you have? Please, Eleanor, think before you act." Alyce hugged her, then returned to the others.

Linen sheets chilled Eleanor's skin, too-sweet roses made her nose itch. The incessant, shrill giggling was enough to make her clasp her hands over her ears.

The door burst open, almost crushing a hapless woman behind it. A throng of men swirled into the chamber amidst laughter and stomping feet.

Richard looked as grim as she felt. He removed his enameled collar and short velvet tunic, placing them on his wood chest.

"Look at that. Let's see what else he's got beneath those hose," a woman said.

The other women laughed.

"What about the beauteous bride? Is she naked under there?" More laughter.

Eleanor clutched the sheets to her neck, hiding as much as she could for as long as she could. She couldn't stop trembling. How mortifying to be forced to display yourself to everyone you knew. Yet when the time came, she'd stand proudly before them all.

The earl, clad now in his silk pourpoint, approached the bed. His shoulders were truly broad, not enhanced by padding as she had assumed. The contours of his chest were impressive. His hose outlined powerful thighs.

His physical perfection changed nothing. If their marriage were consummated, having it annulled would prove even more difficult. But what were the consequences of refusing him? What had he meant earlier by "defiance leads to hardship?" She licked her dry lips.

"See how the bride hungers for the groom!"

"Eleanor wants to eat him up."

The men cheered.

The earl studied her. He turned to the crowd, hands poised to untie his hose from his undertunic. Some women were like to drool, their mouths hung so far open. He undid one tie. "Our thanks for your friendship. But you have seen all you're going to see. Return to the music and drink. Enjoy."

"I need some good luck. Her garter is mine!" A portly man stumbled forward, arms outstretched.

Eleanor recoiled.

Richard stopped the man with a hand to his chest. "Out. Now. Every last one of you."

Disgruntled moans and groans ensued, but in the face of his hard stare the onlookers slowly took their leave. With a sympathetic smile, Alyce closed the door behind her.

The silence after the revelry was both welcome and strained.

Richard's back flexed as he untied his hose. "I received training to be a knight and land owner. You were taught how to be a chatelaine. Some information on how to be husband and wife would've proved useful."

She relaxed a bit. "You're right. I was told only to be obedient. And that by law, advantages convey to the husband. Not very encouraging." Had her mother lived, would she be better prepared for this moment? Being alone with a man while disrobed, husband or not, and carrying on a conversation felt awkward to say the least. If they'd had time to know each other, better yet, being in love, would mitigate such things.

"I suppose each couple learns together. And makes their own rules."

"A nice thought. If both members of the couple wish to remain wed to each other. You didn't want to wed me. Nor I you." Nakedness left her feeling uncomfortable and insecure. Weak. With the sheets still clutched to her, she reached for the silk robe draped across the bottom of the bed. She slipped it on. "The new king needs powerful lords to support him. He aims to have our lands united, not you and I. I fear my father has misled you about the size of his coffers. If you release me, you can seek a trustworthy father-by-law." She slid off the bed and walked to him. "Would that suffice?"

❧ ❧

The rich, well-sauced foods Richard had eaten churned within. So much for his good fortune. On his wedding night his bride asked, nay, begged him to release her. To another man.

If he complied, he'd lose all he'd just gained. If he didn't, she could resent him for the rest of their days. He couldn't survive that.

"I understand your confusion and dismay over all of the sudden changes." She wasn't rejecting him personally, so his manly pride should remain intact. Her insistence on dissolving their union rankled nonetheless. Yet in a strange manner, it also bothered him that he couldn't accommodate her. "But the answer is no. The king gifted me with more than your holdings. I don't need them, or your father's coin."

Delicate fingers clung to her linen night robe. Her flowing golden hair tempted him to touch it despite everything.

"How can you want a woman who loves another?"

"Far sharper weapons than your tongue have sought to wound me." Yet Richard steeled himself against the prick of her words. "Marriage isn't about love, but duty and honor. We're wed in the eyes of God, king and man. So we shall remain." He'd come to his senses. The flash of yearning for anything beyond that had disappeared. He stepped closer and waited until she looked at him. "You are mine now, and what is mine I keep. Do not think to betray me."

Her violet eyes widened, but she said nothing. He knew he sounded harsh. How else could he let her know he wouldn't tolerate disloyalty?

He wouldn't divulge his own foray into love and subsequent disillusionment, nor the perfidy of his mother. He'd learned not to trust women he knew well who'd professed love. So how could he trust Eleanor?

"I believe in familial love, the deep caring one has for siblings and parents, which grows over time. That's what I hope we can someday share. Much of life is either restraint or sin. People of our station have duties to fulfill and can't afford to succumb to every yearning. Why should life be different for you?"

"Because…because…." Her face fell and her shoulders sagged. Had the long day taken its toll, or was this a new womanly strategy to avoid him? "Because we just met."

Richard folded his clothing until his sympathy subsided. He couldn't let her reluctance sway him. "I thought for certes you'd send me on a merry chase tonight by hiding. Or are you waiting until I fall asleep so you can climb out the window?"

He earned only a faint smile. "My thanks for the excellent ideas. Perhaps on the morrow." Eleanor returned to bed, still wearing her robe.

Though stunningly beautiful, in her unhappy state Eleanor didn't arouse him. If her lack of enthusiasm wasn't enough to demolish desire, he couldn't seem to forget that she wanted his friend.

Their marriage had to be consummated or it wouldn't be as binding. Perhaps if he touched her soft flesh, inhaled her woman's scent, enticed her with his caresses....

He sat beside her. She smelled sweet and fresh, like lemons. After waiting a moment to let her adjust to his nearness, he stroked her luxurious hair as he'd longed to since he saw her. Smooth as the finest samite. She allowed him to run his fingers through each golden lock, but he sensed her skittishness. He'd tame her with utmost patience, akin to the way he'd succeed with an unbroken horse.

Richard bent toward her, seeking the delicate skin on her neck. His finger pushed away the edge of her robe, exposing a thin gold chain. He kissed her neck just above the chain and she shivered. An expected response from most women of his acquaintance, but did Eleanor shiver with desire or distaste?

He pressed on, kissing his way toward her mouth. His lips met hers, then again, but she didn't kiss him back or open her mouth. Either she was completely untutored in the ways of men or she primly refused his advances. Her eyes were closed.

Never had he expected such complete disinterest.

Richard worked his way down Eleanor's neck, then lower still, tugging the sheet from her reluctant fingers. He opened her robe to reveal her breasts, lush and magnificent. A key dangled from the gold chain shimmering between them. What did it open? What was so important to his wife that she wore the key beneath her clothing and close to her heart? But this was a time for touch, not talk.

As his fingers roamed her smooth curves, he started to respond. So did she. He smiled. Her nipples firmed beneath his questing fingers, arousing him fully. Her head tipped back and her lips parted, clear signs she was starting to welcome, to enjoy, his touch. His erection pulsed as he continued gentle strokes, biding his time, enjoying the anticipation.

Until something splashed onto his cheek. Eleanor was crying. Whether her tears were feigned or real, his interest withered.

"I believe I'm still bound to Arthur," she whispered.

He swore. Anger seethed through his veins. She was a woman grown and needed to face her responsibilities. As he faced his.

"You are married to me. No other."

Eleanor drew her robe tight. Her glorious hair fell forward to cover her face.

There'd be hell to pay if he failed to consummate their marriage. How could he convince her? Uncertainty didn't sit well with him. As a soldier, one acted or died. Even in his new role as an earl, he felt comfortable with the decisions he'd made thus far.

"I am sorry, but I…I just can't…." Eleanor put her head in her hands and sobbed quietly.

His anger dissolved like snow in the sun. There was but one course of action to follow.

Richard walked to one of the chests delivered by his squire. He lifted the lid, revealing his daggers strapped beneath. Sliding a weapon free, he admired the sleek blade as it gleamed in the firelight.

He strode toward the bed, dagger in hand.

Eleanor looked up and screamed.

❧❧ ❧❧

Eleanor seized the bedcovers as if they could protect her from the fear surging within. And Richard.

One minute he was kissing her, the next he brandished a dagger. He strode toward her, weapon held high. Candlelight accented his broad chest and well-muscled arms, making him seem a warrior on the attack.

She scrambled to the far side of the bed, tangling her foot in the covers. She kicked off the offending cloth.

"Help! To me!" She sped across the room.

Richard ran after her, feet pounding the floor. "Eleanor. Stop! What are you doing?"

They reached the door at the same time. He slammed his hands against it as she struggled to pull it open. His powerful arms trapped her between them.

"Let me go!" The iron handle chilled her fingers while the heat of him scorched her back.

His breath came in a rush above her. She choked when she tried to loose another scream.

Summoning all her courage, she bit out, "Hurting me will gain you nothing."

He spoke softly into her ear as he had earlier, making it tingle once again. "Eleanor, stop before someone hears. I'm not going to hurt you. I'd never hurt you," he vowed. "The dagger is for me."

"What?" Eleanor turned.

Richard's chest almost touched her nose as he breathed. She could smell him, her herbal soap mixed with an intriguing scent she couldn't define. His strength, clearly carefully restrained, no longer frightened but impressed her. His eyes narrowed behind his tousled hair.

"The dagger is for me," Richard repeated. "To cut myself so I can smear blood on the sheets. That way all will believe we are well and truly wed."

"Oh. Oh." Eleanor nearly collapsed in humiliation. She couldn't look at him. "I saw the dagger and panicked. I'm truly sorry. It's been a long, trying day."

Alyce had been right. Perhaps she did need to think before she acted.

Being so near him unnerved her. He fascinated and drew her against her will. She ducked under his arm and hurried back to the bed.

"Blood on the sheets. 'Tis an excellent idea," she said. "Why didn't I think of it?"

Because she'd been immersed in Richard's touch. When he kissed her neck, the shivery thrill spreading through her so surprised her she hadn't thought to pull away. His hands on her breasts, which no man had ever touched before, had been so gentle, yet made her hope for more. His touch calmed her while inspiring a traitorous stirring deep within. For a brief moment, she'd wanted to touch him, to feel how different his flesh was from hers. To see if she could elicit a similar reaction.

How could Richard affect her so when Arthur's kisses hadn't? The shock of her body's response had made her cry. And her tears convinced Richard to grant her a reprieve.

Eleanor had bought time to find a way to get Arthur back. When she did, she'd prove her marriage to Richard had never been consummated, notwithstanding any "proof" on the sheets. If necessary, she'd submit to an embarrassing examination to show she remained pure. Using Richard's good deed against him bothered her, but she had no choice. Guiltily, she glanced at him, glad he couldn't read her thoughts.

He stood by the bed. "I'm giving you the opportunity to adjust to the sudden changes in your life and to me as your husband. 'Twill be a challenge, for I believe in honesty. Nor am I a good dissembler."

A small spiral of remorse twisted Eleanor's stomach. They'd been married less than a day and already he'd violated his principles for her.

"I admire honesty, as well. But events beyond our control brought us here. It's only for a short while. And for a good reason, to protect ourselves." This would be best for him too. Someday he'd realize that. Still, she hoped niggling guilt would fade. "Let us be honest with each other, at least. You deserve a bride who doesn't love another man."

Richard stiffened. A gleam lit his eyes as he leaned close. "What if I could make you want me?"

At that moment she believed he could do anything.

Against her will, Richard captivated her, like an exceptional jewel. He acted the polished lord, yet danced with cheerful enthusiasm. He exhibited tactful authority when clearing the chamber during the bedding. When angry, he had the presence of mind to rein in his emotions while revealing an exciting, untamed edge. She'd never forget the tenderness in his gaze when he touched her. And she wanted to see it again.

She'd seen more aspects of Richard's personality in a day

than Arthur had revealed in the years she'd known him. She couldn't recall Arthur raising his voice or bursting into laughter. He was ever mellow. Why should that bother her? 'Twas far better to have a calm, predictable husband who'd be content to follow where she led.

"You're a soldier. Why fight a losing battle?" she asked.

"The king made your hand part of my recompense for excellent service."

"I've no doubt such recompense is well-deserved. From what I can see, you're honorable and kind, yet carry yourself with the presence and confidence of a leader. Those qualities combined with your wealth and physical attractiveness yield a man most women would be overjoyed to wed."

"Such praise makes me wonder if you know your own heart." He placed his hand on her chest.

Eleanor wished his fingers would move lower to cup her breast. No. She wouldn't succumb to his tempting ways. She slid under the covers. With a devastating smile, he returned to his side of the bed.

"Most women would be overjoyed to wed," she repeated. "Not I."

He shouldn't be left without a bride just because she'd been promised to another. Perhaps she had a friend who would suit. A friend who didn't cringe every time she heard the words alchemy, transmutation or quintessence.

Yes, yes, yes! She wanted to shout with glee. Here was the solution to her problems. She would find Richard a better bride so he'd agree to relinquish her. A new bride, more comely, wealthier and even more talented than she, to serve as greater reward. Both Richard and the king would be appeased. Only her father would be unhappy. But after his recent actions, she had no need to worry about him.

Joyous enthusiasm filled her until harsh reality took its place. Finding this new bride would be no easy task, for she'd have to be a better prospect than Eleanor herself. All her life she'd been complimented on her beauty. She could read, write and do sums in addition to the womanly abilities of running her household, needlework, dancing and the like.

How to find the woman Richard deserved, the perfect bride?

There was nothing she loved better than a challenge.

Eleanor blew out the candle and pulled up the covers, staying as close to her edge of the bed as possible. She didn't dare ask Richard if he would sleep on the floor by the fire. He had given, now she must.

Richard pulled back the covers with one hand, dagger poised again in the other. She didn't want to watch, but couldn't force her gaze away. After all, he was doing this for her. He raised the dagger to his head and cut his scalp.

She gasped. Unconsciously squeezing the blanket, she waited to see what he would do next.

"Do not fear. Even minor scalp wounds bleed profusely. No one will see this, not even my squire," he said, his voice flat.

He seemed strangely well prepared. Had he anticipated her reluctance to consummate? Or had he sliced himself to protect a woman before? The answers should make no difference. But she couldn't help wondering how many women he'd made love to. If she, who had no intention of being seduced by Richard, was sorely tempted, there must be women who'd been willing or even pursued him.

Richard spread his hair away from the cut. He tilted his head until a few drops marred the pristine sheet, then smeared the blood into the fabric. Without a glance at her, he wiped his hands clean on a cloth, then dabbed his head. After throwing the red-spotted cloth into the fire, his eyes burned with an emotion she couldn't describe. Not anger, not sorrow, but something in between.

Eleanor sensed that he expected her to say something. What? *Thank you? I'm sorry?* Neither seemed appropriate.

Her education had taught her how to handle every situation, every task she'd faced. Until today. Everything that lay before her was unfamiliar. She needed some control over her future. She'd take charge by finding Richard a new bride. By keeping alchemy far from her life.

His hands went to his hips and he finished untying his hose.

Eleanor shut her eyes.

The well-stuffed mattress gave slightly as he got in. She felt the movements of the covers as he arranged them. Time passed as she listened to his breathing and the crackling fire, but she couldn't compel her tense muscles to relax. How would she ever sleep with him in the same bed, even far away?

She wouldn't think of him, but of women she knew who might be worthy of consideration as his new bride. There was Lady Howes—

"Are you a virgin?"

All thoughts of suitable acquaintances flew from her head. Surprise made her sit up. "What?"

"You heard me. Is that why you refuse to consummate our marriage, because you have no virgin blood left to shed? You were betrothed for many years. That's akin to marriage. And you profess love for Arthur. Have you made love with him?" He sat up. The covers fell to his lap, the glow of the dying fire outlining his muscular chest and arms. "Have I been played for a fool? Do you refuse me, your lawful and rightful husband, to honor your lover?"

Eleanor gasped. His accusations stung. "Does your concern stem from the fact that I might not be a virgin, or that I might've made love with your friend?"

Could Richard be jealous of her past?

Richard stood and rounded the bed with no obvious regard to his nakedness. She refused to look anywhere but at his face. He looked furious.

"Answer me." He loomed over her.

"How dare you doubt me?" Eleanor flopped onto her back, tempted to pull the covers over her head. "I am pure."

His lack of trust stung sharp as a bee. How, in such a short time, had he managed to gain enough power over her that it mattered what he thought of her?

Silence. Endless silence.

"How do I know you speak true? You were betrothed and wanted to marry Arthur, so why wait? You said we should be honest, but are willing, nay, eager to lie about the blood on these sheets." He bent over her, so close his hair tickled her cheeks. "How do I know how many more lies you'll tell?"

He smelled wonderful, enticing. She had a sudden urge to

touch him, to feel the molded muscles of his substantial chest. She held her arms tightly by her sides to keep from doing just that.

"You know there's but one way for me to be certain you tell the truth in this," he whispered.

If he moved another inch, their lips would meet. Eleanor held her breath. Her heartbeat quickened. He slid a finger down the side of her face, pushing away a strand of hair. A delicious shiver coursed through her. His warm hand lingered on her neck. She hoped he'd kiss her.

But she couldn't give in to this strange curiosity, this unwelcome need.

"I have spoken true. Believe what you will." She forced a steady, cool tone.

Richard didn't move. She couldn't either, held in thrall by nervous anticipation. She feared her reprieve had ended, all too soon. Would he have his way with her to prove her purity?

Why did part of her want him to? He was her husband, after all. No. He wasn't.

At last he stood and turned away. She let out a sigh of relief. If he'd looked at her that way one more minute…. She'd hoped to taste him again, to feel her flesh against his. Never before had she been attracted to any man but Arthur, nor thought it possible another man could interest her. Richard so easily awoke unfamiliar desire.

Her few kisses with Arthur had been pleasant, scattered over the years between his fostering and warring. But she hadn't yearned for more the way she did with Richard. What was happening to her?

She had to return to Arthur a virgin or not return to him at all.

It was a good thing she'd be free of Richard soon.

❧ ❧

Richard returned to his side of the bed, wishing he'd built up the fire so he could've read the truth in her eyes. Had she used tears to trick him into rescuing her? All knew she was clever.

Eleanor had a seductive way about her he doubted she knew she possessed. That combined with her beauty had interested him from their first meeting. Now, having touched and tasted her, he wanted more. His lingering arousal was proof. Had she felt so right because she was his wife?

How close had she and Arthur been? Visions of them passionately entwined paraded through his head. He relived the moment in the alcove when he found Eleanor in Arthur's embrace, feeling again the annoying, sharp jolt of possessiveness. He imagined them together, smiling and happy. They laughed as they undressed each other, then Arthur put his hand....

He would not think on this.

Eleanor's occasional sigh told him she was still awake. What thoughts beset her?

Why did he care?

Even in the most harrowing situations, truth had served him. Yet less than a day into his marriage, he was caught up in a grievous misrepresentation. For a brief moment he thought of going back on his word just to get the deed done. But then he'd lose any chance of earning Eleanor's trust. She had to come to him voluntarily or she'd make the rest of his life—their life—miserable.

He had to make her understand her duty and choose to fulfill it. If he was fortunate, she might come to want him for himself. At the very least, she'd have to realize that her best choice was to accept him as her husband.

His best choice was to make her accept him. His physical attractiveness and ease with women were gifts he'd never used to attain goals the way he used his intelligence and strength. For the first time in his life, he was going to have to court a woman. His own wife. As skilled as he was as a warrior, he had little idea how to woo. He'd approach Eleanor as he did a battle, strategizing with care, analyzing all potential weaknesses.

Then he'd besiege her walls as earnestly as he attacked a rebel's castle.

All he truly needed from Eleanor was acceptance and fulfillment of her duty, obedience, and above all honesty.

Mayhap if he repeated that enough he would come to believe it.

CHAPTER 4

leanor tossed and turned as Richard slept beside her. Would she get used to having a man in her bed? After all that had befallen her, when would she feel comfortable again?

She touched the key she'd worn around her neck for almost fourteen years, but found no comfort as she oft had from the symbol of her hopes for the future. Even her source of solace was lost to her now.

She lifted herself on one elbow. Richard hadn't moved for some time. Carefully, she climbed out of bed. She lit a candle with glowing embers, then held it toward Richard. Good. His eyes were still closed. Shielding the fragile flame, she hurried to two wood chests on the other side of the room. The larger, plainer chest held her clothing. But the smaller one, with its ornate carved border, held greater treasure.

After another glance at Richard, Eleanor set the candle down. She pulled the chain over her head and used the key to turn the lock before lifting the lid. Her favorite scent of lemons now seemed stale and bittersweet as her fingers trailed over linens and cloths she'd spent hours embroidering, many with the initials A and E elaborately entwined in thread of precious silver. Near the bottom rested her wedding gift for Arthur, a tapestry depicting his favorite hound, as fine in her eyes as a costly cloth of Arras.

She bid a temporary farewell to the past, to things that had meant so much to her. On the morrow, she'd have this chest moved to the storage area, where the trappings of her disrupted life would molder with her dream of what should have been.

Until she could make it so.

Dawn had barely broken, but she had to talk with Alyce before joining the remaining wedding guests.

Eleanor knocked on her sister's door. "Alyce! Let me in."

Never would she have admitted she hastened to escape Richard. Though they'd remained on opposite sides of the bed, his mere presence did strange things to her. Surely her sleepless night was due to enthusiasm for her new project.

Alyce opened the door and rubbed sleep from her eyes. "Is aught amiss?" Her face brightened. "Or have you come to tell me about your wedding night? What was it like?"

"Naught is amiss and one choosing to give herself to the Church shouldn't be concerned with what takes place in the marriage bed." That took care of Alyce. Now she only had the rest of the castle to deal with. Eleanor closed the door behind her.

"This could be my only opportunity to learn of such things," Alyce persisted.

The rising sun peeked through the arched window, highlighting her sister's delicate beauty. With her pale skin, luminous azure eyes and hair almost as shiny as gold, she looked like an angel. The lone flower in the withered garden of her stark room.

"Every time you're here, you make that face," Alyce said. "How else can I prepare for my future? But I would like to hear of your wedding night."

"We'll talk of that anon," Eleanor said with a dismissive wave. "Alyce, I have a project."

"Oh, no, Eleanor. No." Alyce gasped. "Not another project. You promised. The last one almost cost a year's crop from our herb garden."

"Adding nourishment to the soil to make plants grow faster and bigger remains an excellent idea. I must've miscalculated the proportions. Or had the wrong mix of ingredients."

"And before that, I feared the wool would never grow back on the sheep."

"I hoped to make shearing easier and faster. I almost succeeded." Eleanor hopped onto Alyce's bed. "This time is different, you'll see."

Alyce shook her head. "I'll hear you out, but make no promises." She picked up her comb, climbed onto her bed and began unwinding her long braid.

Eleanor wanted to dance with joy. "We are going to find Richard a bride!"

"He already has one. You." Alyce's hands dropped from her hair.

"I'm going to seek an annulment. If I get it, Richard will be left with nothing. No bride, none of her lands or gold, none of the prestige of a highly ranked wife. Whether I get it or not, if I find another bride who'll satisfy both him and King Edward—a better bride—he'll be happier with her and end the day ahead. We'll all be happier. Then I can marry Arthur." And finally be alchemy free.

Alyce stared at her, hands dangling at her sides, mouth agape.

"Close your mouth," Eleanor said. "Everything happened too fast yesterday for me to think. How could I meekly accept a change in grooms, after years of waiting?"

"It was cruel of Father to keep it from you," Alyce agreed. "But women like us don't have the luxury of choosing their husbands."

"Just because we don't know of many marriages based on love doesn't mean there aren't any. Else why would there be so many books written and tales told of romance? Why should people spend their lives stuck with someone they don't want?" Eleanor sighed.

"Marriage isn't about love."

"You sound like Father. Last night I began a list of unwed women we know." Eleanor couldn't tell even her sister that between the unfamiliar sounds of Richard's soft breathing from the other side of the bed and concern about falling asleep and rolling toward him, she hadn't slept a wink.

She started pacing. "First is Lady Howes, wealthy but not beautiful enough and only two small manors to her name. Obviously this better bride needs have more lands than I."

Christ hanging on a large cross on Alyce's wall interrupted her recitation. His sorrowful, compassionate eyes haunted her. Was it a sin to find your husband a new bride? She pivoted and kept walking.

"Katherine de Sutton is of excellent lineage, but spiteful. Richard would never be comfortable with her. Alice Poynings has wealth, but six children from her first husband. I don't know how he'd feel about that." She shook her head. "As you can see, the available brides lack the necessary qualifications."

"Better bride? Qualifications?" Alyce's voice cracked. "Have you lost your wits?"

"I've never been more serious." Eleanor halted. The dazed expression on Alyce's face proved she hadn't grasped how clever the plan was. "I'll let you think. When you agree that helping Richard to another bride is the way to help me and him to happiness, nod."

Alyce combed her hair, but Eleanor could tell she wasn't counting the strokes as she usually did.

"What do you think?"

"I said I would hear you out and I have. I think you are ill." Alyce stared at her as though she had three eyes. "The shocking events of your wedding day must've disrupted your humors. Your blood, bile, choler and phlegm are clearly out of balance. I shall send for the physician. Perhaps you need a bloodletting."

"Don't even think it," Eleanor warned. "I am well."

"How can you be?" she asked. "You were sorely tested yesterday. But you must do your duty."

She sounded just like Richard. "Duty." The word left a taste in her mouth worse than sour milk. "Why do men have more freedom to do as they choose? Why must women obey men's demands?"

"'Tis the way of the world. Richard and Arthur didn't have much choice, either. From king to peasant, we all must obey a higher power." Alyce set the brush on her trunk and began to make her bed.

"I have to try." Eleanor pivoted again, skirts swinging. "Here's how my idea will work. What is my favorite tale?"

"*The Odyssey*," Alyce answered.

"I put the two together, and voilà!" She clapped her hands. "Aren't I brilliant?"

"What has *The Odyssey* to do with finding Richard a bride?"

Eleanor spoke as patiently as she could. "Odysseus's wife Penelope waits twenty years for him to return from his voyage. She can't keep her suitors at bay, so she holds a test of skill. A husband test. She'll marry the man who can string Odysseus's bow and shoot through twelve axes."

Alyce held up her hands as if warding off disaster. "Oh, Eleanor, no."

"You see? Brilliant."

"You have gone mad. You mean to hold a bride test."

"Exactly." Eleanor raised her arms with glee. "Wait...why have one test when we can have several? I know! We'll hold a tournament. A bridal tournament." She skipped around the room.

"Stop this instant. Or I'll be certain you have the dancing mania and will send for the physician." Alyce hurried toward her. "Finish the tale. Penelope believed Odysseus would return, so she made the contest impossible for anyone but her beloved husband to win."

Eleanor froze mid-step.

"Is that what you're going to do, Eleanor?" Alyce asked, her voice softer than usual. "Set the bar so high only you can prevail? You are all the things you say Richard deserves. Are you but giving yourself time to see if you could care for him? Or if Arthur remains true?"

Slowly, Eleanor turned. Could Alyce be right? Of course not. "The only fair way to have Arthur is by providing an excellent new bride for Richard."

"Didn't Odysseus kill all the suitors after he won?" Alyce crossed her arms.

"'Tis like you to be absolutely literal," Eleanor said.

"Plan or not, perhaps Arthur will prefer the bride Richard offered. How do you know he still wants to marry you?"

The question hung in the air like unwelcome fog.

"Arthur says I should accept Richard," she admitted. "I don't believe he means it."

"Has Richard agreed to this lunatic scheme?"

The thought of discussing this with him made her uneasy. "I'm not sure he'll need to. Once he meets the winner and sees how much better suited she is, the means of finding her won't matter. Richard seems perfect in every way but two. He's not Arthur, and he's pursuing alchemy. Yes, he's handsome. Yes, he seems honorable, kind, intelligent and many more good, manly things." Including inspiring stirrings of what she had to admit was desire." But I want to marry Arthur."

"You sound like a spoiled child. I half expect you to stomp your foot."

Eleanor stiffened. "I'm not upset over being denied a mere sweetmeat or toy. Mayhap I am a bit stubborn. Nay, persistent. I won't give up on the one thing I've always wanted."

"You're a married woman now and have—"

"Here it comes. Your 'I'm the younger but because I'm going to the Church wiser sister' voice." Eleanor hated when Alyce talked in that superior fashion. Because she was almost always right.

Alyce took her hands. "Sometimes we can't have what we think we want. But then what we get is actually better. If you have faith, if you trust in God, perhaps what you must do can become what you truly want to do."

Tears of frustration and sadness welled in Eleanor's eyes. She kept her eyes open until a fat tear was ready to roll down her cheek. Then she blinked, sending the tear on its way.

What good timing.

Alyce smoothed back Eleanor's hair. "Ellie, please don't cry. I don't agree with you, but if this is what you think is best, you know I'll help."

Eleanor bit her lip to keep from smiling. A surge of guilt erased her satisfaction when Alyce's eyes also filled with tears.

"Promise me that for once you'll carefully consider all of the consequences," Alyce ordered. "What will happen if you fail? What if you succeed?"

"Stop fretting. 'Tis action that wins the day."

At least she hoped so, for she had no answers to Alyce's questions.

ॐ ॐ

"You don't have the satisfied smile a man should have the morn after his wedding. I saw the bloodied sheets," Blanche said, resting her hand on Richard's arm. "What could be amiss?"

She'd cornered him on his way to the great hall where guests gathered to break their fast. The clamor of conversation mixed with laughter.

He shook her hand free. "You've outstayed your purpose and your welcome."

"Does your unpleasant disposition this morning reflect on her?"

Richard wouldn't let her goad him, but she was right. He hated the emptiness he'd felt when he'd awoken and realized Eleanor wasn't beside him. He'd quell such feelings and reinforce the armor around his heart. No sense caring for a woman who didn't want him. No sense caring for a woman at all.

Keeping his voice low, he said, "I'll have the guards bar the gates should you visit any of our holdings." He raised his voice as they neared the tables. "Farewell, Lady Latimer. I bid you safe journey."

"Blanche, must you leave? I haven't had the chance to speak much with you. Or others deemed important enough to be guests at my wedding, unbeknownst to me."

Eleanor. She looked lovely in a high-waisted, green velvet gown with tight sleeves. A headdress with a turned back brim and sheer veil covered the thick blond hair he'd so enjoyed seeing and touching.

Could he tell her the whole truth about Blanche this soon? She didn't need another unpleasant surprise. Yet they'd agreed to be honest.

"Lady Latimer was just about to bid us farewell. It's time for us to move forward now that the festivities are over."

"I agree," Eleanor said. "And forging new friendships is one way to do that."

Blanche smiled one of her cat-has-got-the-cream-now smiles.

"Eleanor, I'd enjoy remaining at Middleworth for a day or two. My obligations can wait."

Arm in arm, the two women strolled into the hall, skirts swishing over the floor, leaving him to follow. Blanche's trilling laugh grated on his nerves.

She clearly wanted to work her way into Eleanor's affections and sought a means to remain close to him. What mischief was she up to?

If he told his new bride about his past, she'd likely wish to be rid of him all the sooner. But better that the news come from him than Blanche.

Later today, then, when he and Eleanor were alone.

🙚 🙘

"You left before I awoke," Richard began as he sat beside her. He spread butter on a thick slice of the costly manchet bread only served to those at the high table.

"I didn't want to disturb you," Eleanor said. "I needed to speak with my sister."

She didn't want to be reminded of how handsome Richard was, but couldn't help noticing. He wore a tunic of fine wool the color of leaves in the deep of the forest, which brought out the green in his eyes. Similar to the shade she'd chosen today. Did they like the same colors? Books? Anything? She wasn't sure she wanted to know.

Best she not find more reasons to esteem him before she obtained an annulment. If only she could stop wondering what their life together would be like.

"This cheese is delicious." He took a bite, then licked his lips.

Startled by the intriguing memory of his lips on hers, she turned to her own cheese.

"We don't know very much about each other," he continued.

Apparently they thought alike. A good quality to have in a spouse...that one planned to keep.

"How could we? We just met yesterday."

"True. So let's start with something simple. What are your favorite foods?" he asked.

"*Pain perdu* is one of my favorites, and anything fried in butter. I confess to a fondness for crystallized ginger."

"Ah, so you favor sweet stuffs."

"What do you like to eat?" The question was out of her mouth before she could call it back.

"Venison stew and roasted meatballs."

"Very well. I can have Cook prepare roasted meatballs for supper." Why was she trying to please him? What purpose would getting to know Richard serve? Best not to think of him and how nice it was to converse and think about something other than their awkward situation. Best to focus on her plan.

She worried her bread into a pile of crumbs as she assessed the female guests. Could the potential bride be right in front of her? Most of the women were already married, others wouldn't suit. Except perhaps for Blanche. The vibrant beauty seemed intelligent. Some men had openly admired her. Perhaps Richard would, too. Eleanor was glad Blanche was staying so she could learn more about her.

"I'd hoped today you'd give me a tour of Middleworth," Richard said. She couldn't escape the warmth of his gaze. "Then I thought we'd ride into the village so you could introduce me to the villagers."

He had, at least, said "hoped" and "thought," instead of issuing orders. Sometimes his tone reminded her of her father's, cold and distant. Yet a few minutes ago and last night, he'd sounded as if she were the most important person he knew. And she'd liked that.

How much time did he expect to spend with her? Getting to know him, sharing things, becoming friends could endanger her plan. But being ill-mannered or churlish wouldn't get him to agree to it, either.

"'Tis a fine day for a tour." True. "I'm sure the villagers would love to meet you, their new lord." Also true.

"I look forward to both events, and to spending the day with you," he replied.

Because he wanted to or because he had to? The answer shouldn't matter.

What did she want? Eleanor busied her mouth with a large

bite of cheese. She didn't have to bare her soul or convey every thought in her head, or feign emotions she didn't feel.

"I haven't spent much time in Northumberland. Is the North Sea coastline as beautiful as they say?" he asked.

"It is. I have happy memories of walking along the beaches with my mother." Her heart swelled. If she were still alive, what would she advise?

"We shall have to go, then."

"No. Yes," she blurted. "Yes, we shall." Would doing more things as a couple reinforce her wish to be free, or tie her to him all the more? If only she had more time to be sure.

Near the end of the meal, when naught remained but scraps too small for the almoner, a messenger wove his way through the crowded hall. Richard opened the sealed parchment and scanned the contents.

"I'm needed at court," he announced. "King Edward wishes me to join him at Windsor Castle."

Eleanor felt torn in two. She'd get to meet the king. And court would be the perfect place for her bride contest. Where else would so many eligible women gather? Perhaps Arthur would be there, too, trying to gain favor with the new king. Seeking information about how to pursue her annulment would also be easier.

But if she left, she couldn't interfere with her father's alchemy experiments. With its goals of transmuting base metal into gold, unlocking the secrets of Nature and immortality, she didn't understand how the king could support the sacrilegious "science."

First resolve my marriage, then deal with Father.

She breathed a sigh of relief when the messenger handed her father a similar parchment. He'd be going to court, too.

"The timing is unfortunate. I'd hoped we'd have time to get to know each other." Richard took her hand. His warm palm was unexpectedly satisfying. "I'll endeavor to conclude my business quickly. If you prefer, you may remain here with your sister instead of waiting for me at Glasmere Manor."

Would any man simply ask what a woman preferred? Wasn't she capable of knowing whether she wanted to travel with him or not? At least he'd offered her a choice again.

She didn't want to wait at his home, alone except for servants she didn't know. Nor did she want to stay here, for this no longer felt like home. A lump formed in her throat. Where did she belong?

"You intend to leave me behind," she said. "But I intend to go with you."

"Why?" His eyes narrowed. He didn't trust her.

"Why wouldn't I want to go to court? I haven't been in years. And didn't you tell our wedding guests, 'Let it not be said I would neglect or abandon my new wife. I will have you by my side?'"

"Your memory serves you well," he said with a nod. "But you said you'd remain at home. 'Tis best I go alone."

What could she say to make him agree to take her? The right words formed a lie. Thus far, she'd been painfully honest, whether he believed her or not. In the deep recesses of her mind, she heard her mother cautioning, "A single lie never fails to beget more."

The achievement of her goal was worth any means, because her plan worked to his benefit as much as hers.

"Your memory also serves. What if I've changed my mind?"

"What changed your mind in such a short span of time?"

The line between truth and deception was slim. She didn't want to cross it. She wouldn't break her promise to be honest, she couldn't lie. That didn't mean she wouldn't do her best to influence him.

"How long will you be away?" She pitched her voice low, as sultry as she could make it.

"A month, at least."

"Such a long reprieve," she whispered. She met his gaze boldly and traced a finger down his sleeve. "Longer than I expected without you to warm my bed."

The slight narrowing of his gray-green eyes told her he understood.

❧ ❧

The hum of conversation continued around them. Richard

saw only Eleanor, even more beautiful today then yesterday, when shock and dismay had paled her skin and dulled her violet eyes.

She wanted to go to court with him. Her not so subtle hint about their lack of consummation was unconvincing, however. The more sincere a woman seemed, the deeper the betrayal likely to follow. He'd allowed himself to be beguiled by Blanche and had learned caution from his mistake.

Mere hours ago Eleanor stood firm in her love for another. She couldn't have changed her mind, developed feelings for him so quickly. What was her ploy?

"Do you hope Arthur will be at court, too?"

"He's not my main concern," she replied. "As you've said, you and I are wed. We should be together." As she rested her hand on his sleeve, her wedding ring sparkled.

The first time she'd touched him of her own accord. He liked that.

"I don't believe you're going just to be with me."

"You're right. There is another reason. I can't stay here with my traitor father. This is no longer my home," she continued. "And since I haven't yet been to Glasmere, that isn't my home, either."

If she joined him, he could be escorting his wife to the man she said she loved. Not a pleasant prospect. Blanche would likely return to court as well. He didn't want Eleanor anywhere near her, either. Between his business with the king and his and Eleanor's former betrotheds, he'd have his hands full. And he'd have to postpone his search for his father's missing alchemy scrolls.

But he wanted his bride to get to know him better, and he had to well and truly consummate this marriage. Neither could occur if they were separated.

Which was least selfish, to bring her or leave her behind?

CHAPTER 5

"I can't go to court!" Alyce cried. "Now that you're finally wed, I am for the Church. 'Twasn't only your life affected by delays. Politics and war kept you from Arthur and me from following my path."

"Now who sounds like a spoiled child?" Eleanor demanded.

They walked to the small chapel where Alyce would spend the rest of the morning in prayer. Regular services weren't enough for her devout sister.

"Obviously you haven't made up your mind about what you truly want," Eleanor said. Morning sun set the sapphires on her ring aglow. She dropped her hands to her sides. "Remaining here was an excuse. You could've gone to the convent at any time and returned for a visit. You kept putting off your departure. Why?"

"I—"

"Your chamber reflects your interest in taking the veil, but your words and actions don't. Who did I catch eavesdropping on two of the maids last week as they engaged in frank discussion not meant for a maiden's ears?"

"You listened with me," Alyce said.

"I needed to know, as a woman about to become a wife. We have no mother or aunt to explain such things. But you, only this morning, wanted to hear about my wedding night." Eleanor could have kicked herself for bringing that up again. "This journey could help you make your decision. Going to court will give you a taste of the secular world. If you enjoy it overmuch, mayhap the life of a nun is not for you."

"It's what Mother wanted."

Their footsteps echoed on the stone floor of the chapel. Sun filtered through a round stained glass window of Mary and child, enhancing the quiet reverence.

"But is it what you want? What harm can a few more weeks do?"

"None, I suppose."

"You say marrying Richard is my duty. To whom do you owe yours?"

"God?"

"Ha. If you have to ask, mayhap you need to think on it a bit more."

Alyce tapped her fingers against her chin, which meant she was tempted.

"I can't do this without you," Eleanor admitted.

Her sister tilted her head back and closed her eyes, as if asking God to help her choose. "Since you need me, I will go."

Minutes later, she reached her—and now Richard's—room to change into her workaday gown to spend the afternoon tallying supplies. Eleanor paused in the doorway. Daylight poured through open windows on the wall opposite the bed, revealing Blanche on her knees beside one of Richard's chests.

"Blanche. What are you doing in here?" Eleanor was glad that her trunk filled with intimate goods had already been removed.

Blanche closed the lid and stood. "Richard borrowed something of mine long ago. I sought to learn if he still had it."

A weak response. Mistrust seeped through the walls of her new friendship. Had Blanche slipped anything up her wide sleeves? Eleanor caught of whiff of her perfume, sickly sweet as an overripe pear.

"Did he give you permission to enter our chamber?" A sudden streak of possessiveness made her emphasize "our."

"I didn't want to trouble him with a trivial matter."

"Let's ask Richard whether he has this item, instead of you prowling through his belongings."

"That won't be necessary. He's been busy, with the wedding and preparing to go to court," Blanche hedged.

She was hiding something.

Richard and Blanche's shared looks and subtle undertones and the way she constantly watched Richard had made Eleanor wonder what they'd been to each other. Not that she cared. 'Twas but natural curiosity as his present wife.

"I gather you've known Richard for some time," she began.

"Yes. 'Twas years ago," Blanche replied. "But he was very much in love with me." Her smug smile grated on Eleanor's nerves. "We were betrothed."

The remnants of her morning meal curdled in her stomach. Yet Richard hadn't seemed pleased when Eleanor invited her to stay on at Middleworth. Last night, their wedding night, he'd let her talk about Arthur, about wanting to end the marriage, without saying a word about Blanche. What if both bride and groom wanted to be with other people?

He'd remain married to her for the sole purpose of discharging his duty. To Eleanor, no obligation was worth a lifetime of suffering. Not after what had happened to her mother, Maud, and most other women she knew, forced through the sacrament of marriage to live with and bed a man they didn't want.

Why did women have to accept their fate so blindly? She would be different. She'd choose the man she spent the rest of her life with.

Thank goodness she'd taken matters into her own hands and thought of her bridal tournament. 'Twas the only way for both of them to be free.

"Yet you wed Lord Latimer," Eleanor said. The key protruded from the chest's lock. She turned it with a satisfying click, then put it in her pocket. "Why?"

"Why do most women marry? Because they must. As you did." Blanche took a breath as if she was about to say something else, then worried her lip between dainty teeth.

Eleanor's curiosity had taken on a life of its own. "And after your husband died? Did you and Richard still love each other?"

"By then Richard was too engrossed with the Duke of York's

death and Edward's struggles to gain the throne to consider marriage. As you'll learn, he lives to carry out his duty. After Edward became king, he made Richard an earl and commanded him to marry you," Blanche continued with a shrug. "Richard had no choice."

Why did those words burn hot as fire?

At least Blanche wouldn't travel with them to court. Eleanor would be spared days of wondering about hidden meanings behind every word or glance she and Richard exchanged. Not that it should make a difference to her what they said or did.

Richard meant nothing to her. Nothing at all.

Inspiration struck after Blanche left. If she and Richard once loved each other, perhaps their feelings could rekindle if Blanche was one of the potential brides.

That way, all four of them could end up with the spouses of their dreams.

🐝🐝

As she hurried back to her chamber, Blanche's heart sped faster than Thistle, her favorite mare she'd had to sell.

Caught by Eleanor searching Richard's things…what a disaster. She'd been so busy fuming over Richard's marriage she hadn't heard his new wife approach. Had Eleanor accepted her excuses?

Well, she'd tread with more care. And cultivate Eleanor's friendship so she'd have more reasons to see Richard. And find ways to win him and his father's alchemy secrets.

🐝🐝

"Here's my plan," Eleanor whispered to Alyce.

They sat in a corner of Middleworth's large solar, the deep blue silk gown Eleanor would wear to court spread across their laps. Each worked a needle with costly silver thread to form a glistening flower border along the hem. The same thread she'd used to embroider her and Arthur's initials. She wished she had gold, instead.

Richard and her father sat on a cushioned bench on the opposite side of the room, entrenched in conversation. Congratulating each other on their success at wedding her off, no doubt. They'd best not be plotting the best approach to extract quintessence, thought to be the fifth element after earth, fire, air and water.

Eleanor said, "You'll help choose six promising contenders from the available unwed ladies. You write faster and more neatly than I, so I'll rely on you to keep track of each lady's qualifications and progress."

She bade herself focus on her delicate stitchery, yet found herself looking at Richard. Why did he have to be so handsome? Why did his smile warm her heart?

"What if they don't want to participate? What if none of them wants to marry Richard…in general, or in particular because he's married to you?"

Eleanor forced her gaze from her husband to Alyce. "What woman wouldn't want to marry Richard? Except me, that is. And he won't be married to me for long. Alyce. I must tell you something. We haven't yet…consummated."

"What?" Alyce's squeal drew the attention of Richard and her father. "I thought—"

"All's well!" she called before lowering her voice. "I don't know how much longer I can hold him off." *Or how long I'll want to.*

"Are you sure you want to?" Alyce annoyingly echoed her thoughts. Her sister knew her far too well. "Eleanor, please, stop this foolishness." She set her needle aside. "How did you get Richard to agree to—never mind. You're letting what you think is your right to marry Arthur blind you to what must be."

Eleanor's needle paused. "I need time to plan. I can't feign illness, nor can I think of another way." She smoothed a stray thread from a shimmering flower.

"You can't choose a trail of deceit."

Eleanor raised her head in defiance. "It was chosen for me by our father and our king who attainted Arthur. I but follow in my own way. For the greater good."

Richard was looking at her. Her heart beat faster as he walked toward them.

He bowed and handed Eleanor an engraved leather pouch. "For you, my lady. This belonged to my father's mother. He would want my wife to have it."

Alyce gathered up the yards of silk as Eleanor took the pouch.

"My thanks." She lifted the flap. "Oh, my," she breathed as she pulled out the most stunning brooch she'd ever seen. Made of embossed gold, the heavy piece boasted nine large cabochon rubies.

"I hoped you'd like it. 'Your mouth provokes me, Kiss me, kiss sweet!' Each time I see you so it seems to me," Richard said.

A sweet frisson of delight shot through her. She couldn't help but remember the heat of his kiss, the surprising need he evoked. She felt herself blush.

"'Tis a quote by Charles d'Orleans," he added.

The thoughtfulness of his gift touched her. She couldn't dissemble in her thanks, no matter that she might encourage his pursuit. With a smile she couldn't suppress, she said, "This is the finest gift I have ever received. I refer to both the brooch and the quote."

Richard smiled back, clearly pleased. His eyes gleamed, now more green than gray, making him even more striking. "I shall see you anon." He bowed again and left the solar.

"Don't you see? You're the most fortunate of brides," Alyce said. "Your husband thinks to court you!" She smiled wistfully as she ran a finger over the rounded stones.

First the wide sapphire wedding band and now this. Two spectacular pieces of jewelry from Richard in as many days. She couldn't help but be flattered. Suddenly she wished she had something to give him in return.

"What are you doing for him?"

"The most thoughtful thing of all. Finding him a better bride."

"Hmm. I wonder what else he has planned," Alyce said. "Surely he doesn't think even a beautiful gift will sway you from Arthur."

"Exactly what I was thinking," Eleanor answered. She pinned it to her gown and admired the glow of the rubies.

In all their years of betrothal, Arthur had given her but two presents, both of which she had treasured: a pair of hawking gloves and a rather plain belt. Gifts didn't make the man. She was churlish to compare Richard and Arthur based on generosity.

She shouldn't compare them at all.

"You can't keep it, you know," Alyce said.

Instinctively her hand flew up to cover the brooch. "Why ever not? You saw Richard give it to me."

"And you heard him. He gave it to his wife. You'll have to give it to his new bride when you choose her," Alyce said matter-of-factly.

❧ ❧

That night, Eleanor stayed on her side of the bed as Richard packed. He'd removed his tunic, and moved about the room in his hose and shirt. The fabric clung to his broad shoulders as he added a few items to his baggage.

His sword leaned against the wall beside his chests, some of his clothes hung on her pegs next to her gowns. His presence dominated the space. The novelty of having a man share her room hadn't worn off. Nor had the trepidation of having to spend another night with Richard in her bed.

"Has Blanche mentioned that she was in our room earlier?"

Our room. How strange that sounded.

His head snapped up. "Blanche was in here?"

Eleanor relaxed, glad to have found a topic unrelated to their marriage. "I came upon her searching through one of your chests. She said you'd borrowed something long ago and she wanted it back."

"Did she say what?"

"No. I wondered if she was telling the truth. She behaved suspiciously, so I locked all of your chests and took the keys."

"Good. Be wary of her," he warned.

"Why?"

He sighed. "I hope the day will come when you do something simply because I say so. Be on your guard."

Getting information out of him was harder than pulling weeds from a parched garden.

"Blanche said you were betrothed. That you were in love with her." Just repeating the words set off a strange uneasiness.

Richard froze. "What of it?"

So Blanche had spoken true, in this at least. The thought of him caring deeply for another woman pierced deeper than it should have.

"Why didn't you marry her?" she asked. "Because the king didn't command you to? Or wasn't she high-born enough for a man with aspirations such as yours?"

"What makes you think that?" He flew across the room as if he had wings. Sparks of anger flashed in his eyes. "What else did she tell you?"

"That she had to marry Lord Latimer and you had to marry me."

"As usual, she left out crucial parts of her tale. Can any woman be trusted?" He sat on the bed, brushing against her because she was so near the edge. "I don't want to discuss Blanche."

Eleanor burned to know the whole truth. Had their love been tragic, like hers and Arthur's, kept apart against their will? Despite Richard's obvious reticence, he'd revealed a key fact: he didn't trust Blanche or women in general.

"I want to discuss us," he said, his voice low. He reached for her braid and unraveled it. His fingers combed through the strands, soothing yet sensual. "On second thought, I can think of better things to do than talk."

He kissed her, a multitude of feather light pecks. Then his mouth grew insistent, claiming hers.

The way he stroked her hair sent delicious shivers down her spine. His light, sweet kisses set her blood racing. Where would he venture next, what new sensations would he ignite?

His gaze held hers as his fingers roamed across her neck and over her shoulders, awakening the skin beneath. Her nipples peaked as he gently circled them.

Eleanor wanted more. She wanted him. Sudden need made her tremble.

He withdrew his hands. "You're shaking. What you said this morning as we broke our fast about me warming your bed...I thought you were ready."

Better for them both that he think she was nervous. She was, but not for that reason. Well, some of that, also. "I thought so, too. I'm sorry. I still need more time."

"How much more?" The warmth faded from his eyes.

Guilt lanced her. How could she utter the truth, yet mislead him at the same time? No wonder he thought women couldn't be trusted. But as she'd told Alyce, she was doing this for the greater good.

"Soon."

"We must do our duty. I'll give you until we arrive at court."

That wasn't long enough. She kept her thoughts to herself.

He turned his back to her and drew up the covers. In minutes his even breathing told her he was asleep, clearly not tormented by a racing mind as she was. Tonight the sound didn't soothe. Each inhale was a hiss of ire, each exhale an admonishment.

Hours later, Eleanor bit back a curse as she rubbed her calf to ease a sudden cramp. She'd crouched so long beneath the window outside her father's alchemy workshop that her limbs protested. Her shoes and the hem of her old gown were soaked from the evening's rains, clinging and uncomfortably clammy against her legs.

She peeked inside, fury stinging her veins as she took in two long, polished wood tables with an array of oddly shaped glass containers for distillation and other processes. Scattered about were pages and pages of notes covered with mysterious diagrams, symbols and elaborate drawings.

This was her last chance before they left for court to put an end to his experiments. Her father's obsession to find a way turn inexpensive base metals into gold came from the devil and would be his ruin, just as her mother had said.

He proved it by spending vast sums on tools and implements when the mania overtook him. The need to make himself the richest man alive, more powerful than the king, trounced reason.

He worked ceaselessly despite the late hour, first heating something that looked like salt over the fire in the raised hearth against the back wall, then pouring colored liquids from one flask into another, pausing to write every so often. Soot covered his apron.

When the fire dwindled and Eleanor's eyelids drooped, he yawned. Her father stacked the pages of notes and carried them toward the hearth. Her heart leapt with hope that he was giving up and would toss the pile of vellum in the fire. Instead, he set the pages at his feet. Her jaw dropped as he worked several stones free from the wall, placing each on the floor. He stuffed the notes into the hole he'd exposed, then returned each stone until the wall looked untouched.

Satisfaction revived her. Her persistence had been rewarded. She'd never have uncovered that hiding place on her own.

She ducked as Edmund de la Tour exited, locked the door and headed toward the castle. Obviously he didn't know another key hung on her key ring. From her mother.

She turned the key and slipped inside. Memories of her last visit flashed through her, when she'd searched for anything resembling a formula. Her goal had been destroy part of whatever she found to make him think he'd misplaced any missing pages. If she burned the lot, he might suspect her.

"What in God's name are you doing here?" He'd slammed the door. A glass jar had tumbled off the table and shattered, silvery liquid slithering into the dirt floor. "There go several hours, wasted."

Eleanor had shaken off remorse at being discovered. "You promised Mother you'd stop this foolishness!"

"She's no longer here to protest. Leave me to my work." He picked up kindling from a basket and carried it to the hearth.

"I speak in her stead. Do you even have a license?"

He didn't answer.

"I thought not. Why do you refuse to see that the quest to turn base metals into gold can only bring ruin to all involved? Men have killed and will again to gain the secret for themselves."

He looked up from his notes. "You're but a woman. What can you know of men's ways? Whoever is the first to bring the true formula to the king will be rewarded beyond belief. And will know he has achieved a miracle."

"Or be murdered to prevent him from creating endless amounts of gold for himself."

Her father's eyes glowed, so lost was he in his reveries. "That man's fame will live forever. That is what I seek, a legacy."

Eleanor shivered, remembering. Driven by greed, her father would work himself to death if she didn't stop him.

It could take years to recreate any work she destroyed. He'd be furious, especially if he figured out she was the culprit, but any guilt would be mitigated by his betrayal of her, the need to fulfill her mother's last wish and the belief that she was doing the right thing for him and her family.

The dying fire shed just enough light. Standing on her toes to reach the stones, she grasped the first one her father had removed. She tugged 'til her fingers were raw, but it didn't budge. To gain better purchase, she dragged a bench to the wall.

"Let me help you."

She jumped at the sound of Richard's voice. Her hands dropped to her sides.

He stood in the doorway, one arm raised as he leaned against the frame. The fading fire emphasized his high cheekbones and deep-set eyes.

Her heart thudded painfully. Had he seen her reach for the hiding place? Had she made matters worse by revealing the location of her father's work, so Richard could claim it for Edward?

"What are you doing here?" she demanded, sounding oddly like her father.

CHAPTER 6

"I could ask the same of you," Richard said.

Eleanor quickly masked her surprise and sat gracefully on the bench he'd watched her drag to the hearth.

"I awoke to find you gone," he said. "Again. As I searched for you, I saw your father heading toward the castle from this direction. And spotted your footprints."

What luck. Eleanor's midnight wanderings had led him to the very place he sought, saving him hours of fruitless searching.

He closed the door behind him. The dimly lit workshop was so similar to his father's, bittersweet memories of working by his side flashed through his mind. But of course it would be similar, with its numerous alembics—glass vessels required for distillation—since his father and Eleanor's had been partners. Disagreement over the best ways to proceed, over who owned the work accomplished thus far, forced them to go their separate ways.

Mere months later, his father and his new partner were murdered. Two of his many scrolls of notes disappeared. Richard suspected Edmund de la Tour, but neither he nor the authorities had uncovered any proof. But he'd never been granted access to Edmund's workshop.

Until now. The proof he needed, had sought for years, could be in this very room. He itched to pull those stones free to learn what they concealed.

"What brings you here?" he asked.

She shrugged. "I needed peace. Our healer once lived in this cottage. As a girl I visited often."

That sounded plausible, but the way she cast her eyes down told him there was another reason.

"So your father still plays at alchemy," he said, eager to hear what she knew of her father's activities, past and present.

"More like pursues with a vengeance."

"Is he near success?" Richard's heartbeat sped. Was her father benefiting from his father's labors or his own?

"I don't know. 'Twas only recently I learned he'd returned to this workshop."

Richard wanted to be the first to provide King Edward with the means to obtain much needed wealth to fund his new kingdom, if doing so were possible. He needed to give meaning to his father's years of work. First he had to find the missing scrolls to see if his father had in fact succeeded.

His wife stood in his way. If he didn't search the cottage now, he wouldn't have another chance until they returned from court. Who knew when that would be?

He lit and held up a candle. Eleanor's unbound hair gleamed golden as the light passed over her. He had a sudden urge to take her in his arms, to start his seduction anew.

"Your father was also an alchemist," Eleanor said, her face unreadable. "My father told me. And I know you seek his formulas for the king."

Did she know they'd been partners, that her father had betrayed his? "No one knows when Edward's alchemists will come up with the mix of ingredients needed to complete the process of transmutation," he said.

"The philosopher's stone." Disgust laced her voice.

"And there's also *elixir vitae*, the elixir of life." He couldn't keep excitement from his. "Such discoveries could change the world. Not only could we turn base metals to gold, wondrous enough on its own, but prolong life. Science and medicine melded for the good of all."

She jumped to her feet. "It's heresy."

Unfortunate that their views on such an important aspect of his life were so far apart. "Do you believe in Communion?"

"I see what you're trying to do. That's religion, a ritual passed down through the ages. Faith. Not the same at all."

Arguing would get him nowhere. "What do you know of your father's experiments?"

"Not much. He wouldn't tell me when I asked." A shadow seemed to pass over her. "The hour is late. Perhaps we should return to our room."

He bit back frustration. He'd get nothing from her this night. Not information, not consummation. "You're right, Eleanor. This place is peaceful. I'll stay for the nonce."

Richard moved to the bench, close enough to inhale her sweet lemon scent, and sat.

"Then we shall share the peace," she said, sitting beside him. "While we can."

She wasn't going to leave him alone in her father's workshop. He'd have to find a way to borrow her key.

He smiled. "Let us share that and more."

ॐ ॐ

Richard's smile was so compelling Eleanor was nearly tempted to stay. But she had to get him out of here. Out of her way.

He seemed uncommonly interested in her father's workshop. His gaze had probed every shelf crammed with books, every nook and cranny. Did he want to know if her father was farther along than his had been, or did he seek something specific? She hadn't mistaken the gleam in his eye nor his determination when questioning her. Had the mania attacked Richard also, driving him to steal her father's knowledge?

Fortunately it didn't matter if he himself played at melting base metals, for she'd not be wed to him for long.

"I'd leave you to your peace and seek mine elsewhere, but I must lock the door," Eleanor said.

"So your father won't know you were here? I'll do it. Give me the key."

Richard did want something. If she gave him the key, he might press it in wax to fashion his own for later use.

He stood, then leaned back against the wall and crossed one leg over the other, but she sensed tension beneath his nonchalance as he held out his hand.

As far as she could tell, everything of value lurked behind the stones. Clever though Richard was, she doubted even he'd find the hiding place. Unless he'd seen her pull on the stone.

Did he approve of the quest, or was he just following orders? She dared not ask. Like as not he wouldn't answer, for there was no trust between them. Nor did she want to reveal her own hand. In any case, his goal was pursuit of the transmutation formula.

"A good chatelaine keeps her keys close," she said, indicating the chain dangling from her waist.

In an instant he was off the bench and had her pressed to the wall. "Was that an invitation for me to try to take them from you?"

"No." She couldn't get out another word with his hard body against hers.

Sliding slowly down her arm, his hand left a tingling path. His fingers closed around her wrist, his mouth inches from hers. She tightened her grip on the keys as he moved his fingers in a gentle circle over her shoulders, again and again, stroking her, lulling her.

Slowly, he lowered his head to kiss her. She was appalled to find she wanted him to. Eleanor broke away before he could wreak more havoc on her senses, the wool of her gown sticking briefly to the stone wall.

"You've already proved you're stronger than I. But you won't control me, I'll see to that." She marched to the door and swung it open, exasperated by her response to him and her failure to destroy her father's notes. "If you want me to be ready to travel this morning, we'd best prepare."

"'Tis obvious you're trying to get me away from this cottage. It suits my purpose to go with you. Never fear, I'll find out what's in this place and what it really means to you."

She'd alerted Richard's suspicions, as he'd alerted hers. There was no way she'd escape his vigilance to return to the cottage before they left for court.

But then, he'd not escape hers either.

๛ ๛

'Twas two days into their journey to Windsor. The horses plodded along the road, keeping pace with carts laden with bedding, clothing and supplies. At this rate, combined with frequent stops, the trip from Northumberland to Berkshire would take weeks instead of days. Though she chafed at the delay and was unaccustomed to long hours in the saddle, Eleanor couldn't help but appreciate the respite from her worries.

She wouldn't let her father's watchful, disapproving eye affect her, and did her best to avoid and ignore him. There was nothing left to say.

Thank goodness she and Richard were rarely alone. Due to the scarcity of rooms at inns along their route, she shared with her maid Mary and Alyce, while Richard stayed with his squire, Reginald.

That didn't stop Richard from finding dozens of ways to torment her. Like when he'd hold her hand—so she didn't trip on rough ground. But his warmth and strength made her less steady than she was on her own.

He was proving to be the most eminently attractive yet disconcerting man she'd ever met. As he rode beside her, more than once her gaze strayed to his mouth, remembering his kisses and wishing he would try to kiss her again. Wishing....

She held her head high, as if enjoying the afternoon sun's warmth and the lovely setting. In the space of a week she'd been wed to a man not of her choosing and wrenched from the comforting safety of what she'd once called home. Home, where she'd been queen of her domain and few dared say nay to her. Now she was under her husband's thumb.

At court she'd be a newcomer, with no authority despite being a countess. She'd have to share a chamber with Richard again, surely the most frightening prospect of all. The solution was to organize her bridal tournament posthaste.

"We shall rest the horses here," Richard called out.

No, not again. She couldn't bear any more of his "rests." "Surely we're not far from the next inn?"

Richard bestowed one of his slow smiles upon her, the kind that set her insides to melting fast as butter in a hot pan.

Why did he inspire her desire? Why did she yearn to see Richard again as soon as he left her sight? She shuddered. If this was how really caring for someone felt, she didn't like it. She'd never felt this way about Arthur. For the first time, she wondered if she truly loved him.

Of course she did. Not missing him constantly was her way of handling his lengthy departures.

The group stopped beside a sparkling stream. Water splashed as it flowed over the rocky bed. Bright yellow gorse dotted green, rolling meadows.

Richard reached up to lift her from Saffron. She tensed, knowing he'd slide her against him as he did every time he helped her dismount. His hands closed about her waist, followed by a brief sensation of weightlessness as he plucked her from the saddle, then came the slow, intimate descent while his green-eyed gaze held hers. He smelled clean and fresh despite their long hours on the road. The feel of his hard body unsettled her yet again.

"Do you hunger?" he whispered.

Not for food. "No."

His closeness made her uneasy. Choosing that moment to rumble, her stomach defied her.

He laughed. She wished the sound didn't please her.

"Come then, I have sweetmeats in my pack." He grabbed her hand, leaving her little choice but to follow.

The horses drank from the stream and nibbled on greenery while the eight men accompanying them reclined on the ground nearby, some eating, some resting.

Richard settled a short distance from the others on a flat rock surrounded by waving grasses. He seemed perfectly at ease. In a russet tunic, tight brown hose revealing powerful thighs, a hardy traveler replaced the elegant lord. He stretched, arm muscles flexing, broad chest expanding. He watched her with a slight smile, making her suspect this display of maleness was solely for her benefit.

Eleanor remained standing. Being near Richard weakened her resolve.

"Alyce," she called. "Come join us."

"We'll sup alone," Richard said softly.

Not if she could help it. But Alyce chatted gaily with Richard's squire, clearly without concern for her sister's welfare. Eleanor opened her mouth to call again.

"If Alyce shares our meal, there won't be enough food for you," he said.

She seethed. Richard couched orders in kindness. She glared, but he munched on an apple as if he didn't have a care in the world.

To eat or not to eat, that was the question. Give in to Richard, or preserve her dignity. Dignity prevailed over her growling stomach. She'd starve before she let him win, before she let any man order her around like she was a witless fool. She stepped away.

Two steps later, a tug on her skirts jerked her to a sudden stop.

"Sit, dear wife." His voice was deceptively pleasant.

Eleanor twisted. The expression on Richard's handsome face was full of challenge. He released her skirts and with a wave of his hand indicated the spot beside him.

She sat across from him, but he smoothly shifted his large frame until they were so close their thighs seemed as one. His heat burned through her clothing.

He displayed a piece of crystallized ginger between his thumb and forefinger. "Here."

He'd remembered their conversation about favorite foods. Was he being thoughtful or trying to tempt her into liking him? She reached for the sweet, but he pulled back.

"Open," he said as he leaned forward.

She held out her hand.

"Your mouth," he whispered so near her ear the warmth of his breath tickled.

Her mouth dropped open in surprise. He popped the sugared date between her lips.

She bit his finger.

He yanked his hand back. Then he smiled, the most seductive smile she'd ever seen. A shiver raced up her spine.

"Ah, a most agreeable form of love play, my sweet. Are you so eager to eat me up?"

Eleanor snatched another comfit from his pack and ate it. "No, I hunger only for your food." She sat up straighter, peering over the grasses. If only Alyce would look her way.

Richard's finger brushed her cheek. Her hand hastened to cover the spot.

"You had some sugar near your mouth," he said.

After they'd eaten, Richard raised his hand, catching his squire Reginald's attention. The lanky blond lad jumped to his feet, ran to one of the carts and pulled something out.

The youth returned with a lute. Richard accepted the instrument and a small piece of quill for plucking the strings. After strumming a few chords, he launched into a song.

What new torture was this?

"Le souvenir de vous me tue,

Mon suel bien, quant je ne vous voy.

Car je vous jure sur ma foy,

Sans vous ma liesse est perdue."

She translated the French as he sang the sweet melody, "The memory of you kills me, my only love, when I cannot see you. For I swear to you by my faith, without you my joy is gone."

Her chest tightened as his long fingers moved over the strings. His rugged face seemed softer as his soothing bass caressed words meant only for her. The final phrase faded into the warm breeze.

She couldn't look away.

He began another song. The familiar tune seemed strangely fitting here, accompanied by: the grasses' soft chorus and subtle beat of the rushing water.

"Sing with me," he said.

Her throat felt suddenly hoarse. She feared the joy of their voices blending, her heart warming toward him further....

She'd already given into him more than she'd planned by sharing meals as they traveled. Allowing him to ply her with tender morsels and engage her in witty conversation. What would he want next? Thank goodness he didn't know she played the harp, the perfect instrument to complement his lute.

How else would he seek to control her? "Open," when he wished her to eat. "Sing" when he desired a tune. Surely "Spread," as in "Spread your thighs," would be next.

Never. Not for this man, no matter how handsome, how appealing. Richard didn't fool her. He sought to control her, so arrogant he thought persistent wooing would win the day.

"Do you truly believe my weak, feminine sensibilities would make me yield after a few sweet songs and treats? Ha."

He smiled knowingly. "You know you enjoyed them."

Alyce often said God tested people to prove their faith or devotion to a cause. Clearly Richard was her test. Could Eleanor remain devoted to Arthur despite Richard's temptations?

Soon they'd be at court with the king, where she could inquire about the steps she'd need to take with the church court. Where she could find Richard another bride.

She wouldn't let him affect her. She wouldn't fail.

※§ §※

Richard set aside the lute, well satisfied by the meal, the fine day and his progress with Eleanor. As he'd hoped, courting seemed to be the key to winning his wife. She'd eaten from his hand. She'd swayed with the music's rhythm and even smiled, proving his songs had weakened her resistance. At one point he thought she might swoon at the loving words he spoke.

Was it fair to entice her to succumb? Once he'd fallen victim to words such as those.

He'd made the hugest mistake of his life more than ten years ago when he was but a knight with limited hope of rising higher. He had fallen in love. With Blanche, then Blanche Fastolf, daughter of parents of modest means, and asked her to marry him. She'd professed her feelings for him. They set a date for their wedding. He'd been happy.

Until the night his dreams were crushed. Before returning to his chamber after a meeting with his overlord, he'd passed Blanche's room. Her door had been slightly ajar.

He'd heard laughter, her laughter. "Kiss me, John."

John? His heart had all but stopped. Blanche, bedding another man, mere days after plighting her troth to him.

Betrayed by his betrothed. The pain had been worse than when an enemy's sword slashed his calf during a battle. He'd learned that enemies lurked even in the guise of lovers.

He'd surged forward, but Blanche's next words halted him.

"Yes, John, I will wed with you." Another laugh, sultry. "I was meant to be the wife of a nobleman. My children need to be born of noble blood."

That instant, his heart had closed. A portcullis slammed down, the iron gate locking his emotions inside as securely as it kept in a castle's inhabitants. The harsh ache of Blanche's betrayal had diminished with time, but the concern over not being worthy remained. Now he was a powerful, wealthy earl. No one would deny him. Especially not his wife.

Richard would practice his wiles, learned from a master, on Eleanor. But, wise to their effect, he'd remain aloof.

His beautiful wife sat quietly, for once, at his side. How delectable she'd looked with the dusting of sugar on her cheek. How he'd yearned to taste the sweetness of her skin.

Desire for her was safe and natural. Caring for her could prove more dangerous than facing a battlefield with the enemy in full armor.

He didn't need to love Eleanor to fulfill his duty.

CHAPTER 7

Eleanor couldn't wait to reach Windsor Castle so Richard could attend the king. Having him near from dawn 'til sunset, then hours of fitful sleep by his side, exhausted her. Because she constantly battled the part of her that wanted to accede to his wooing. But the goal she fought for was worth the effort.

At an inn the night before they reached Edward's court, all savored a delicious meal of blawmanger with rice and chicken. Laughing travelers cozily crowded the place, creating a friendly and welcoming mood. Alyce, worn out by the excitement of the journey, nearly dozed in her bowl. Mary took her off to bed.

"The air is pleasant," Richard said. "Will you walk with me?"

Yes. No. Eleanor didn't trust herself to be alone with him. All she had to do was say she was tired. But she wasn't. Despite her earlier need to be free of him, she didn't know how many more opportunities she'd have to share his company. At court Richard would be surrounded by desirable prospective brides. Anticipation and reluctance vied within as they went outside. She'd revel in these few minutes.

The hush of the moonlit night contrasted with the patrons' boisterous conversations. The scent of spring flowers floated on a refreshing breeze, mingling with familiar smells of the nearby stable.

He led her to a small bench, his hand on the small of her back. She stiffened, leery of his intentions.

❦ ❦

As he put his arm around her, Richard caught a whiff of her lemony scent. Another woman would likely guess his intent or have one of her own, but Eleanor didn't react to his touch. She didn't even look at him. He put a finger under her chin and gently turned her head.

Their gazes met, sending a flicker of desire through him.

"Eleanor, over the past few days you and I have had the chance—"

She rose and walked to a flowerbed. "I'm looking forward to meeting the king, though the prospect makes me a little nervous." Eleanor picked a rose and sniffed it. "Out of my element."

He wasn't fooled. She hadn't left him on the bench because she had a sudden need to pick a flower. Nor did "out of her element" refer only to meeting the king. Being alone with him made her uncomfortable.

"I have another confession to make. Isolated as I was at Middleworth, I haven't paid much attention to recent changes in our land," she said. "How can Edward even be king? The former king, Henry VI, has a son to inherit his throne."

He sighed. Eleanor tweaked his vanity and made a mockery of his prior successes with women. He knew he'd seen glimmers of attraction in her eyes during the past few days, as if she wondered what it would be like to relinquish her staunch devotion to Arthur and give life with her husband a chance. She had seemed to enjoy, even anticipate his touch and their time together. Given this romantic setting, the semi-privacy of a moonlit garden on a pleasant evening, he was sure no woman but his reluctant wife would choose the most unromantic topic possible.

Unwittingly she had raised the stakes. How would he find a way to entice her while discussing politics?

"The situation is somewhat confusing," he began. "Ordinarily Henry's son would have succeeded him. In this case, the question of who should rule depends on whose reasoning you accept. The Act of Accord in 1460 made the Duke of York and his sons successors to the throne and displaced Henry's son."

"How can men make laws as to who should be king? How could they disinherit an anointed king's son, a prince of the realm?"

Richard rose and stood behind her. He clasped his arms around her, enjoying the way she fit against him. He wanted to kiss the side of her neck but instead spoke softly into her ear.

"York believes Henry VI and the other Lancastrian kings before him usurped the throne from the true Yorkist heirs," he began.

Eleanor turned to face him, then stepped back. When he loosened his hold to accommodate her, she moved to the other side of the narrow flowerbed.

Advance and retreat.

"King Edward is descended from sons of Edward III on both his father's side and his mother's." He rounded the flowerbed. "By this logic, Henry VI has a lesser claim to the throne, being a descendant of a younger son of Edward III than York. EIV, 5Thus, York believes his line should resume its lawful and rightful place. York convinced the lords this was true, hence the Act of Accord."(ross, wotr 49)

The intent way she looked at him, the slight flick of her tongue as she moistened her lips, her delicate scent, aroused him. Made him want to kiss her and more. She made even politics exciting, all while he was supposed to be enticing her.

Consummation could wait no longer. He'd desired her from the first. As he came to know her, he wanted her all the more. He admired her defiance and pride, which made her more attractive to him.

His attempts at chivalrous courting had made inroads, but he still sensed reluctant resistance. As if she desired him but wasn't sure she wanted to. He would make her sure. He would make her forget Arthur.

He'd been uncharacteristically lenient, allowing her time to adjust to their "situation" as she called it. But they were married, there'd be no annulment. She had to learn that a union with him could be quite pleasant. He could think of only one way to teach her. Of only one way to imprint himself upon her and make her forget all other men.

Slowly, letting her see the desire he refused to hide any longer, he walked toward her.

She backed away, matching him step for step. The waist-high garden wall stopped her retreat. Their gazes locked, hers defiant, his intentionally determined. He'd never do anything she didn't want him to do. He had to make her see that she did want this, as much as he did.

"The Act of Accord," she repeated softly. "So what becomes of Henry and his son?"

Still he moved forward until their bodies pressed against each other. She didn't move, didn't push him away. As if she waited to see how far he would go. He lifted her onto a low ledge. Her hips were now flush with his. Their breaths mingled. He felt the rhythmic rise and fall of her chest.

"And what of Henry's queen, Margaret of Anjou?" Her voice faded to a whisper.

He took a deep breath to quell his need. Wanting her had taught him patience.

"Henry and his son, Edward, still hope to regain the throne. The former queen gathers support for Henry's cause," he whispered into her ear.

He kissed her neck, then the delicate skin behind her ear. At last. She tasted better than their meal. He moved his hips in a circle. Again and again. Three tiny, gentle rotations against her and he was hard. Her slight gasp revealed that she sensed the change in him, even through their layers of clothing.

"Wh-why are you doing this?"

"You wanted to know how Edward could be king," he said, placing another gentle kiss on her neck. By the saints she smelled good, more pleasing than the rose garden surrounding them.

"I meant—"

"Sssh."

Eleanor drew in a breath and leaned against the wall. Her eyes widened. "I think...."

"Don't think." He kissed her neck again. "Feel." Another

lingering kiss, then he made his way toward her mouth. "Feel me. Us."

His hips continued their slow movements. He wouldn't be able to take much more of this. To secure her consent, he needed to arouse her gently. To allow her sensuality time to blossom.

With great care, as if she'd crumble to dust if he moved too quickly, he linked his fingers with hers. She didn't object. He lowered his head, stopping when their mouths were mere inches apart. Her lips parted.

Yes, he thought, just so.

Eleanor was his wife. He had the right to kiss her, and much more. Only to earn her trust would he go to such lengths to woo her.

Slowly, so slowly, he bent closer. He paused a hairsbreadth before their lips met, waiting. Then he kissed her, a careful, light touch to test her willingness, though he burned to possess her.

"Richard," she whispered.

He kissed her again. Deeper this time, a true kiss. Need seared him as she clutched his shoulders. He pulled back slightly, afraid she was pushing him away, rejecting him again. But she drew him down to her, violet eyes gleaming with desire.

"More."

The single word promised victory. His heart leapt.

She kissed him back, matching his intensity. He slid his tongue into her mouth and felt her lean into him. The thrill of her response added to his. Desire soared as their mouths fused, tongues teasing, hands roaming.

Staggered by the passion igniting between them, he broke away. They stared at each other, breathing hard. Her lips were slightly parted, rosy from his kisses. Inviting.

His groin pounded, demanding release. But their first joining couldn't be in a public, albeit secluded, place. He took her hand, determined not lose this opportunity...but where to go? Not the woods, not the stables, nor their shared rooms.

"Well, what a coincidence."

Arthur. Richard's desire melted faster than snow tossed on a fire.

Eleanor pulled away, obviously embarrassed. Embarrassed by

being caught in her husband's arms by her former betrothed.

A fine stew. His gut churned.

"On your way to see the king, I presume, as am I." Arthur's face was placid, his voice welcoming rather than sarcastic. Did he still want Eleanor, or did he accept his new lot in life?

"Arthur," she said.

Eleanor looked at Arthur, then at him. She seemed uncertain how to proceed.

"The two of you seem to be faring well," Arthur said. "I can only hope my marriage yields such success."

What did Eleanor see in him? Obviously wealth and position meant little to his wife. Arthur had neither. Did she prefer blond hair and an angelic face to his darker, less refined features? The former earl was the precise vision of a chivalrous knight from a romance, while he looked the hardened warrior. Women had oft praised his features and form, but what if he wasn't to her taste?

He wished he didn't care.

"What brings you to court?" Eleanor asked. He was pleased that her face revealed curiosity, nothing more.

"I hope to curry Edward's favor," Arthur replied. "To prove I no longer support the Lancastrians."

Perhaps he spoke true. Or perhaps the man endeavored to follow Eleanor. To steal her away.

"A worthy goal," she said.

Richard had a sudden urge to prove his worth, to please his wife. Despite their hasty nuptials, despite the fact that he needed her lands and funds and that marriage to her fulfilled his duty, it wasn't enough to know she had to stay with him.

What idiotic vanity was this, to want his wife to admire him, to want to stay with him? He was naught but a weak fool, returning to the road he'd traveled long ago and vowed never to revisit.

"I wish you success," Eleanor added.

His love for Blanche had commenced just this way. With him hoping and endeavoring to please her. With him caring what she wanted. Just like Blanche, Eleanor wanted another man to succeed.

Of its own accord, the portcullis guarding his heart had lifted ever so slightly as his interest in Eleanor grew. He slammed the heavy gate back into place and added another lock.

Arthur and Eleanor stared at each other. She'd never looked at him, Richard, quite that way. He burned to know what they were thinking.

As the moment stretched, awkwardness increased. How to break the spell that seemed to hold them all immobile? A horse whinnied, as if echoing his discomfort.

Would Eleanor ever stop loving her erstwhile betrothed? Would he and Arthur ever regain their easy friendship?

"I've sent for Margaret," Richard announced. "She should be joining us at court within the week."

Arthur nodded, but his expression didn't change. Eleanor looked at the blossom still in her grasp as if each petal held its own unique fascination. A breeze brushed the flowers at his feet.

Perhaps that hadn't been the best subject to raise. If anything, the mood grew more strained.

"It's late, and we need to get an early start on the morrow." He held out his hand.

For an instant he feared she wouldn't take it. Worse, he thought she might request a moment alone with Arthur.

Eleanor took his hand, but handed Arthur the flower.

A gesture of friendship, or something more?

❧❦ ❦❧

Could there be a more awkward set of circumstances? Eleanor's fingers trembled as she lit a candle.

"Arthur is here," she told Alyce, who'd awoken when she entered their small, but surprisingly clean, room. "He found me kissing Richard in the garden."

Richard's kisses had enthralled her, weaving her in a content spell of desire. He'd been a panther stalking his mate, sleek and purposeful. Powerful. Her body had burned to explore the sensations he aroused. To learn what came after kissing.

Until Arthur arrived.

Alyce sat up, her silvery hair glistening in the candlelight. "What happened?"

Eleanor set the candle on the only table and removed the veil from her new hat with a flat crown. "I stood between the two of them, wondering if each was going to grab an arm and pull."

Even as guilt tore her apart. Wanting to make love with Richard made her disloyal to Arthur. The strain on Richard's face as he glared at Arthur provoked additional guilt that she hadn't done her duty and consummated their marriage.

"And before that you were kissing Richard," Alyce said. "Did you enjoy it?"

Eleanor sighed. "I did," she whispered.

"Hmm. Eleanor, which man do you really want?"

She wasn't sure how to answer that question.

CHAPTER 8

The king gave the council a reprieve while he shared a private meal with his queen, Elizabeth, so Richard decided to find his wife and do the same. Finding her in the vast castle took some doing, but his efforts were rewarded in the moat garden beneath the central tower.

She sat on a bench amidst clumps of white-flowered bushes. A dozen or so children sat on pillows in front of her, rapt expressions on their young faces. Several adults stood nearby.

"And the dragon's red eyes gleamed in anger," Eleanor said. The sun sparkled off her wedding band as she raised her hands. "He reared back and drew in a huge breath—can you show me what that would sound like?"

All of the children drew in huge, loud breaths. He hid a laugh behind his hand.

"Yes, just so," Eleanor said with a smile. "Well, the dragon was just about to breathe fire on the maiden Meridwen. His green scales glinted in the firelight as she struggled against her bonds, fearing the end was near."

What a pleasant surprise. His wife was an expert story teller.

"'Help, help!' the maiden cried, though she knew no one could hear. Suddenly a knight appeared at the entrance to the dragon's lair. A golden light surround him, making his armor shine. He drew his sword—" Eleanor stopped. Her smile widened. She'd seen him. "Oh, look! Here's the brave knight now. Richard, come join us."

The children turned. Some gasped with glee. One little girl hid behind a larger one.

A dark-haired boy stood and bowed. "Please help us save Maid Meridwen from the dragon, Sir Knight."

Eleanor's eyes twinkled with obvious delight. "Oh, yes. Please do."

The last time he'd played with children he'd been one himself. Could he relax enough to participate? He didn't want to disappoint Eleanor. What he did want was to share this with her. Richard drew an imaginary sword with great flourish, and raised it high. "Maid Meridwen, I shall rescue you!"

Eleanor rose, putting her hands behind her back as if she were tied to a stake. "Oh, thank you, most generous knight."

Richard addressed a bush. "Dragon, I shall defeat you!" He swiped the air, back and forth. "Victory is mine!" He sheathed his sword as he ran to Eleanor and swooped her into his arms.

"My hero," she cried.

The children laughed and applauded.

Richard laughed, too. When had he had this much fun?

Suddenly he saw himself and Eleanor at Middleworth with three children, two with dark hair and one with blond. Theirs? Longing pierced him.

With his wife smiling up at him from the comfort of his arms, anything was possible.

🐝🐝 🐝🐝

"Your Grace," Eleanor said with a graceful curtsy despite a smile that wavered. Her ceaseless chatter as they made their way to the king's private apartments in the Upper Ward had conveyed her nervousness. "It's an honor to meet you."

The skirts of her pale blue gown with its long train pooled on the tiled floor. She'd only looked lovelier alone with him. In their bed, with her hair down....

A mixture of pride and confusion swept him as the king, in a short tunic with jeweled chains across the chest and black hat, raised her. Her tall headdress almost poked Richard in the eye.

Edward bent over her hand and did her the additional honor

of kissing it. "A pleasure to meet you, Countess. I hope you enjoy your time with Us at court, though I'll be keeping your husband busy. I'm certain you'll find many friends among the ladies." He dropped her hand. "What news, Richard? Have you found your father's scrolls?"

Eleanor's smile instantly became a frown. Her gold and pearl necklace caught the light as she folded her arms.

What was this? Richard hadn't expected Edward to bring up alchemy while meeting Eleanor. He felt torn in two. Do his duty to his king, or prevaricate to avoid Eleanor's distaste for the subject? "I...."

"Ripley wrote that he's working on another treatise...this one based on the search for the philosopher's stone," Edward said. "I'm eager to learn of his latest experiments."

George Ripley, a prolific alchemist. The Wheel, his drawing of the planets corresponding to essential alchemical elements, had sparked much dialogue in the alchemy community.

He had to say something. "I look forward to reading his treatise."

His wife's frown morphed into a full glower, but mercifully she held her tongue.

Edward pulled a scroll from a pile on his desk and unrolled it. "I've been wanting to show you this alchemical table depicted as a genealogy, drawn by one of my alchemists. Do you see how he traces the path from souls of kings to the elements?"

Eleanor drew in a breath.

He continued, "Ingenious, though I'm not sure how this furthers the quest. It seems more a paen to curry my favor." The king perused the scroll covered with rows of circles connected by lines and decorated with an elaborate sun and moon. "The possibilities of new scientific developments are unlimited."

A thrill ran through Richard. So true. If he shared his enthusiasm with the king, he'd give Eleanor more fodder for her dissatisfaction with their marriage. If he didn't, he'd be disingenuous and fail to serve to his best ability, and would disappoint himself.

"Fascinating." Richard took a step closer to the beautiful,

complex image. "I think this illuminates the relationship of your lineage to the ultimate success of the alchemical process."

"Hmm. Yes. I think we're getting closer. Finally," Edward said with a smile. "I'll have the true recipe soon. Lady Eleanor, what do you think?"

"'Tis a wonderful drawing, Your Grace. Such delicate details reflect remarkable talent." His wife pursed her lips, as if keeping the words she really wanted to say in her mouth.

The king's smile faded as he rolled up the drawing. "Quite the politic reply. I know your father and Richard's were partners. What do you know of Edmund's work?"

She sent Richard a pleading glance.

He wished he could help and sympathized with her obvious struggle. She didn't want to disparage alchemy to the king's face, but didn't want to lie, either. Why hadn't he thought Edward wanted to meet Eleanor to learn what she knew, not merely because she'd newly wed a noble on his privy council?

Eleanor had to tip her head back to look at Edward, several inches taller than Richard himself. She opened her mouth, then closed it again.

The awkward silence stretched. He knew she wanted to say something like, "My father wouldn't even tell me I couldn't marry my betrothed. Why would he tell me about his alchemy?" Or, "My father is obsessed with the 'science' I think is heresy."

"Your Grace. My father didn't share his pursuit of alchemy with me." Her lovely face didn't convey a hint of her distaste for the topic or her anger at her father. "I was unaware until recently that he'd begun experimenting again after promising my mother on her deathbed to give it up for good."

Richard released breath he hadn't realized he held. His esteem for his wife increased several notches. Though often more outspoken than most women, she'd managed to speak true yet knew when to keep to herself thoughts that could cause trouble.

"Ah. I see. Well, I'll ask him later today." He turned to place the rolled drawing into a bin with other rolls. "Hearing the latest from all alchemists in the realm is most exciting. Don't you agree, Richard?"

Fortunately Edward didn't see Eleanor roll her eyes.

⁂

As she prepared for bed, Eleanor told herself she was glad Richard had been too busy to attend her after their meeting with the king. The focus on alchemy tarnished the honor·done to her and her enjoyment of the privilege while fueling her hatred of the "science." And didn't bolster her good opinion of the man she was still married to, either.

Was no man safe from alchemy's siren song? No matter her true feelings, she'd known better than to share them with her liege lord, whose face had born the obsessed look she'd seen on her father. So she'd quickly learned to play the courtier's part, though it didn't sit well. Yet she needed Edward's help, not his displeasure.

Richard returned so late he didn't even check to see if she was asleep. She wasn't. She hadn't intended to wait up, but she couldn't seem to sleep without him there. Or accept that she missed his soothing breathing and warmth by her side. Most annoying.

His preoccupation with the council left her free to begin her search for his better bride, determine how to pursue the annulment and keep conversation about or dealing with consummation at bay.

The next morning, Eleanor gathered five of the most promising single women at court in a room in the old Round Tower, telling them she had an interesting proposition to present. When two of their original choices declined to participate, she and Alyce put their heads together again and selected additional contenders.

The final five now sat on stools in a circle, obviously wondering why she'd asked them to this a small but elegant room draped in colorful tapestries.

She referred to the list Alyce had prepared in her precise handwriting on a sheet of vellum.

The Challengers

1. Lady Blanche Latimer, widow, no children, 33
2. Lady Isabel Buntyng, widow, 27. 2 boys 6 and 10.
3. Lady Anne Gryffyn, unwed, 18
4. Lady Rose de Breyne, unwed (betrothed killed in battle), 20
5. Lady Mary Whyte, widow, 30. 2 boys 10 and 12, 1 girl 8

All, as far as she knew, were sufficiently wealthy and of high enough birth to be matched with an earl. And there was a pleasing variety of ages, appearance and children.

"Ladies, my thanks to all of you for meeting with me," Eleanor said. "This is a most unusual situation and opportunity. Should any of you choose not to participate once you learn of it, you are welcome to leave."

The women leaned forward almost as one.

"There is a wealthy, quite handsome nobleman high in the king's favor who needs a bride."

A mélange of gasps and sighs followed, accompanied by raised eyebrows and widening eyes. Lady Anne, the youngest and prettiest with her fair skin and bright blue eyes, looked stunned, while Lady Rose, owner of the largest breasts, appeared close to drooling.

"To speak plainly, this man is already wed." Eleanor held up a hand to quell the comments and questions she could tell were ready to burst forth. "But he needs a better bride than the one he has now. One of you could be that bride."

Isabel gasped louder than before. "Lady Glasmere, what are you asking? That one of us commit a sin and destroy a man's marriage? Why?"

The widow's reddened cheeks displayed her outrage. The sturdiest of the group, she wore a cream, high-waisted gown that didn't suit her sallow complexion.

Richard had noted details about her own gowns. He'd even suggested she acquire a new kind featuring a rounder skirt. Had she made a mistake inviting this woman to join her select group?

"Are you promoting bigamy?" This from Lady Whyte, who

appeared so shocked Eleanor jumped up to fetch her a cup of watered wine.

"No, of course not." Eleanor handed her the cup, then returned to her seat. "When the nobleman is presented with this better bride, he will choose to relinquish his present marriage and wed anew. I assure you, all will be legal and in accordance with the Church," Eleanor replied.

"An annulment could take ages," Lady Isabelle complained. "If you even succeed. Why not seek him a new bride when the old one is done with?"

Eleanor bristled. "Let me worry about that. Now. There are five of you and but one of him. To determine which of you is best suited for this man, we're going to hold a bridal tournament."

More gasps from the women. Whispers flew.

Anne stood. "This is an outrage. I don't want to be in involved in such a scheme." The train of her pale blue gown with ribbon trim fanned out behind her as she paced.

Mary nodded, making the row of jewels on her headdress sparkle. Her eyes were darker and grayer than Anne's. She was the tallest and thinnest of the lot. "I agree. 'Tis not seemly. Playing games to win a husband, indeed."

"Ladies, your attention please." Eleanor clapped her hands. This meeting wasn't going quite as she had anticipated. The women were wary, or worse. Even as she spoke, doubts nagged at her, too. "At least listen to all I have to say before you decide."

Anne sat and crossed her arms, a skeptical expression on her comely face.

"If you disapprove of my plan, return to your lives and your beds. Your empty beds," she added. "Anyone who does not wish to continue, to have a chance at wedding a wealthy, highly ranked, attractive man, please leave now."

The women exchanged glances, but not one moved.

"As to the tournament," she continued. "Men hold them to demonstrate their prowess to earn prizes. So shall you display your skills. Don't fear, we're not asking you to ply lances in a joust or engage in a mêlée with swords and pikes. But we shall keep to some standard tourney rules. For example, four judges will choose the victor." She paused, making sure she had the full attention of each woman. "I'm sure you are all wondering who the prize is. The winner will receive Richard Courtenay's hand in marriage."

More gasps.

Mary's mouth gaped in a very unattractive manner. "But he's married to you."

"What's wrong with the Earl of Glasmere? Why don't you want to keep him?" Isabel demanded.

Questions like these Eleanor had anticipated.

Before she could reply, Blanche said with a sly smile, "Nothing is wrong with Richard."

Eleanor couldn't stop her eyes from narrowing. What was that annoying, harsh ache deep in her chest? Surely not jealousy.

Blanche, who looked annoyingly beautiful in a green gown with fur cuffs, sounded so...knowing. They'd been betrothed. How intimate had they been? A shudder rippled through her. Surely because of an errant breeze.

"Eleanor isn't arranging this tournament because of a flaw in Richard," Blanche continued. "She still wants to marry Arthur Stafford, the former Earl of Glasmere. She was betrothed to him for years, as some of you may recall."

Five heads turned, looking to Eleanor for confirmation. She hadn't wanted to discuss her reasons for seeking a better bride, but now had no choice. Or did she? Blanche was a tricky one. Mayhap Richard had been right when he warned Eleanor not to trust her. Mayhap Blanche sought to undermine her.

Blanche smiled. "The king sent Arthur off on a mission soon after he arrived at Windsor. With so many former nobles trying to gain Edward's good will, that was quite an honor."

Eleanor bit her tongue, striving to keep from revealing her surprise. She hadn't known Arthur had left court. How had Blanche learned of it? At least she understood why she hadn't seen him, why he hadn't tried to contact her. She swallowed to clear her mouth of the sharp taste of blood, wondering if Richard had a part in sending Arthur away.

"My reasons are of no import. All that matters is whether each of you wants to be a countess." She stood tall, her gaze encompassing all of the women. "That each of you thinks she would make a better bride than I and is willing to participate in my tournament with hopes of winning Richard for herself."

For an instant, brief and sharp as a flash of lightning, Eleanor wondered if she was making a mistake. It pained her to think of any of these women as better brides, whether they were better in general or specifically better for Richard. Richard, her handsome, kind, powerful, wealthy husband. The man whose kisses made her yearn for more.

But staying wed to him would make a mockery of her lifelong dream of marrying for love, of choosing her husband. She'd join countless woman denied the opportunity to make decisions.

And how could she countenance his involvement in alchemy, deal year after year with the same lunacy and devilry her father had put her and her mother through? Eleanor had overheard her mother crying too many times to risk a similar outcome.

This was the moment of truth. Either she laughed and pretended the whole thing was a delightful prank, or she proceeded with her plan. She took a deep breath, feeling as though she teetered on a precipice with a stony ravine yawning far below.

"Does anyone wish to leave?" she asked.

Silence.

"Very well then." Eleanor fought back unexpected tears as she picked up the parchment on which Alyce had written the tournament rules.

She had made her decision.

"Here are the areas in which you will be judged. One: Wealth. I shall need a verifiable, detailed listing of your gold, lands, rents and other income. Please include any significant jewels and plate. The next area is Beauty, for which you'll don your finest attire. Three, Embroidery. You will have an hour to—"

Lady Rose interrupted. "Money can be counted, lands documented. How can you measure beauty?"

"'Tis in the eyes of the judges. They shall choose the woman they feel most suitable based on her appearance and the way she presents herself," Eleanor said. "May I continue? Three: Embroidery. You'll have an hour to stitch the design of your choice using fabric and thread we will provide. Not that I don't trust you, but Richard's hand is a prize of great value, perhaps worth trying to sneak in someone else's work."

"Hm." Lady Rose sniffed, either upset that her integrity might be questioned or because she'd be prevented from partaking in such a deception.

"Four is Music. Richard greatly enjoys music." The memory of him playing the lute and singing to her flashed through her mind. How she'd melted and smiled. Yet she was handing the opportunity for future songs to another. "Thus he values considerable skill in this area. You'll each perform two songs, singing or playing the instrument of your choice. The judges may award an advantage to the woman who both sings and plays.

"Household Management is next. This is also a difficult skill to measure. You may choose three witnesses to offer proof of your ability to run a household via a verbal report.

"The last area is 'Overall.' The judges may consider the best bride overall, though she may be lacking in a particular area."

"That's all? What about falconry?" asked Isabel.

"Or hunting?" This from Rose.

"You must include dancing," Blanche said.

"And what of religious devotion?" Mary clasped her rosary.

Clearly each woman promoted her finest talent. "There are countless womanly skills we could examine. I have chosen these based on what I know of Richard's preferences," Eleanor answered.

"Have you?" asked Blanche, her voice low. "Have you, really?"

Mary paled. Isabel actually licked her lips. Eleanor felt herself blush, but couldn't think of a reply. Because, even though she was his wife, she didn't know.

"Shouldn't you take that into account? A man of his...talents...and enthusiasm is likely to prefer an eager bride."

Blanche intimated that she knew Richard's desires. Disgusting.

No matter. For she, Eleanor, would soon be free of him. One

of these women would soon share Richard's bed and suffer any mistresses.

"Here is how we shall proceed."

❦❧ ❧❦

At last Richard had a break in his grueling schedule. Though his meetings with Edward and his council proved fruitful, too much sitting made him restless.

All he wanted to do now was find Eleanor. Their conversations made him want to spend more time with her. Even their sparring made him feel more alive. He felt sure they'd consummate their marriage any day now. If only he hadn't been so exhausted of late. He'd considered waking her each night he saw her sleeping so sweetly, one hand curled under her chin, but knew he, and she, needed rest.

He'd packed a basket for an impromptu meal. But he couldn't locate his bride. She wasn't in their room, nor in the main garden. Nor could he find Alyce, and he knew the two were inseparable. Windsor was a very large castle, with Upper, Lower and Middle Wards. He'd squander his respite in fruitless searching if he didn't find her soon.

As he passed the Round Tower, feminine laughter rang out from a room above his head. He hurried up the stairs. Through a partially open door he saw Eleanor, Alyce and five other women seated in a circle. Eleanor spoke softly but intently. The women he could see from his vantage point listened with quiet concentration.

He stepped forward. "Well met, ladies."

All eight heads turned. All eight faces bore varying degrees of surprise and guilt, especially those of Eleanor and her sister. Blanche also looked smug.

Richard waited in the doorway, hands on his hips. He'd come upon a clandestine gathering spearheaded by his wife.

"Have I interrupted something?" he asked.

A woman he didn't recognize, with a tall headdress, giggled. Two who looked vaguely familiar pressed their lips together as though secrets could not be pulled from them even under torture. One looked as if she might burst into tears and clutched a rosary so tightly he thought the beads might leave permanent impressions in her palms. Blanche laughed. Alyce looked to Eleanor, who, for once, was speechless.

He'd pursue the matter when he had his wife alone.

What was wrong with him? He faced a room full of beautiful women, yet his thoughts were only of Eleanor. Never before had a woman drawn him so. But then, he'd never been wed before. Marital instinct, legal and religious claims must be what drew his attention to his wife.

"My lady wife, I have but a short time free from my duties." He indicated the heavy basket he carried. "If you would grant me the pleasure of your company, perhaps we could stroll in the gardens and partake of a light repast?"

Alyce jumped to her feet. "Oh, yes. A most excellent suggestion. We can finish," she paused, "this later."

Why was she so nervous?

A mixture of sighs and giggles told him the others approved of his interruption, perhaps wishing they too had a gentleman with whom to stroll.

"Ladies, I shall see you all anon," Eleanor said. She walked through the circle toward the door.

Blanche blew him a kiss behind Eleanor's back and flashed a come-hither look.

What was she up to now? And his wife?

CHAPTER 9

Eleanor had frozen the instant she heard Richard's voice and hadn't thawed. He was sure to do one of two things as they walked: ask questions she didn't wish to answer or pursue her with sweet words and even sweeter kisses. She wasn't certain which approach unnerved her more.

Denying her interest in him was all the more difficult when they were alone. All he had to do was smile, and she yearned to while away the hours listening to him talk. Trying to make him laugh. All he had to do was kiss her and she yearned to succumb to the wonders of his mouth. And more. Which was wrong when she'd pledged herself to Arthur and vowed to find Richard another bride.

Knowing he'd want to continue where they'd left off as soon as they reached a private corner of the gardens and enduring her body's traitorous enthusiasm at the thought, Eleanor knew she had to choose.

Kiss, or tell Richard her plan.

Tell. Though he believed duty obligated them to remain wed, as a reasonable man, he had to appreciate the awkwardness of their situation. When offered a bride who'd be better for him and for the king, surely he'd be satisfied.

"I suppose we are equally stubborn," she began as they strolled into the Upper Ward's bright afternoon sunshine. She took a deep breath of fresh air and let it out slowly, also releasing the castle's dankness and the strain of persuading the candidates to her cause.

"In what way?"

"You want me to be your wife as much as I want to…not be."

He pressed his lips together, which she now knew was his habit when annoyed, revealing the appealing dimple in his right cheek.

"Eleanor, why do you work against me? Why not give us a chance?"

"You know why," she whispered. Though recently fond feelings for Arthur had been few and far between. She needed to see him again.

"If only we could work as hard together to make everything turn out for the best," Richard said.

"I hoped you'd wish that," she said. "I think we can. May I tell you how?"

❧ ☙

Eleanor's cautiousness warned Richard he wasn't going to like her idea.

After several moments of walking in strained silence, he gestured to a secluded, sun-dappled spot beneath an ancient oak tree and set down the basket. She helped him spread the blanket.

Eleanor made a lovely picture as he opened the bottle of wine, sitting before him with her green skirts spread about, the gauze veil on her tall headdress floating gently in the breeze. The brooch he'd given her gleamed in the sunlight. It pleased him that she wore it every day. He wanted to please her enough to drive thoughts of everything but him from her mind.

As he poured, she arranged the food: strawberries, cheese and more sweetmeats like those he had fed her on their journey to court.

"As an earl, you need a bride equal to you in status," she said. "As a noble, the king wants you bound to a wealthy family. As a man, you desire a beauteous, gentle wife. How can you satisfy all of these needs?" She took the proffered cup. "My thanks."

"I thought I already had," he said. "With you."

She made a face. Flattery didn't seem to impress Eleanor.

"There is one thing more. Wouldn't you also like a wife who wants you?"

Still she harped on that. "In the best of all possible worlds, yes. But as you well know, one can't always have all one desires."

"What if you could?" Enthusiasm brightened her eyes to purest violet.

He watched her sip the wine, followed the movements of her mouth on the cup. And wanted to kiss her.

Eleanor continued, "What if you could have a wealthier bride, one who is even better connected, more beautiful and more skilled than I?"

"Why do you ask? I told you on our wedding day and night I had no interest in another bride."

"I want to do this for you, Richard. For us. I'm going to find you a better bride."

If he looked at her hard enough, maybe he'd see something to help him understand.

"When I succeed, you'll be richer, have superior political connections and be happier than you are with me. Don't you see? No one loses, everyone wins."

"I—" He wanted to say, "I think this is a horrible idea," but was so astonished the words stuck in his throat. He grabbed his cup and gulped.

"You're a wonderful catch," Eleanor admitted. "I would want you if I hadn't been pledged for so long to another."

He choked on the wine, then recovered. Every sentence yielded new surprises. "My thanks for the kind words and thoughts. But we are already wed."

"Marriages end for many reasons. Need I list them? While you were ensconced with the council, I made arrangements to start annulment proceedings. I was forced to wed you, as you recall. And my betrothal to Arthur was annulled without my consent," she persisted.

Finally Richard understood why her father waited so long to tell Eleanor who she'd wed. For certes she would have found a way to avoid wedding with him at all. His stomach churned. "You've obviously thought on this a great deal. Who else knows of your idea?"

"Only Alyce, at first. I needed an assistant."

"An assistant," he repeated. Maybe that would help him follow.

"To take notes. To keep my records of the potential brides."

"There's more than one?"

"Well, of course. You just saw them."

The five women. Potential brides, for him. And Blanche, the woman most eminently unsuitable to be his bride, was one of them. He hadn't seen through her skillfully crafted façade all those years ago when he thought he knew her well. Eleanor couldn't hope to do so on such short acquaintance. The other women had been passing fair, but none as attractive to him as Eleanor.

He shook his head. Was he actually taking this lunatic scheme seriously?

Eleanor picked up a strawberry by its stem. It dangled enticingly from her fingers. He wanted to feed her the fruit and lick the sweet juices from her lips. And other places.

He adjusted his position.

"How could I be sure which woman would satisfy you?" she asked. "I settled on five contenders. A nice number from which to choose. Four would be too few, I think, to offer sufficient variety. More would be difficult to keep track of."

"How long have you been planning this?"

"Since our wedding night. I pondered making the decision myself, based on a specific set of characteristics you might like. I decided four judges would be better, as in a tournament. Perhaps you'd care to help to select the winner? What man wouldn't want five excellent prospects from which to choose?"

So caught up in her scheme was she that she didn't even look at him. If she had, she couldn't have missed the maelstrom of emotions surging within him. First swarmed sadness that she refused to realize he had no interest in a better bride. Why couldn't she see that if you already had what you wanted, something different, even more, wasn't necessarily better? Next followed fury, oddly mixed with admiration she'd go to such lengths to be rid of him. Her keenness, the efforts she had made, showed him this was what she truly wanted. To leave him, but at least not in the lurch. That she was willing to take such steps to see to his happiness made him want her all the more.

If only she'd turn her considerable efforts toward him and their marriage instead of searching for answers in every direction except in front of her. Why couldn't he make her see that? He hated failure.

His final emotion: acceptance. Their conversations obviously meant little to her. The extraordinary kisses they'd shared hadn't swayed her from her cause. Mayhap in her inexperience, she thought she could find such wonders with any man. He knew better. He'd done his best to convince her, but maybe his persistence had pushed her farther away. Mayhap, as she said, he fought a losing battle.

Was she right? Should they go their separate ways, for both their sakes? Even though he'd be the one to pay the highest price...a life without her beside him. Without the joy of raising their children.

Unless...maybe there was a better way. *His* way.

⁂

Eleanor couldn't bring herself to look at Richard. If she did, she'd burst into tears or throw herself into his arms. Or both. She'd gone too far to back out, yet encouraging him to seek another wife was far more difficult than she'd expected. Each word added another weight on her heart.

What was she to do? She wanted her husband, yet had pledged her devotion to another. Her mother always told her a woman of honor never went back on her word. And that a woman's word was all she had to give.

The way Richard had looked when she told him about the better bride, much the same way Alyce had when she unveiled her plan but tinged with pain, almost undid her. Only by staring into the distance or into the burgundy depths of her wine could she continue.

Maybe he'd refuse to accept her scheme. Maybe she wouldn't have to hold the bridal tournament. If so, would he forgive her for trying?

Richard drained his cup and poured another. Though she'd toyed with the strawberries, neither of them had eaten much of the food she'd spread at the edge of the blanket. With a smile she could tell was strained, he leaned forward. He was so close she could see emerald flecks in his eyes, make out each of his long lashes.

If he kissed her, she'd want more kisses. He'd be more than happy to provide them, and more. Which might lead to consummation. And make getting the annulment all the more difficult if not impossible.

Was Richard giving her one last chance to choose him?

She couldn't move.

"Eleanor. Are you very, very certain this is what you want?"

She nodded slowly, even as her body urged her to say no.

He leaned away, resting on one elbow as if he didn't have a care in the world. Was the sudden chill actually in the air or just in her?

"Very well, then. You've convinced me. Why shouldn't I study these 'better' brides? I'd like to get to know each of them before the tournament. As you said, forging friendships is one way to move forward. I have a lot of moving forward to do. Thanks to you."

She felt her mouth drop open.

"What have I to lose? And to ensure your tournament's success, I'll talk with the king about having the archbishop hasten the annulment proceedings."

Her throat went dry. "You want to involve the king?"

"Otherwise we'll have no way of knowing how long it'll take until our marriage is officially ended. Why wait?"

"Why indeed." Eleanor thought she might vomit.

Why, why couldn't she be sure of what she wanted? Why did every option feel like a mistake?

❧❧ ❧❧

"What are you doing here?" Blanche shrieked. "You nearly scared me to death, lurking by those bushes."

Sir Hugh FitzWalter disrupted her solitude near a hawthorn

thicket in the moat garden. The balding son of her landlady reminded her of a spider and made her skin crawl.

"I but sought a respite from the pressure you've put me under. Now you deny me even that," she said.

"Sit with me."

Mindful of her second-best wool gown, she eased herself to the ground. He waved her closer. Reluctantly, she hefted her skirts and complied. An excess of spicy scent emanated from his gangly frame. The short tunics and tight hose of the day mocked his too-thin legs.

Hugh rested on his elbows, clearly at ease, despite the dour expression on his long face. She held herself straight and stiff.

"As I hadn't received any of the information you've promised, I came to see for myself."

"There've been no reports because I haven't learned anything of use," Blanche said. "Yet."

"Ah, but since my arrival at court, *I* have. Should I be angry with you, Blanche? You wouldn't dare betray me, but I hear you've set your sights on winning Richard back. That you're part of this bizarre tournament everyone is buzzing about." Hugh rolled to his side, propping himself up on his elbow. "Your enticements couldn't hold him before, why should they now?"

He reached out and pinched her chin. The sun, pleasantly warm until his arrival, bore down on her with a vengeance. Sweat dripped down her neckline. She swiped it before it could stain her bodice.

"'Twas I who left him." And what a mistake that had been. She twisted her head until Hugh released her. "'Tis merely an act that I seek his favor now. His stupid 'wife' offered me the opportunity to get closer to him, so I took it. How better to find what we seek? Thanks to her absurd tournament, I'll have access to Richard almost every day."

"What good is that? Think you he carries his father's alchemy scrolls on his person? You're moving too slowly. Time is running out," Hugh warned.

Her heart thudded. "What have you heard?"

"My sources inform me that another alchemist is close to success. And rumors abound that several others have joined in the race. We must be first to bring the formula to the king, or all of our efforts will have been for naught."

"I'll work harder, if only to prove you wrong. I tell you again: Richard doesn't have his father's scrolls or know of their existence." Blanche emphasized each word. "It's been years since his father died. If Richard had them, being the honorable man he is, either he would've destroyed them or given them to Edward. Then all would know of their existence."

Hugh took a deep breath, then spoke with great care as if talking to a dim-witted child. "What does Richard's father's folio of notes say?"

She knew the ugsome book nearly by heart. "'Most revered Lords, Readers of this Epistle, let it be known that with assistance from God I am Guardian of the most secret Essence, the Philosopher's Stone.'"

Saying the words sent a spray of needles up her spine. Never in her life had she thought to be involved with alchemy, the mystical science of transmuting base metals into gold. Anyone who knew how to combine ingredients into such a quintessence as the Philosopher's Stone would command more power and wealth than the king.

"And he writes that he shall secure the decoction through his heirs," Hugh said. "So Richard either has the formula or has memorized it."

"You search with me," Blanche suggested. "I've tried to encourage Richard to discuss his father's work. He won't. He barely talks to me these days. Obviously I can't tell him what I'm really after.

"If the formula is written, we don't even know what form of writing to seek. The missing scrolls, another folio of scribbled notes, or perhaps a scrap of vellum? Even if we knew which castle or manor to search, each has too many possible hiding places."

Hugh's frown made her regret her outburst. She couldn't afford to offend him or his mother. No one but they knew the dire financial straits she faced. Her presumed wealth had earned her admittance into Eleanor's tournament, but she'd have to falsify records to participate in the actual event.

She had no home. Her dower lands had been sold to pay her debts. Hugh had purchased the clothes on her back. At the moment, he too lived in fear his resources would dwindle, relying as he did on his mother's charity.

She had to turn the tables. "I'm surprised the guards granted you admittance. Has Edward reversed your attainder?"

"No, 'tis another reason why I came. Never hurts to try to convince Edward of my loyalty in these times of strife. My presence should reassure him I've changed sides."

"Unless he thinks you a spy."

"Which brings us back to the beginning. That's why I must be first to bring the Philosopher's Stone, the elixir of life, the means to transmute metal to gold, to the king. 'Tis the only way to convince the king to return my properties. The only way to regain wealth in my own right." Hugh scuttled closer and put his arms around her. "Come to my room. I've missed you."

"Hugh, stop." She forced herself not to recoil when his strong scent made her gag. "We shouldn't even be seen together, unless we're arguing, or I'll be taken out of the running. Richard doesn't trust me as it is."

Disgust washed over her as he took her hand. But she wouldn't let it show.

"Perhaps you're right," Hugh agreed. "But you'll still come to me in secret. Whenever I like. Secrecy will serve to heighten our pleasure. You'd best not make me beg or I'll make you regret it."

Blanche bit back a sharp retort. She had no one but herself to blame. Her mistakes, her need to rise ever higher, had led her to this sorry pass.

All she had to do now was the impossible: find the formula for the Philosopher's Stone, something alchemists had tried to discover for centuries with or without their secular or religious leaders' permission. Something King Edward desired. If she did, she'd be free of Hugh. She'd move far away, where no one knew her past. Never again would she be any man's whore. She'd start anew.

But for now, she must play her part, distasteful as it was.

After making sure no one was nearby, she ran her hand down his chest to his nether parts and fondled him. She succeeded in raising a small bulge. 'Twas all this maggot of a man could produce.

His breathing was already heavy. "Not now. Later. Blanche, leave me."

For now, she obeyed.

⁂

Later that night, Richard lay awake. How could he sleep with Eleanor beside him?

He'd tried not to care for her, to stop wanting her, but her beauty and unique personality drew him. Her intelligence. Her only flaw was her refusal to want him. Perhaps that reluctance heightened his interest….the thrill of the hunt. Each time he thought he might breach the wall she'd built between them, she put up another defense. Cunning as a lord defending his castle under siege.

He could make out her profile in the light of the dwindling fire. He enjoyed watching her sleep, the only time she was still enough that he could admire her beauty. Her hair spilled over the covers, almost touching him. As he reached for a glistening lock, bringing it to his nose, he knew himself for a lovesick cow. Dropping the strands as if they'd burned him, he cursed his body's response. Just looking at her, merely catching a lemony hint of scent, aroused him. And wasn't enough.

He closed his eyes. Why did he want a wife who hoped to wed another man and wished him to marry another woman? Who despised his work? There was no way they'd consummate this marriage now. How could he stay married to her as he needed to? As he wanted to?

The sheets rustled. Richard opened his eyes to see her facing him, eyes closed beneath the hair draping her face. Taking care not to disturb her, he slid closer.

Eleanor's movements had disrupted the tight cocoon of coverings she wrapped around herself each night, as if the doing of it could protect her from him. Her thin linen nightgown hinted at the tempting treasures that lay beneath.

He wanted Eleanor. And he would find a way to have her.

CHAPTER 10

"You've been married for several weeks without any love-jousting?" Richard's brother Owen slapped his thigh and burst into laughter. When he recovered, he asked, "Is aught amiss in your nether regions?" That spawned another gale of laughter.

Richard didn't appreciate being on the receiving end of his brother's sarcastic wit. As soon as Owen arrived at court, they'd taken advantage of a break from work to ride out for this peaceful, private glade in the Great Park, as far from the courtiers as he could get. The tranquil, sunny day opposed his stormy mood.

He stretched out on the grass, hands folded behind his head, and closed his eyes. Not even his brother would see how Eleanor's recalcitrance troubled him. "She won't lie with me."

Owen's laughter rang out again, echoing in the quiet. "This is why you sent for me, dragging me away from a liaison with a most pleasant and accommodating widow? I rushed here, fearing trouble afoot. Never did I imagine you needed assistance with a woman."

"Not just any woman. My wife. I hoped the master of seduction would yield some secrets," Richard replied, his voice rife with mockery. He was tempted to grab his sword and show his brother who was the better man, in swordplay at least. But he needed advice first. "I assumed either duty or interest would make Eleanor accept our marriage. Neither has."

Telling his brother the details of his unusual situation rankled and made it more embarrassing. He was a powerful, intelligent, wealthy man. How could he allow a second woman to bring him to doubt his worth? He thought he'd learned his lesson.

Richard opened his eyes to get his brother's reaction to the worst of it. "I know why. Because she hates alchemy and thinks it the devil's work. Because she still loves Arthur, her former betrothed."

Silence.

"What, no witty retort?"

Owen's expression was serious for once. He toyed with a leaf. "Have you looked at this from her point of view? I can't imagine the shock of waking up planning to marry one woman and ending the day wed to another." He winced. "Or even the shock of being told whom to wed. My selection of a willing wench for even a nightly romp is a careful process, much less a woman who'd be bound to me for the rest of my life."

"I fault her father for not informing her of the change in grooms. Naught can be done to change that," Richard said. "There's more. Eleanor has further defied me, her father and Edward. She seeks to find me a better bride."

Owen stared. Then his eyes narrowed. "You're not usually this amusing. Tell me you jest."

"If only I did." The awkwardness of his plight hit him anew. He tipped his head back, allowing the sun's warmth to assuage his tension.

"Your wife is going to find you a bride."

"Your ears work well."

"Unbelievable." Owen remained silent for a few moments.

He and his younger brother were similar in so many ways, from appearance to temperament. But their differences made them need each other to achieve balance. Owen's ability to analyze a situation and come up with creative solutions was unmatched. On the field of battle, Owen strategized while he, Richard, led the men. If left to his own devices, Owen would wallow in pleasure and mirth, while Richard preferred work over enjoyment.

"Do you want Eleanor, or might you be happier with a different bride?" Owen asked.

"I want her."

"Because you can't have her?"

"No, nor because I must stay wed to her. Because I desire *her*."

Owen tilted his head, as he always did when he was about to make a proclamation about Richard's character. "Just desire? Nothing more?"

"I hold true to the vow I made after the Blanche debacle."

They recited in unison, "Women are fickle, not worthy of trust. Never to love but desire when you must."

Richard laughed with his brother, but melancholy shadowed his merriment. He'd never forget the pain loving Blanche had caused. Never.

"I enjoy being with Eleanor, as I haven't enjoyed other women," he admitted. "She's different. She doesn't profess to care for me, nor is she trying to snare or flatter me."

"Quite the opposite. Aye, she seems to be honest in her disdain of all you have to offer."

"For once I believe some of what a woman says to me. But how can I sway Eleanor from the man she thinks herself in love with?" he asked. A vision of her laughing with Arthur flashed through his mind. "Yet she must have some care for me. She selected each woman—"

"There's more than one?" Owen was nigh on choking.

Richard handed him the wineskin he'd brought. He sighed. Best get it all out. "There are five. Eleanor is arranging a bridal tournament."

Perhaps he should've waited until Owen swallowed. Red wine spewed forth, most of it dripping onto the grass and not his clothing.

"You get five women?"

Richard retrieved the wineskin. "She wanted me to have a choice. As I was saying, she selected each of them with my likes and dislikes in mind."

"How thoughtful. You could forbid it," Owen suggested as he dabbed at a wet spot on his hose. "The king gave her to you and you want her. Why indulge Eleanor if you intend to keep her in the end?"

"I want her because she's different. Her determination to achieve her goals impresses me, even if this goal seems a foolish and frustrating one." He sat up and took a drink, admiring their peaceful surroundings as he wished for peace in his heart. "Better to let her play her hand but see to it I emerge the winner of the game. Should I refuse, if I strong-arm her into staying with me, her stubbornness would keep us from ever having a marriage that thrives. I know that as surely as I know the sun will rise on the morrow. Every time she came to me, I'd wonder if she did so because she had to.

"Eleanor must choose me of her own accord. Then, knowing her as I do, she'll never let me go. She holds on to what is hers with fierceness. In that we are alike."

"More fool you to fancy such devotion. She's already your wife. Why risk losing her to another?" He reached for the wineskin. "And what if you change your mind? What if you prefer one of the other brides in Eleanor's stead?"

"I won't." Richard sensed she was the only woman who would satisfy him. "But should one of them truly prove better, how can I lose?" Just saying it made him feel ill.

Damn Eleanor. Why did he have to care for her? He thought of his attempts to woo her, how each time he kissed her she seemed to concede a little more ground, seemed a bit more attracted to him. The battle was far from won. He'd have to work faster, harder to make her cancel the tournament.

"What of the others?" Owen asked. He leaned forward on his elbows, enthusiasm for the concept seeming to win out over his original doubts. "Can I choose after you?"

Richard smiled. Owen looked eager as a youth about to get his first pup. "Why not, should you find one to your liking. All are wealthy. Some already have children, some more lands, some more gold. Each is prettier than the next, but none as fair to me as Eleanor."

Owen laughed again. "Despite your fine vow, you seem a lovesick fool. A sight I never thought to see. Next you'll be on your knees serenading her like a minstrel."

Richard wouldn't give his brother the satisfaction of learning he'd done just that. Nor would he tell Owen about the poem he'd recited or the supreme efforts he'd made to take things slowly with Eleanor while restraining his interest.

Owen rose to one knee and sang a bawdy lay. The horses nickered at his discordant sounds, not even close to the actual tune.

"Despite your tendency to annoy me and the fact that you sing like a braying ass, I value your opinion above all others. I want you to be one of the judges."

❧ ☙

Eleanor held her borrowed copy of René d'Anjou's *Livre des Tournois, Treatise on the Form and Organization of a Tournament*. She forced her gaze from glorious paintings of knights riding sumptuously caparisoned horses to concentrate on his advice. Alyce sat opposite her at a long wood table, her pen flying across pieces of parchment, pausing only to dip in the ink.

Richard sat beside her. Since he was to be the recipient of the winner, she couldn't find a way to say him nay when, despite his busy schedule, he'd asked to be part of the planning. She wouldn't let his intense gaze or nearness bemuse her. Not at all.

Did she imagine the glint of sadness in his eyes?

She continued reading aloud. "The king of arms must say to the judges, 'Noble and redoubted knights, honored and gentle squires, I have come before you to advise, request and notify you on behalf of the very noble and very powerful princes and my very redoubted lords that if you wish to please them you will take charge of organizing, and be judges, of a very noble tourney and bouhort of arms that has recently been undertaken by them.'"

"Slow down," Alyce said. "I'm only at 'very noble and very powerful princes.'"

"I'd be happy to write a summary of tourney rules for you," Richard said.

"My thanks, Richard, but I'd prefer to take them straight from the source. I'll ask for your preferences in certain areas, if you like, but I'd not trouble you with mundane administrative issues."

"Since my future is at stake, 'tis no trouble. But proceed."

"My thanks again." Was he trying to bait her? "'These lords have agreed together to choose you over all others on account of the great fame of your valor, the renown of your intelligence and the praise of the virtues that have long endured in your noble persons.'"

"That's quite a long book. Do I need to copy every word?" Alyce set down her pen and shook her hand. "I'm not sure how long I can keep this up, so—"

A page approached and bowed. "Your Grace, the king has requested you to join him."

Eleanor managed to hold back a sigh of relief.

Richard rose. "Since time is of the essence, Eleanor, I'll not ask you to wait to continue until I can return. May your plans meet with much success." He kissed her hand, then her cheek, and left with the page.

His warm breath, the soft brush of his lips, his fresh scent set her blood racing.

"Eleanor. It's not too late to stop this foolishness," Alyce said. "I've seen the way Richard looks at you. And the way you look back."

Alyce could be quite annoying.

"Be that as it may, mutual interest isn't love. It's not enough for my marriage." Eleanor returned to the treatise. "The judges choose the day and place of the tourney. Then 'one of the pursuivants of the company of the king of arms, who has a very loud voice—'"

"How do you know your feelings won't grow with time? Does Richard delight you? Do you want to live with him instead of Arthur?"

Alyce's questions made her squirm. Unfortunately, the more she came to know him, the more she liked him. Richard was wonderful in all aspects save one. Could she come to care for him the way she had Arthur, despite his pursuit of alchemy? She lacked sufficient time to be sure.

Focus on the task at hand. "'Who has a very loud voice ought to cry, taking three great breaths and three great pauses: Hear Ye, Hear Ye, Hear Ye. Let all princes, lords, barons, knights and squires of whatever marches that are in this kingdom and all other Christian kingdoms, who are not banished—'"

"Enough!" Alyce cried.

Eleanor looked up in surprise. There was yet so much work to do. "I can easily adapt these rules to meet our needs, but you must help me."

"End this folly and stay married to Richard. Once the tourney is cried, the entire court will know you don't want him. If you change your mind after that, it will be too late. Have you thought about how all of this makes him feel?"

Yes. He needed their marriage, for duty and personal gain. But what of his efforts to woo her? "Are you with me or against me? I need your support." Not only her assistance in preparing for the tournament, but also her belief that Eleanor was doing the right thing.

"I want what's best for you," Alyce said. "And what will make you happy."

"Both require having the power to choose my husband. One who isn't caught up in alchemy."

"It seems Richard cares for you, and you enjoy his company." Alyce set down the pen and capped her inkwell. "Mayhap you can have all you desire. Mayhap you can choose. Make Richard your choice and all will be well," she pleaded.

Eleanor closed the heavy treatise and pushed it aside. If only her troubles were as easily displaced. "I confess I'm not sure what I want anymore. When I'm with Richard, it's exactly as you say. I come alive. I savor our time together, then think of when I'll next see him. But he's too deeply entrenched in his vow to help Edward achieve alchemy. You've seen what the quest has done to Father, heard tell of others. It's like a disease that consumes all sense and reason. And for what? These supposedly smart men, including the king, are not only wasting their time and money, they're endangering their souls. Don't you agree?"

"Our priest says some priests are alchemists. And that Mass involves transmutation...."

"He would say those things. Father wouldn't abide a priest who opposed his 'work.'" She put her hands over her face.

"What am I to do? How will I know if I'm making the right choice? Only after it's too late to change it?"

"Trust in God to provide."

If only she could.

That night, courtiers crowded the great hall at Windsor. Laughter and minstrel's tunes filled the air. King Edward sat on a painted throne on a dais with stained glass windows on either side. Reddish hair fell to his chin. Strands of pearls, each with a gold medallion, crossed the chest of his black and gold brocade tunic.

Her mood and shoulders tense, she stood apart from the gaiety. Edmund approached her. She didn't smile in welcome.

"Daughter. You're looking well." He sat in the empty space beside her. The familiar scent of his soap, which had once represented home, made her skin crawl. "What have you learned?"

"Nothing. Nor will I try, as I told you at Middleworth." She, too, spoke near a whisper. "I won't have anything to do with alchemy. Except perhaps, turn you into the authorities for lack of a license if you continue to pressure me."

The harshness of his hiss stung her ear. "Ungrateful child. Everything you have, everything you are, you owe to me. You will do as I say."

"Or what? I'm a countess now. Above you." Speaking so to her sire made her insides burn, but he'd created a breach too wide to mend.

"So you've given up your foolish notions of ending your marriage? Good. If not, I'll leave everything I have, not only your portion but Alyce's, to the king. For the sole purpose of creating a new Alchemy Commission."

Eleanor gasped so loud people around them began to whisper. She pasted a smile on her face, though her heart ached almost beyond bearing. "How cruel to take out my unwillingness to dance to your tune on Alyce. I'd hoped I could forgive you for my wedding day, for your lunatic demands on me. That we could find our way back to friendship, at least. You've gone farther than too far. I've nothing more to say to you."

For an instant she feared he'd cause a scene. But Edmund left without another word.

What next? If she pursued her annulment, not only she but Alyce would be near paupers, left with nothing but a small estate from their mother and its paltry income. What would they do then, till the fields themselves? If Alyce still chose the Church, who'd pay her dowry?

Eleanor took a deep breath then let it out slowly, imagining that her anger at her father left her along with the air. She was grateful Richard hadn't arrived. She'd appreciate a meal without his company. In addition to his handsome features, which nigh mesmerized her into gazing at him, he was a most courteous and interesting companion. With each passing day it grew harder and harder to imagine him with one of the other brides. And not with her.

The more time she spent with him, the more she wanted to stay with him. Despite all of her plans and dreams.

As if her thoughts had conjured him, there he was. Her breath caught. Why did he have to charm her so just by being, make her want to unburden herself and wonder what would happen if he kissed her again?

"Eleanor, I beg your forgiveness for being late to dine. Again. There's someone I'd like you to meet," Richard said with a welcoming smile that made her sad. For it wouldn't be hers to appreciate much longer. "My younger brother, Owen."

Her husband for the nonce had a brother? What other important information did he withhold? Annoyance mixed with pleasure at Richard's arrival changed to exasperation. "How many other siblings do you have? Why haven't I learned of them?"

"Why would you care? Why would I share things about myself with a woman who is giving me away, especially when I have five women eager to learn?"

Honesty wasn't always the best approach. Not when it hurt.

"Dearest sister-by-law." Owen swept into a graceful bow. "I am most honored and glad to meet you."

"And I you," she said with nod. His natural charm provoked a smile despite her pique.

Owen was almost as good looking as his brother. His hair was as wavy and dark, but worn shorter. His form was leaner than

Richard's and his garments not quite as fine. She wouldn't wonder how he, a second son, made his way in the world. Richard was right. She shouldn't care about or for his family.

"'Tis well you have King Edward's favor. We've already washed our hands and said grace," she said.

"I see you saved a place," Richard said. "Dare I hope it's for me?"

"Despite oft coming late to the table, you haven't failed to make your way here, ever so politely displacing whoever is seated beside me. Out of courtesy, and to avoid having any others move, it seemed easier to hold a place for you," she said.

She should've known that Owen, who so resembled Richard, would act like him. With one of the most magnetic smiles she'd seen, Owen addressed the elegantly dressed noble on her left.

"My lord, I do so despair in troubling you. However, I have only recently arrived at court and would be ever grateful if you would allow me to dine with my family," he said. "Have you met my brother Richard Courtenay, Earl of Glasmere?"

"Sir John Wickham, my lord. 'Tis an honor to meet you both. Of course you may have this seat. I hope to further our acquaintance anon." The man rose, bowed, and left.

"I'm heartily enjoying being brother to an earl," Owen said as he stepped over the bench. "Just in time for the soup. I should've come to court sooner. Only three people to a bowl." He picked up his spoon and dove in.

Richard and Owen maintained a steady stream of banter through the soup, fish and meat courses, reminiscing about their childhood. Eleanor couldn't help but laugh at their tales and appreciate their easy closeness as she ate. But she didn't want to learn about the battle where Richard earned his spurs. She didn't want to be on the edge of her seat hearing about his favorite dog's unfortunate early demise at the fangs of a raging boar during a hunt. Just as she feared, he drew her in against her will.

Owen had included her as family when he asked Sir John to move. She didn't need to be part of their family. She didn't need anyone except Alyce. And Arthur. If only he were here, so she'd know she was pursuing the right course.

As the sweet wafers, nuts and raisins were served, Owen turned to her.

"I'm to be one of the judges in your tournament," he announced. "Will you point out the lucky combatants?"

"What?" Eleanor slammed her hands on the linen tablecloth, narrowly missing the platter of sweetmeats.

"I well know how you and Alyce have studied that tourney treatise," Richard said as he bit into the meat of a nut with exaggerated nonchalance. "You must be aware of all of the rules by now. Each side selects half of the judges. Owen is my first choice."

"Would you like some more wine, dear sister?" Owen asked with a smirk. "Oh, alack, we won't be related for long."

Eleanor fumed. "This tournament is of my making. There are no 'sides.' You also know I consulted René d'Anjou's new treatise to glean how tournaments are run as a rule. Some of his procedures, such as issuing a challenge with a blunted sword and gathering days before to display banners and shields, are not relevant to my event."

"Excellent decision, since women lack shields." Richard munched another nut.

"There are other kinds of shields in addition to those carried in tourneys." Such as the calm mien required to conceal interest in one's temporary husband.

"Too true." His smug expression faded. Was he thinking about Blanche? "We were talking about the rules. Is there a reason Owen can't judge? Of all men, my brother knows my preferences in women." He leaned close and whispered into her ear, "He knows what I truly enjoy. What will satisfy me."

Her entire body tingled.

"In every kind of wifely charm."

She swallowed. Why was he pressing on?

"I have a confession to make," he whispered close to her ear. "There was a time I hoped you'd want to know what I enjoy. Beyond kissing. There are so many pleasures we could've shared. Now I'm glad I didn't waste the effort to explain, since you obviously lack interest in all I want. And all I have to offer you in return."

Torment. Sheer, utter torment. In this moment, Eleanor wanted nothing more than to prove him wrong. He knew just what to say and do to tempt her. But she had set her feet firmly on this path.

And would see it through.

CHAPTER 11

Eleanor's plan was working. Quite well, in fact. So why wasn't she happier?

'Twas the day after Owen's arrival. The scene before her was almost exactly as she had imagined it, as though she'd written a play and all performed well-rehearsed parts.

Richard seemed at ease, content even, surrounded by the five elegant, beautiful, wealthy, intelligent women. They resembled nothing so much as a gaggle of geese parading before the gander. As they waddled around him, their finery reminded her of glistening feathers.

Lady Rose de Breyne tried to feed him some cheese. He turned his head, and she ate it. Lady Isabel Buntyng practically sprawled across his lap. Blanche reclined on a cushion at his feet, revealing more décolletage than necessary.

Owen stood off to the side, a slight smile on his attractive face. The young Lady Anne seemed more interested in Owen than in her potential groom, frequently sending flirtatious glances his way. He, in turn, looked occasionally at Alyce, as always plying her needle.

Eleanor wished she were close enough to hear their conversation, witty if she judged by all the laughter. But she didn't want him to think she was hovering. She leaned against a wall near the door, a glass goblet of hippocras in her hand.

Richard chuckled at something one of the geese said, his

wavy hair flowing as he threw back his head. His smile made her breath catch.

Then he looked directly at her, as if he'd sensed her regard. Their gazes locked. He nodded and raised his glass. She followed suit. In the midst of the crowd, he'd chosen to share a private moment with her. Her heart fluttered.

Edmund approached again. She wouldn't give him the satisfaction of fleeing.

"Eleanor, cease this foolishness." His ruddy complexion betrayed his anger, though he maintained a pleasant expression for the benefit of those who might be watching. "You cannot hold a tournament to find your husband a bride."

"Are you going to cease your alchemy experiments? I'll stop if you will." The words were out of her mouth before she realized what she'd said. Did she truly want Edmund to refrain from alchemy so badly she'd give up one dream to attain another goal? No. The man who called himself her father wasn't that important.

Her father's face grew redder as he drew back his hand. For an instant she thought he'd slap her in front of the entire court, but he caught himself and adjusted his hat instead.

"I'll not bargain with you, daughter. 'Tis not only I who abuse your mother's memory. She'd be ashamed at how brazen you've become."

He no longer had the power to upset or dissuade her. "You're wrong. Mother would be proud of me."

Edmund turned on his heel and headed to the other side of the hall. She shifted her attention to Richard and his flock.

Isabel put a hand on Richard's shoulder. "Would you prefer spermyse or hard cheese? What do you hunger for?" she asked in a voice loud enough to carry.

Richard turned to her with a smile guaranteed to make a woman weak in the knees.

What was that ache in her chest, the coiling pain? If it worsened, she'd need to visit the physician. And why did her stomach constrict as if she'd eaten something foul?

Suddenly she knew. She wanted to be the recipient of Richard's seductive smiles. She wanted to be the one to make him laugh and share his mirth. Even the one to feed him cheese.

No, that couldn't be true, for she loved Arthur.

But it was. When had her affections changed from the man of her past to the man of her present? She wanted to be with Richard. Mayhap only because she was forced to watch other women fawn over him as though he were the most sought-after man in England.

Which, except for the king, he was.

Eleanor gasped at her own foolishness. Her selfishness, her insatiable need to have her own way combined with her hatred of alchemy and fear of what it could do to those who engaged in it, had led her to this.

How could she make Richard care for her after the way she'd behaved, rejecting him again and again? When she'd gone so far as to find him another bride? Unwanted tears stung her eyes and her stomach sank faster than an anchor dropped off a ship. These women were so wonderful, so perfect. She could never hope to keep his interest now.

A startling fear gripped her. What if Richard fell in love with one of the women she'd chosen? What if Arthur found romantic bliss with Margaret? If her plans went awry, leaving her with neither man, she wouldn't be able to bear the failure. The emptiness.

The bridal tournament had seemed like a most excellent idea. She hadn't been able to think of anything that could go wrong. But as Alyce had said, many of her projects had seemed like good ideas before they too went astray. Like the time she...no, she wouldn't think on that now.

She was the unwitting victim of her own scheme. The joke was on her. She was jealous. Miserably, agonizingly, unable to stop thinking about Richard jealous.

Was there a way out?

❧ ☙

Richard knew every other man in the room, married or not, wanted to be him at this moment. For how often did a man have five wonderful women, one literally at his feet, tripping over themselves to please him, bring him sweetmeats and drink? At least one was clearly prepared to offer more.

Lady Rose sat on his lap with her arm around his waist and whispered bold sexual invitations in his ear. Some of her suggestions were tempting. Especially when she offered to show him what she could do with a peacock feather. But he wanted to try these things with Eleanor, not her. And not only because Rose had onion breath. He smiled. Eleanor would be perturbed to know one of her candidates had a slight flaw.

He knew Eleanor pretended to be studying the goblet she held. Did it upset her to see him cavort with these women as he hoped? Or did his feigned interest please her, because soon she'd be free? A few feet away, Owen raised his cup in approval, perhaps favoring the woman who now sat by his side or eager for the tournament so he could choose between the remaining four. Well, three, for he'd never want Blanche.

Rose stuck her tongue in his ear, which made him cringe and lean back.

Richard had to expedite Arthur and Margaret's wedding. Arthur was due back any day from his travels for the king. If he were wed, Eleanor might call off the tournament. She might cancel the annulment proceedings in the church court and resign herself to staying married to him. Better than not having her at all. Then time would be on his side.

He stood abruptly, almost dumping Rose to the floor. "Ladies, I must take my leave."

A sorrowful chorus begged him to stay.

"'Tis early. Stay just a few moments more, my lord," Isabel said. She bumped into Mary in her eagerness to get close to him.

"I beg pardon, but duty calls, my beauties. Duty calls."

His duty to his wife.

As he strode to the door, he couldn't resist a glance over his shoulder at Eleanor. Her eyes were wide and her mouth open slightly, as if she were stunned. The costly glass goblet dropped from her fingers and shattered into myriad pieces.

❧ ☙

Certain that all could read her face and see jealousy mixed with embarrassment, Eleanor didn't wait for a servant but bent low to pick up the shards amidst concerned murmurs of those nearby. A sliver sliced her finger, her blood crimson bright against the pale glass.

Before she could blink, Richard knelt beside her, a pristine cloth in one hand. With the other, he took her hand and examined the cut. His fingers felt hot as brands against her skin. She couldn't help but be pleased that despite the attentions of five willing women he remained attuned to her. That he'd come to her.

"No glass remaining that I can see," he said. "Does it hurt?"

"No." She shook her head.

Gently he held the cloth over her wound, then wrapped it around her hand. He helped her to her feet, but she wavered, leaning against him.

"It's nothing, truly," she said. "But thank you. Thank you for caring."

He lifted a hand as if to touch her cheek. She leaned closer, then pulled back. Her body followed her thoughts, toward him and then away.

He dropped his hand.

"Why did Richard run to her aid? He has us to care for now," Isabel whined loudly.

"She told us she was giving him up, but maybe she wants to keep him," Blanche said with evident scorn.

Richard put a finger under her chin and raised her head until she met his penetrating gaze. "Do you? Do you want to keep me as your husband?"

Despite his low tone, it seemed everyone present heard. The silence in the room was absolute, every ear awaiting her answer.

A moment ripe for change, suspended in time.

She could call off the bridal tournament. All she had to do was agree with Blanche. She could laugh and say, "Ah, yes, you promising brides have shown me the error of my ways." She could apologize sincerely for her indecisiveness and say at last she'd chosen the husband she wanted. Or she could flee, avoiding any answer.

Those options would make her look the fool. Should she care what others thought if she ended up with what she wanted? What, who, was that?

Her interest in Richard was too new, too raw, to abandon her elaborate, and now very public, plan. If she gave in to jealousy, she might regret it later. Then, with the tournament cancelled, if her plea for an annulment failed, she'd be trapped in an unwanted marriage.

If only Arthur were here. If she could see him, talk to him, she'd know if he remained the choice of her heart. She closed her eyes, willing him to appear in her mind's eye. There he sat on her favorite bench in her garden at Middleworth, with his familiar straight blond hair, blue eyes, and welcoming smile....

But wait, who was that sitting next to him?

Richard. Holding out his hand.

"Eleanor, are you well?"

Her disturbing vision burst like a bubble. Her thoughts crowded her tighter than the avid courtiers surrounding her. The sensation of Richard's arm sliding protectively across her back unsettled her. His hand closed around her waist, holding her securely in place.

"No," she whispered. "I don't think I am."

❧ ☙

Another night without sleep. Richard threw back the covers, appreciating the cool breeze on his skin. The strain of his new marriage combined with the urgency of his obligations to the king and his new estates sent thoughts racing through his mind swifter than his fastest steed. Eleanor's steady breathing should soothe him, but served as a reminder of the distance between them.

Moonlight streamed through the windows and set her aglow. Her fair hair gleamed. The sheet clung to her, outlining soft curves he yearned to touch.

Eleanor was truly beautiful in any light. If only she wanted him as he did her, wanted him as her husband in truth. He'd had no choice but to wed this woman who yearned for another and for whom he was now cursed with ever-present desire.

She stirred, dislodging the sheet. The moon revealed the contours of her breasts and their gentle movements as she breathed. He grew hard remembering the feel of them beneath his fingers.

Shadows concealed her beauty, taunting him. Closer he slid, then closer still, wanting to be near her. Her scent of sweet lemons floated up. Once again the moon illuminated his delectable wife.

Whose eyes were now open.

Her gaze locked with his, jolting him. Her eyes widened slightly and her mouth dropped open. Richard's body responded anew. His skin prickled as if he could feel her stare moving over his thighs up to his chest, then down again. Her eyes widened as she focused on the evidence of his desire. When she met his gaze, hers was replete with invitation.

Unable to resist, he bent his head and kissed her. A faint sigh escaped her as his mouth moved over hers. He felt her sleepy warmth beneath the fine linen gown.

Eleanor clutched his arms, then ran her fingers through his hair. His tongue explored her mouth. With each heartbeat, he needed her more.

Then she put her hands flat on his chest. To stop him?

He broke their kiss to look at her and saw confusion mixed with passion.

"Why am I so drawn to you?" Her voice was a mere whisper.

He smoothed her hair. "Desire knows no reason. Nor can it be forced. Thus when found, should be cultivated like the rare flower it is."

"Is that another quote?" she asked with a smile.

He loved her smile. "'Tis mine own, but I'd be honored should you wish to repeat it." He bent to kiss her again.

"But why you?" she persisted before his lips met hers.

She meant, he presumed with annoyance, instead of Arthur.

At least she found him attractive, though she fought it with all her might. He had to transform her attraction into ardor strong enough to bind her to him. If only he had more time alone with her without the flurry of court life combined with her preparations for the foolhardy tournament.

He'd make the most of the moments they had, while she was where she belonged. Next to him, in their bed.

"This can't be right." Eleanor shook her head. Yet as if of their own accord, her hands slid up to clasp his neck. Her fingers threaded into his hair. Holding him close. He liked that. "We shouldn't."

"We're married," he countered. "This couldn't be more right. It couldn't feel more right."

Richard tilted his hips against her so she'd know his need. He caressed her shoulders, then ran his hands down her back, slowly, soothingly. She didn't resist.

He had to taste her again. Their mouths blended in a deep kiss, hard and demanding. Their tongues met, hers tentative at first, then growing bolder, exploring. He held her close, then his fingers sought her breasts through her gown, stroking the undersides. He squeezed gently, appreciating how her breasts filled his hands. She was so soft, so tantalizing.

A gasp escaped her as he toyed with a firm nipple. She arched her back, yielding to his touch. Her eyes were open, wide with sensual surprise.

"You like that."

"I, well, yes," she admitted.

Her arousal heightened his. Richard appreciated the irony of his success. He'd tried to woo her, to court her as gentleman should court a lady, and had only fallen deeper under her spell. To awaken her interest, all he'd had to do was take off his clothing. Kiss her. Touch her.

Hunger surged through him. But he didn't want to pounce like an overeager youth. Patience, he cautioned.

Before she could protest, he tugged her gown up and over her head, eager to see all of her. Her eyes had darkened to deepest violet, her smooth, white skin and gentle curves completely exposed to him for the first time. She lay still as he gazed upon her, from her ankles to the golden hairs between her legs, up from her perfect breasts to her reddened lips.

"You are so beautiful," he said.

The urge to kiss her breasts was overwhelming. He bent his

head to each soft mound with reverence. His tongue meandered. When he reached the peak, his mouth closed over her.

Eleanor jumped, dislodging him. She sat up, hair aswirl. She scrabbled for her sleeping gown, then tossed it over her head. Staring at the linen folds as though they contained answers to her every question, she gripped the fabric close.

"We can't do this," Eleanor said hesitantly, as if she searched for a valid reason. In an instant, the glow disappeared from her eyes. "'Twould not be fair to the other brides."

"I don't care about the other brides." Richard bit back a variety of curses. "I'm married to you." He'd been so close to success. "You mean to continue with your tournament, even now?"

"Yes?" Her answer sounded like a question.

"I know you enjoy talking with me. I know you enjoy my kisses," he persisted. "Why do you fight me?"

"You know why. Don't make me say it." Her fingers tightened on the robe.

"Say it. Go ahead, Eleanor. Make me believe every word that comes out of your mouth."

"Because I still plan to wed Arthur."

"Exactly as I thought." Her statement should've stung, but didn't. "I don't believe you. You say that by rote. There's no emotion or conviction. Stubbornness makes you refuse to see the truth." Richard flopped onto his back, unable to conceal a grimace of unsatisfied desire.

"I shall do what I set out to do," Eleanor said. "Why is that so difficult for you to accept? You look ill of a sudden. Shall I fetch you a compress?"

Despite his aching flesh, he smiled with satisfaction. She did care for him, even if she couldn't admit it yet. And her obvious ignorance proved she'd never lain with another man, never before experienced the intimacies they'd shared. Not even with her beloved Arthur. As it should be, but among long-betrothed couples, often was not.

Eleanor clearly tried to resist the wondrous sensations he evoked in her. Refused to accept their marriage. He could be just as stubborn as she. Richard determined to renew his gentle assault on her until he satisfied needs she didn't even know she had. Then she would be his wife in truth.

Then she'd cry off her tournament.

Tomorrow night couldn't arrive soon enough.

❦ ❦

Eleanor returned to bed, but rolled away from Richard. She couldn't face her husband, partly from embarrassment at her response to his caresses. Her entire body hummed the way her harp resonated after the strings were plucked. That she wanted more made her cheeks burn.

Surely she wasn't so shallow as to fall for his attractive form alone. Yet when she'd opened her eyes and feasted on his bare chest, the way it tapered to his waist, his flat stomach, his—she felt herself blush—his maleness standing proud, strange yearning flooded her. She'd wanted to press herself against him and feel his skin against hers. To know what it would be like to have him inside her. Even now, all she wanted was to curl up close and have him hold her as they slept. To feel safe and secure in his arms.

Thank the Lord she'd found the strength to stop before they'd gone any further. Was this a test to see if she could remain loyal to Arthur even as Richard tempted her? Everything had changed…too much, too quickly.

Earlier in the day on her way through the bailey, she'd watched a group of boys playing with marbles. She understood the poor toy's plight: being slammed by another marble, knocked about against your will, landing somewhere you never intended to go but couldn't stop yourself, having to adjust to your new situation before being smacked again when you least expected it.

How could she keep Richard and her increasing desire for him at bay until she knew for sure what she wanted?

CHAPTER 12

Encouraged by Eleanor's response to his kisses, Richard spent the day half-hard anticipating the night to come. Never before had he been so enthralled by a woman. Because he couldn't have her? Owen would laugh for hours if Richard confessed how much he yearned for his wife. Perhaps any man would want a woman who so frequently tempted but had yet to fulfill her sexual promise. How much was Eleanor the woman, and how much was needing to consummate in truth? The need to be in control?

He couldn't be sure.

By the time they were alone in their chamber, he was more than ready. Had she spent her day in the same state, or had her thoughts been of the tournament? Of Arthur? He prayed not as he stood, waiting, clad only in tight hose.

His wife looked at everything but him, as she had on their wedding night. She peered into her clothes chest, then arranged the contents. Yet the silence wasn't awkward, but tinged with anticipation. Next she focused on the ewer of water and brass basin for washing as she prepared for bed. If she didn't stop, she might rub her skin raw on the linen towel.

Richard crossed to stand behind her. She started, but didn't turn, rigid as a soldier on watch. He sighed. Clearly they wouldn't pick up where they'd left off. He'd have to melt her resistance afresh.

She tested his patience. But waiting so many years to resolve his father's alchemy achievements or lack thereof had honed it. Persistence would prevail in both cases. The prospect of another night of unsatisfied need prompted him to augment his efforts.

Richard brushed her hair aside and ran the tips of his fingers down the side of her neck. So smooth. He placed a row of tender kisses from her collarbone up to her jaw. Ever so slowly he rubbed her back with long, languorous strokes. Her closeness, her fresh lemon scent ensnared him. When she relaxed, he slid his hands past her ribs to cup her breasts, appreciating their weight. His thumbs teased the peaks to tautness.

How he wanted to touch her again. How he wanted her.

He placed his hands on her shoulders and turned her to face him. "Tell me now. Should I stop?"

No answer.

His erection throbbed. "Eleanor?"

She looked at him, her eyes darkest amethyst. "You intrigue me," she whispered. "I want you."

He exulted in her reluctant admission. "Then you shall have me. I'll show you many things I know you'll enjoy. We both will."

"But we can't."

"Why?"

"I can't seem to help myself, Richard. I don't feel in control."

Concealing a smile, he said, "This isn't about control. It's about feelings. And being open to having them."

He kissed her. The first sweet taste of her spurred his need. His mouth moved over hers in a multitude of soft kisses, tempting her to respond. She sighed, then kissed him back with surprising fervor. His tongue met hers as he deepened the embrace, as he encouraged her heady responses.

She couldn't know what her kisses did to him. Each time he was with her and grew more familiar with her body, his desire increased. Imagine what it would be like to be inside her.

He pulled off his hose. Her nightgown was the final barrier. He slid the garment up and tugged it over her head. She did not protest, but raised her arms to assist him. As it dropped to the floor, he clasped her close. The fullness of her breasts met his chest, his thigh instinctively slipped between hers. He was lost in the sensation of her body touching his.

But he wanted more. "Touch me."

Her expression yielded a mixture of uncertainty and desire.

He put her hands around his waist. Tentatively she explored his back. With greater confidence, her questing hands moved to his arms, lingering over his biceps, then across his chest, teasing his skin. The sight of her small, pretty fingers touching him added to his desire.

Eleanor wanted him, at last.

Richard had planned to make their first time together a leisurely experience full of deep, sensual kisses. He meant to allow her time to get acquainted with his body, his touch. But he was about to explode and her alluring sighs indicated her eagerness.

Capturing her mouth in a potent kiss, he guided her to the bed. Her golden hair spilled in glorious disarray as she lay waiting. Waiting for him. He moved over her and pushed the shining locks aside to expose her full breasts, then took one hardened peak into his mouth, sucking gently. He tweaked the wet nipple as he tongued the other. She squirmed beneath him.

The waiting, the constant thoughts of Eleanor had aroused him more than he had thought possible without release. He could wait no longer.

Richard slid his hand between her legs and discovered sleek moisture. She was ready for him. Instinctively her hips lifted, sending his fingers gliding over her tender flesh. She moaned as he found a sensual rhythm.

Soon he'd sink into her and her hot wetness would surround him. The anticipation was almost enough to send him over the edge.

A low cry from Eleanor made him stop. His heart plummeted. Had he gone too fast? Did regrets beset her?

"Eleanor, sweet, what is it?"

She blushed, a delicate rose spreading across her cheeks. "'Tis only, well, I had no idea it could be this good," she said.

"I shall ensure that you like the rest even better," he said.

"First I want to touch you," she whispered.

She reached for him as he resumed his gentle assault on her. The feel of her hand on his erection made him wild. He couldn't take this. He needed to be inside her. Now. Right now. But her hand moving on him, the pleasure seething inside him was too great.

Then she rose up against his fingers, tilting her head back as she found her ecstasy.

"Richard," she breathed.

That was all it took. His own release overwhelmed him.

He spilled onto the sheets.

❦ ❦

Thank God, she was yet a virgin.

As wondrous, rolling waves of pleasure dissipated, Eleanor controlled her breathing. Richard remained beside her, silent, no longer touching her. She thanked the clouds for covering the moon. She couldn't bear to face him now, either to reveal her embarrassment or to see the look of cocky victory sure to be on his face.

The first sight of his flawless, masculine form last night had weakened the dam of her resistance. Tonight, all he'd had to do was touch her and she melted like snow in the sun. His caresses had released her desire in a flood. The way his thumbs tantalized her nipples made her want to cry out, then the rasp and warm wetness of his tongue on them had actually made her moan aloud. His body pressed against hers had infused her with yearning. She hadn't known for what until she burst into indescribable bliss.

She'd succumbed to her irrational desire for Richard even as she sought another bride for him. She was weak, as her priest often said women were.

'Twas painful to admit Arthur paled in comparison. She hadn't spent much time in his company over the past years. Had she, in her romantic dreams, imagined a better man than truly existed? Perhaps she wanted him out of habit, because she hated change. Take her mother's untimely death. How it had altered her life and her father's moods. What if her determination to choose her own husband blinded her to the truth?

No, 'twas Richard who was blinding her to the truth. He was

the first man who had truly courted her. What she needed was Arthur. She had to see him and let the comfort of his presence obliterate her yearning for Richard.

Her unwarranted attraction to her husband stood in the way. As much as her traitorous body wanted to, she could never kiss him again or she'd risk the downfall of her lifelong dreams.

⚜ ⚜

As if in answer to Eleanor's prayers, the next day Arthur returned to Windsor.

Richard stuck to her like a burr on her stocking, yet wasn't nearly as annoying. She finally escaped his vigilance by encouraging the brides-to-be to whisk him away for a ride.

Just before he left, he said, "I've news. If you're wondering why Arthur is here, 'tis because he'll wed Margaret on the morrow."

Eleanor clenched her fists to control the impulse to scream. "You're worse than my father," she said. "How could you kiss me last night and do—other things while concealing such news? You expect me to trust you, yet you refuse to do the same."

Richard smiled a seductive smile that elicited unwelcome memories. "I meant to tell you. But I had other things on my mind."

"You could have told me as we broke our fast."

"He wants to marry her. Not you. There's nothing you can do."

"Don't ever tell me that again."

"Which part? That Arthur doesn't love you?" He smirked.

"Oooh." To think she'd almost allowed him to consummate their marriage. To think she'd doubted her feelings for Arthur. "I can't wait until the tournament. Then I shall be unshackled from you."

"We'll see." Richard was insultingly smug.

"Richard! We're waiting," Isabel called out in a rather unladylike fashion.

"Come, ladies," Richard called. "Let's enjoy the day."

Let the brides flitter around him like a flock of hungry,

brightly-plumed birds as they departed for their ride. He could have them, every one.

She sought out Arthur.

"Eleanor, what have you done?" Arthur's handsome face displayed uncustomary dismay.

She smiled as he swept her into a niche in the corridor leading to the great hall. For once she'd breached his cool exterior.

"I had to talk to you," she said.

"I came to you only to accept your best wishes on my upcoming marriage," he replied. "Only for that reason."

She fought the urge to snap. This was her last chance to persuade Arthur to her cause. She couldn't let potent anger ruin it, anger toward Arthur for accepting his fate and toward Richard for keeping key information from her even as he tried to make her his wife in truth.

In the dim light from the sputtering wall torch, his expression was grim. Not at all the reception she'd hoped for. "Now tell me of your latest foolishness."

An approaching feminine giggle threatened discovery. Arthur pulled her deeper into the niche. She waited breathlessly as more laughter and footsteps presaged a couple's departure. Ah, to be so happy with one's mate.

No matter, she and Arthur were together at last. He smelled different than he used to, too spicy. Richard smelled, well, fresh and exciting.

She wouldn't compare them further.

"What's this nonsense I hear about a bridal tournament?" he demanded.

"I had to find a way for us to wed without hurting Richard or leaving him without a suitable bride. 'Tis not his fault I was given to him, and he's been so supportive of you," Eleanor explained. "After he has a new bride, he'll be even better off. And when my annulment is final, you and I can be married as we've always dreamed."

Now Arthur would see how much she cared for him, what she was willing to sacrifice and how hard she'd worked so they could be together.

He put a hand to his forehead as though it ached. "You go too far. I can't countenance your behavior. Knowing Richard, I'm surprised he can. He supports this folly?"

Everyone always spoke of Richard and what he wanted. A thought flashed through her mind, quick and piercing. What if Arthur had merely been doing his duty all those years they were betrothed? She hadn't asked. She hadn't thought she needed to.

She forced herself to ask now. "Arthur, don't you love me anymore?"

"Of course I do." He smiled, just as she'd hoped. "I will always love you. How could I not?"

Relief coursed through her. All of her efforts, her indecision, had led to this glorious moment. Arthur had declared his feelings. All would be as she had dreamed.

His straight blond hair shimmered golden, making him a shining knight of valor. She held his hands. They weren't as large as Richard's, didn't promise the same power.

What was wrong with her, that thoughts of Richard hounded her at a time like this? The hands she now clasped were the ones she wanted to hold. Happiness would be hers at last.

"Our marriage would've been one of deep companionship, which is more than many of our kind enjoy. I love you like the sister I never had," Arthur said.

She yanked her hands free. Nausea assaulted her. Her headdress prevented her from leaning against the wall, but she closed her eyes.

He didn't love her as a man loves a woman. As a husband loves a wife. There was nothing, no one to comfort her. All was lost.

"Yours is but a chaste love?" The words tasted sour as bile.

He looked almost sorry for her. "I'd have wed you out of friendship and duty. When did I ever promise more?"

Racing through years of memories, she realized she'd been oblivious to the signs. She'd been the one to initiate their limited physical contact. When she'd asked if he loved her, she'd taken his vague responses as pledges. As if adding enough embroidery to a plain gown could make it magnificent, she'd convinced herself she and Arthur made a perfect match. That's how badly she'd wanted her marriage to be a good one.

A tear dripped down her cheek. The world she'd created in her mind, had let guide her for so long, didn't exist. Arthur was another man who wanted her only to satisfy his duty.

The pain of knowing sizzled in her veins.

"I shall marry Margaret. If I come to love her, all the better. If not, we'll fare as best we can. As many couples do.

"I told you on your wedding day my attainder ended any hope for us. You didn't believe me. Instead of looking toward your future, you wanted to remain in the past, where it was safe. Can you see that now?"

His words smacked her with the strength of actual blows.

He reached for her hand again, clearly a gesture of compassion, not passion. "What I felt for you was real, but it was the love of a youth for a maiden," Arthur said. He released her, as if severing the final tie between them. "Now you can stay with Richard and forego your tournament."

Eleanor felt brittle as an icicle. One more word and she'd shatter into a thousand shards.

Why had Richard readily agreed to partake in her tournament? Arthur, the man she'd waited for, not only didn't love her, he didn't want her enough to fight for her. For both, one bride was as good as another. What man would value and want her?

Insight hit her hard. She'd been a fool to believe what she wanted mattered. In this world of men, women enjoyed only the powers a man granted, be it father, husband or liege lord. She'd hoped to be different from every other woman she knew, but had failed.

Richard had been right to conceal Arthur's arrival. He'd known she'd chase after someone she couldn't have. Did Richard also know Arthur didn't love her?

"Eleanor, are you ill? Shall I fetch Alyce?" Arthur asked. "Say something."

She looked up in surprise. Somehow she'd moved across the corridor into a small room and collapsed on a velvet-covered bench. Her head spun.

Arthur hovered over her. "Do you need a physician?"

He clumsily removed her headdress. As her hair tumbled free, he knelt beside her and put his hand to her forehead.

"Here you are, my lady wife." Richard's face was inscrutable. "And look at the company you keep."

He'd repeated his words from their wedding day when he'd found her and Arthur in the alcove. She was numb. She could only imagine Richard's thoughts at finding Arthur touching her bare head while she lay on her back.

Why should Richard care what he'd seen? Despite the wonderful moments they'd shared, soon he'd move on to a different, apparently eagerly anticipated, bride.

"Eleanor isn't feeling well. Richard, Eleanor, I'll see you both anon. As you might imagine, I've numerous tasks to attend to before the morrow." Arthur hurried away as she sat up, her head continuing to spin.

"Nothing happened. We were saying our farewells when I felt faint," she said.

"Of course," Richard replied. "Why would I think otherwise?"

"What are you doing here? What happened to your ride?"

"I didn't want to leave on such a discordant note. Halfway to the stables, I sent the ladies ahead without me." He handed over her headdress. "They weren't pleased."

She collected a couple of wayward pins before accepting it. "Oh. So you weren't checking up on me."

"That as well, Eleanor. I feared you'd run straight to Arthur the first chance you had. 'Man is his own worst enemy.' That's not a quote from me, but Cicero."

He turned and left her. Alone.

❧ ☙

Arthur's wedding passed in a blur. She barely noticed the beauty of St. George's Chapel. Richard and Alyce hovered protectively on either side, as if afraid she might do something rash. When the priest asked if there was any reason why the bride and groom should not be wed, Richard's hand rested on her waist. To comfort, claim her, or prevent her from interfering?

Margaret was a thin, pale wisp of a woman who looked

young for her age. Arthur revealed no sign of distress or happiness.

The kiss that sealed their marriage didn't even hurt. Thankfully, Eleanor felt nothing.

Arthur was duly wed. But he planned to make the best of it, while she'd made the worst.

Why go forth with the tournament? There was no one she'd rather wed than Richard. Mayhap living with another zealous alchemist was the price she'd have to pay to salvage the mess she'd made of things. Maybe he wouldn't let alchemy rule him.

Why hadn't she made this decision yesterday or this morning? Because it would've seemed as though Richard had conquered her. Because Richard, like her father, had kept knowledge from her.

Another wedding feast, and again she had no appetite for the delicacies placed before her. Again music made her head ache. Richard sampled every course, oblivious to her misery. She waited for him to ask her to dance. That would make her feel better, to smile at him and hold his hand. To enjoy a few moments as if they were a true couple. As if her dream of being happily wed to the man she chose could come true.

Alyce had been right. She just had to choose Richard.

How could she explain her changed outlook? She'd wait until they were alone. Where there was no chance of anyone overhearing their conversation.

Now she could eat. She picked up her spoon, ready to dig into the chicken, which she could tell from the aroma was cooked in vinegar and almond milk.

Richard pushed his trencher aside and slid to the back of the bench with a satisfied sigh. "I can't wait. Soon it will be my turn."

"Your turn to what?"

"To be the happy groom, of course. To enjoy my wedding…my real wedding. Not the sham you and I had. When I wed my better bride, as I so look forward to doing. The tournament is a wonderful idea. My thanks, Eleanor, for being so considerate of my needs."

Just what she thought she'd wanted to hear. Yet every word

was like a bee's sting. Jabbing and lingering. Was he teasing her, or did he truly want a different bride, even after the intimacies they'd shared, the efforts he'd made to woo her? His handsome face lacked that slight mocking expression she'd come to know. His eyebrow hadn't risen as it was wont to do. He seemed serious.

"What man has ever been so fortunate, to have a bevy of potential brides from which to choose? Each of whom will demonstrate their skills for me, show me how much they want to wed me?" He took a bite of chicken and sighed contentedly.

Eleanor was glad she hadn't eaten, for the food would've churned in her stomach. How could Richard have held her close and told her she was beautiful, kissed her, said he wanted more, all the while anticipating his new wife? How could he have touched her with what seemed like reverence?

She'd made a dangerous mistake. She'd begun to open her heart to Richard. But she hadn't pleased him. He didn't really want her, only a convenient, well-formed body to warm his bed until he could fill it with the next.

Eleanor bit back a spiteful retort. Her scheme caused more anguish than she'd ever known. Never before had she doubted her own worth. Never had she cared so much about what anyone thought of her, even Edmund. Why did she want to love and be loved…why couldn't she be more like other women who accepted their fates? For the first time she wondered if they were right and she was wrong.

She would cancel the tournament. And do her best to make her marriage to Richard work. She'd show him *she* was the better bride. Hope floated, then popped like a soap bubble. Would he believe her decision was heartfelt?

"Even if you cancelled the tournament, how could I trust I'm the man you truly want to wed? Arthur is taken. If you swore you no longer loved him, or never truly had, how could I not wonder if you'd settled for me? The timing would be too convenient."

Their minds worked as one. Unfortunately.

And if she did call it off, for the rest of their lives he'd give her that knowing look mingled with a hint of mistrust. Which was worse? Watching Richard wed another or watching him doubt her every day? Would she ever be able to relax and stop having to prove her sincerity?

"Since you don't want the one you have, I hope you, too, find a better spouse. And that your evening is a pleasant one," he said with a devastating smile as he stood.

"Are you going to our chamber?" Hope rose.

"No. I'm off to join the revelry, where else? I need to dance with each and every one of my lovely brides to be," Richard said. "At least once. Perhaps more. 'Twill be a long night. No need to wait up."

As her mouth dropped open, he hastened to his first quarry. Lady Rose blushed prettily, then followed Richard to join the merriment. She seethed as he led each prospect to the floor, holding her hand and bowing. Each smiled and laughed as though her life depended on it. Maybe it did.

She remained in her seat. Alone. Abandoned. Richard didn't glance her way, not once.

Two could play at this game. She'd find someone to dance with her. In the midst of the steps, she might wind up next to Richard and have to partner him, however briefly.

The first man she asked, a very attractive baron, said, "I am honored, Lady Glasmere, but you are wed."

"That may be true." She waved toward the dancers and spoke loudly over the sprightly tune featuring a flute. "But you see my husband there, cavorting for all he is worth." She hoped the baron didn't hear any bitterness in her voice.

"An earl can do what he wants, but his wife cannot." He offered an apologetic shrug.

'Twas the same with the second man, and the third. None would risk offending Richard. Another area where men had all the power.

Arthur danced with Margaret. Richard danced with shy Lady Mary Whyte. Even Alyce joined in the fun with Owen. All of them belonged.

She'd made herself an outcast.

ॐ ॐ

It took every ounce of Richard's will not to go to Eleanor. Even as he kept time with the music and passed amongst the dancers, pretending to enjoy himself, he couldn't miss the despair on her face.

He had to do this. She'd created the tournament and all that went with it. He'd play along as though a new bride was his heart's desire until she realized the folly of leaving him. Though his behavior might cause grief in the short term, he hoped his efforts would result in a happier wife, which would make him happier, too. But at this moment, he ached as he could see she did.

When Eleanor had looked at him with those beautiful, violet eyes, expecting him to ask her to dance, he'd clasped his hands behind his back to help him find strength to leave her at the table. He felt her gaze bore into him as he flirted with one woman after another. This was what she'd said she'd wanted.

The intricate steps captured his attention. When he next sought Eleanor, she was talking to Baron Wethington. Jealousy pricked him, but she had as much right as he to dance. The satisfaction mixing with sympathy when the baron declined made him pause, which almost tripped his companion.

His feet started toward his wife. Richard looked down at them in surprise. He was so drawn to her, his body reacted instinctively. He'd hold firm to his plan. Smoothly, he turned back to his partner and bestowed upon her his most charming smile.

When the music stopped, he bowed. "My thanks, Lady Isabel."

She smiled. "I wonder what they'll play next. I so love the flute, don't you? The high tones are so light, the low so moving. Ah, look, they're about to start."

How could he spend years enduring her constant stream of chatter? Eleanor's voice was much more pleasant....

At least there were four other candidates.

"Then I must hasten to another partner."

She pouted.

"'Tis only fair." He turned on his heel.

To find Eleanor standing in front of him. Her lovely, upturned face reflected quiet confidence.

"Eleanor, what are you doing?"

"Asking my husband to dance with his wife." She made a pretty little curtsy.

"I see that. But why? One moment you can't wait to hand me off to another woman, the next you're acting as if we're a true couple. Are you jealous?"

She sucked in a breath. "Certainly not. I just—"

"Just what?"

The musicians struck up a faster-paced pavane. Couples started moving into place, skirts swishing and jewels winking.

"I just...wanted to dance." He could barely hear her over the sprightly tune.

"With me?"

"With you," she admitted, looking at the floor.

Not asking Eleanor to dance after the meal was one thing. Snubbing her would be quite another, now that she'd come to him in front of everyone. He didn't want to be so close to her, touch her delicate hands, smell her. Because his resolve would weaken, and he'd keep wanting what he couldn't have. He didn't want to feel anything for her.

He held out his arm. She placed her slender one on his. The slight weight was reassuring, comforting. If only this meant she was changing her mind.

CHAPTER 13

"What is it, Blanche?" Richard asked.

Blanche sighed. Despite his unfriendly tone and skeptical expression, he had come to her. The narrow, secluded room she'd chosen was perfect.

"Why did you ask to see me?"

Unless she won the tournament, unlikely given her deception and lack of funds, this might be her last chance to be alone with him. She had nothing left to lose. What would become of her if Richard didn't possess the information she needed? Her shoulders clenched.

"I wouldn't have asked if it wasn't important." She leaned against a velvet pillow and ran her fingers through her unbound hair.

"I can't imagine what we have to discuss, yet your missive made your need sound dire," Richard said.

"It is, oh, it is." That was the truth. "I've some of your favorite cheese and malmsey." Blanche cringed as she sliced and poured. She sounded too eager.

Blanche turned, tray of cheese and fresh white bread in one hand, cup in the other, to find Richard sitting on the bench opposite her. She sat so close that her skirts covered his thigh. "Here."

She leaned against him, making sure her breast brushed his arm as she placed the tray on the low table next to the bench.

He ate some cheese and drank a few sips, ones she hoped

were flavorful enough to cover any lingering taste of the love potion she'd added before he arrived.

She sliced more cheese. He quickly ate another piece.

"Well, what do you want?"

How long before the drug started working? *Would* it work? The crone who'd sold Blanche the costly *remedia amoris* swore on her saints' bones that her secret mixture of powdered animal horns, mandrake and sparrow eggs would induce even the most resistant man to desire. Blanche hoped the strange stuff wouldn't harm Richard. But she knew he wouldn't tell her what he knew about the Philosopher's Stone on his own.

And if he wanted her again, perhaps he'd wed her instead of going through with the tournament. All her problems would be solved.

"Thank you for the cheese and wine." He sat back. "Now talk."

"I've been thinking about your father. About his experiments."

"What so interests you in alchemy of a sudden?"

"What interests so many. The possibilities. The ability to turn mere metals into something, into gold. The hope of resurrection." Blanche rested her hand next to his thigh. "You never said what you've seen of your father's writings."

"Why would I tell you?"

His unpleasant tone wouldn't sway her. "I know how highly the old king, Henry, valued his work. The new king will as well," she said.

"All know Edward likes to study the meaning of genealogies and history. What of it?"

"'Tis far more than that. I wondered what your father wrote about and what discoveries he made. Which made me miss you and what we once shared." Blanche used a fingernail to trace a meandering pattern on his thigh. Years ago he'd loved that. Her hand brushed lightly between his legs.

He stood. "Not this again."

"We were so good together. We can be still."

"You endeavor, as you so rightly put it, to make something of nothing. You willingly destroyed what we might have had in your hunger for money and position." He glared at her, his eyes piercing. "What do you really want? Has Lady FitzWalter threatened to evict you? Or did Hugh put you up to this?"

She tried to keep her face calm.

"That's it, then. Do he and his mother hope to use another's work to gain favor and power by giving it to Edward?"

She busied herself pouring wine lest he read more truth in her eyes.

"I must tell Eleanor," he said. "And have you removed from the tournament. I shouldn't have let it go this far."

Her ploy wasn't working. The drug, and she, had failed. If she didn't come up with a new plan, she'd be homeless. And penniless.

Richard had been a fool to meet with Blanche. But she no longer had the ability to entrap him in her webs of deceit.

"Don't try this again. Any notes you send will go unheeded. I shouldn't have acted on this one." His skin prickled from his scalp to his toes. His blood raged as if he'd been enticed for hours. Where had this strange need come from?

His highly arousing encounters with Eleanor must've accumulated into extraordinary lust. His flesh burned, his unexpected erection throbbed. He had to find release. Not with Blanche, despite her practiced efforts. He wanted his wife. He'd go to her, and have her.

Now.

Of a sudden he was tired. So tired. Tired of the search for a "better" bride. He sank back onto the unforgiving wood bench, limbs listless and weak. Why should he have to work so hard to get his wife's attention? Why was he with Blanche, and not her?

"Tell me, Richard." Blanche's hand roamed from his thigh to his erection, cupping him. "Tell me you want me to touch you. You know I can please you."

This was wrong. Yet lust and lethargy urged him to yield to pleasure. She squeezed him through his clothing, gently, then harder. An enticing rhythm.

He closed his eyes. In his befuddled mind, Eleanor caressed him. Eleanor, who knew just the way to arouse him. He moaned, glad she wanted to touch him at last.

Then he opened his eyes. The woman with her hands on his cock was Blanche, not his wife. Blanche looked gleeful. She wanted something. He fought to remember. His father's alchemical knowledge.

Eleanor. He'd go to her.

His head spun, his legs and arms felt heavy. As if he'd been drugged.

As if he'd been drugged.

He shook his head and struggled to stand. "I can't believe you'd go this far." Willing his mind to overpower his body, he jerked her to her feet. "What did you put in my wine? Why? What is it about my father's work that's so important to you?"

🕸 🕸

Shock. Disgust. Misery. The only words fitting Eleanor's feelings about the scene before her.

After a late conference with Alyce about tournament details, she'd taken a wrong turn. She'd been retracing her steps through Windsor's myriad corridors when a familiar moan caught her attention. The moan of a man who sounded like Richard had when she'd touched his erection for the first time. Such a passionate, unforgettable sound.

She turned the corner.

There was her husband, eyes closed. With another woman touching him. Blanche stared at Richard as though her life's goal was to please him.

"Richard, tell me. Tell me what I need to hear," Blanche said.

Hot fury flooded Eleanor. She couldn't watch another second or she'd be violently ill. Not only was she appalled, she was jealous. Exceedingly, achingly jealous.

Look what her plans had wrought.

She ran, away from the sights and sounds of her husband's intimacies with another woman. At last she reached her chamber. She slammed the door and collapsed in a heap on the floor. Powerful sobs burst forth, nearly choking her.

Hearts didn't break, they shattered.

To think she'd begun to feel something for Richard and wondered what remaining married to him would be like. She'd had doubts about going forward with the bridal tournament.

The worst of it was when he kissed her, she'd thought she was the only woman for him. He'd focused on her with such intensity she felt special and cared for. Yet clearly he thought nothing of maintaining his relationship with his erstwhile love. Thought nothing of flirting and dancing with the potential brides.

Then again, why should he remain faithful when she'd rejected him? And offered him other women she'd chosen specifically to please him?

She hadn't intended the tournament to be a test of Richard's fidelity. But that's what her heart was turning it into. More foolishness. Like wanting to choose her own spouse. Like wanting to love him and be loved in return.

All her life her parents had told her marriage was a means to an end, financial or political, or both. Eleanor had refused to listen. Refused to share her mother's fate.

Eleanor pushed herself to her feet and stumbled to the bed. She threw herself face down, pounding the pillows again and again, not certain if they represented Richard or herself and her stupidity in caring for him. A bolster burst open in a swirl of feathers. She sat up amidst the floating fluff, sobbing and sneezing. Feathers clung to her damp cheeks.

"Eleanor, what's going on?"

Richard stood in the open doorway, handsome as always if slightly pale. He hurried, rather unsteadily, to her side. Was he drunk?

Disgusting. He'd come straight to her from Blanche. His hands had just touched another woman. The taste of her would still be on his lips, the cloying scent of her on his clothes, his flesh still warmed by her hands. Eleanor swallowed against a surge of bile. How she wished she had a bucket of bleach to throw at him, as if the harsh liquid could erase her memory of Blanche fondling him.

"Were you in a fight?" Richard picked up a clump of feathers.

"I saw you with her. The door was open. Anyone could have seen you."

He froze.

She held her breath. This was Richard's chance to explain. His chance to make things right.

His expression didn't change. His silence told her more than words ever could. The closeness they'd achieved, which had seemed so real, evaporated like mist in the sun.

"Have you nothing to say?"

"Would you believe me?" he countered. "And why do you care? You invited Blanche to join the tournament. Isn't this what you want, for me to find happiness with another woman?"

Yes. No. One thing was certain. He'd never know how much his being alone with Blanche upset her. Never would she give him such power over her. Still, she used her fury to the fullest. "You've made it quite obvious that you desire another." She peeled feathers from her face. "Perhaps Fortune will smile on you, and Blanche will win. Then you can be together always." Her throat caught, despite her resolve.

Richard sighed heavily. He seemed weary, at a loss for words. "I don't want Blanche to win. Or any of the others. I need to stay wed to you."

Interesting choice of words. "But you haven't spoken a word against the tournament," Eleanor noted.

"'Twas to humor you. I thought you'd come to your senses and give it up."

Her heart soared. She should throw her arms around him and cancel the tournament. But her traitorous head wouldn't follow her heart. "Why do you need to stay with me?"

"Because I am the king's man and must do as he commands. Edward hasn't yet agreed that I can take a different bride," Richard said.

Well, then. She'd get the king's permission somehow.

This conversation was going all wrong. *Tell me you care for me. Tell me I'm the only woman for you.* He needed to say the words on his own.

Richard sank onto the bed, holding his head as if it pained him. "I wouldn't be an earl if not for Edward. I can't go against him in this."

She couldn't take the swift rise and fall of her emotions. One minute Richard said something to make her happy, the next, drop her into despair. She climbed off the bed in a fluff of feathers. How could she sleep in the same room with him ever again? Tears gathered. How could she not?

He didn't want her. He wanted a new bride. And it was her fault. She'd waited too long to know her own mind and find the courage to confess her feelings.

She'd go to Alyce. Eleanor paused, her hand on the latch. "I won't be back."

❧❧ ❧❧

Richard groaned as she slammed the door. Eleanor had left him.

For now.

His head pounded and his legs still felt wobbly. He'd barely made it to their room, tripping several times over his own feet. He couldn't summon the words to explain, couldn't go after her until he recovered.

Richard shuddered. He was in serious trouble on several counts. First and most important, he'd wounded Eleanor. She'd acted as if the incident but angered her, but he could see the hurt in her eyes, hear it in her voice. She must care for him a great deal to be this upset. Unless her concern was possessiveness, defending what was yet hers.

He knew all too well the pain of witnessing one's spouse with another. Even his bemused mind appreciated the ultimate irony of the evening's events.

Second, he wished he could be the one to console her, but didn't know how to repair the damage. How could he explain why he'd been alone with Blanche? He knew how Eleanor hated alchemy and didn't want her involved in anything related to it. Yet they'd vowed to be honest with each other.

Third, Eleanor was right. Anyone could have seen him with

Blanche. How could he tell her he'd made sure the door remained open to prove his meeting with her was innocent, unaware he'd soon be under the influence of some strange drug? The tale didn't sound believable even to his ears.

Never had he felt as though quicksand sucked him under no matter which way he turned. The ground he'd painstakingly gained with Eleanor was lost, possibly forever.

By the saints, he was a warrior, not a sage.

He couldn't lose Eleanor. Not just because he needed to stay wed to her. Because he wanted to. He wouldn't let her go. Even at the risk of his own heart.

For certes she'd use her anger at him, her disappointment, to fuel her decision to go ahead with the tournament. He could refuse to go along, but then she'd feel trapped. The only way for their marriage to succeed on a personal level was to make her choose him.

How could he regain Eleanor's favor?

❦ ❦

Eleanor held out her candle against the deserted corridors. Which way was Alyce's room? She was lost, as in so many areas of her life.

Self-pity would get her nowhere. Never give up, she vowed. Eleanor tried to get her bearings. A few turns later, she found Alyce's room.

She knocked softly, praying only her sister would awaken and not the two women with whom she shared her chamber. But she already knew Fortune was not with her.

From behind the door, an unfamiliar voice asked, "Who's there?"

"'Tis Eleanor," she hissed. "Countess of Glasmere. I need to speak with my sister, Alyce."

The door opened. A yawning young woman walked back to the huge bed and shook Alyce awake. She'd always been a heavy sleeper.

"Your sister's here."

As a bleary-eyed Alyce hurried out of bed, the woman

climbed in. Her sister put on her robe, then joined Eleanor in the hall.

"Whatever is the matter?" Alyce wrapped her robe tightly about her and crossed her arms. "Couldn't it wait until morn? 'Tis freezing out here."

"No, it can't. I saw Richard alone with Blanche. She was…fondling him. And he knows I saw."

"Well, what of it? And why does it upset you?" Alyce asked, keeping her voice low. "Perhaps she'll win the tournament. You'll have succeeded in finding Richard a bride he prefers to you. A better bride, exactly as you wanted."

"Anyone could have seen them. The door was open."

"Oh. So you fear others will know that your husband, whom all know you want to be rid of, might be unfaithful."

"My concern is that the other women might find out. I doubt they'd agree to compete for a groom, despite his fine form, wealth and position, if they knew Blanche had, well, a head start."

"Why are you crying? You should be happy. Soon you'll be free. Of course, Arthur is wed now. But you may still have the chance to choose your own groom."

Eleanor knew why her success was making her miserable. Because she did care. Truly cared. She wanted Richard to desire her, only her. And though she might seem successful to everyone else, she knew she'd failed. Once again her best efforts had produced an unintended result. She'd forfeited control to Richard by coming to care for him.

Did she love him? She gasped. *Please, not that.* Or did she just want him now because the chances of keeping him were so slim? Is that why she'd fought for Arthur?

"You haven't cried as much in your life as you have since you met Richard. And I know why. Because you finally truly care about someone, and caring can hurt."

Her sister was right again. "What's the point of caring if it gives that person the power to destroy you?" If he doesn't want you as much as you want him? Eleanor closed her eyes. "Well then, I shall stop caring for him. Right now."

If only it were that easy.

Perhaps this was why many people accepted arranged marriages. Marriages made for love could yield far more pain than those between strangers. How sad to think she'd spent most of her life wanting a marriage that probably wouldn't have made her happy anyway.

Eleanor hadn't heard a word Alyce had been saying.

"…'twas quite late. And the room, as you said, was not in a well-traveled corridor. It's unlikely anyone else saw them."

"All right, then. The real problem is he is still wed to me," she hissed.

"In name only," Alyce shot back as she hopped from foot to foot on the stone floor. "Eleanor, admit the truth. The reason finding Blanche and Richard together bothers you so is this: You have fallen in love with Richard and want him to love you in return."

Eleanor recoiled. "No. That can't be."

"Are you sure?"

No. Her heart thudded heavily. She wasn't sure at all. Or was she, but too scared to admit it?

CHAPTER 14

"Owen!" Richard hammered his brother's door. "Open the door. Now."

Owen stood in his tiny chamber with tousled hair and half-shut eyes.

"Let me in. Do you have ale?" He needed to wash away the bitter taste of Blanche's drugs and his meeting with her.

"I am, um, occupied at the moment." Owen tilted his head toward the bed, where Richard saw the outline of a body under the covers.

"Ah. Get rid of her," he said as he shoved the door open and strode into the room. "I have need of your counsel."

"What of my needs? Cherie, you must go now," Owen grumbled as he lit a candle. He picked up the gown on his wood chest and held it out. A woman with curly red hair appeared from beneath the sheets. With a petulant frown, she took the garment. As she lifted her arms to slip it over her head, she caught sight of Richard.

Her pretty face brightened. "Oooh, there's two of you. Hard to say which is the handsomer." She dropped the gown and drew back the sheets, exposing her ample breasts. "The more the merrier, I always say."

Richard sighed. Women offered themselves everywhere except in his own bed. The only woman he wanted, and feared he'd ever want, was his reluctant wife.

Owen laughed. "I heartily agree. Perhaps another time."

"I'll hold you to that," she said with a sultry smile. She retrieved the gown and put it on. After giving Owen a brief kiss, she flounced out, closing the door behind her.

"So, brother, what is so urgent?" He piled several pillows on the bed and flopped against them, arms behind his head.

Dizziness washed over Richard again. If he consumed anything, he risked it coming back up. How long would the effects of that cursed drug linger? He grabbed a pillow from beneath his brother and carefully reclined on the other end of the bed.

Richard described his meeting with Blanche and Eleanor's unfortunate discovery. "I believe Hugh put Blanche up to this. He wants Father's alchemy writings."

Owen jumped off the bed. "By my troth, do you have Father's scrolls? Did he discover the formula for the Philosopher's Stone?"

"I don't know," Richard said. "I have eighteen of Father's scrolls. The other two and his folio of notes are missing. I spent hours studying his numerous drawings of the alchemical process, but couldn't come up with a workable formula. If it exists in the scrolls I have, 'tis so well hidden Father's own apprentice couldn't find it. The secret could be in the other two scrolls, or elsewhere. Or nowhere."

Richard's thoughts wandered to Eleanor. What was she doing? How could he ease her mind?

"We must search for the missing scrolls so we can give all twenty to Edward," Owen said. "I've heard his alchemists work night and day. For certes they could use Father's information."

"I need to tell you something," Richard said, heart heavy with memories. "You were away in service to your lord, unaware of the unusual circumstances surrounding Father's death. About the day Father believed he'd discovered the mixture for the Philosopher's Stone."

"What? And you never told me?"

"You'd have abandoned your duties to join me if I'd told you." He continued, "I overheard Father and his new partner, Sir Thomas Cromer, celebrating. They were certain they'd finally created the remedy to restore the long ill King Henry's health. While I shared their joy, I also feared for them. What if they failed to cure him? What if he took a turn for the worse, or died? Their reputations were at stake.

"They never had the opportunity to present their discovery. Father and Sir Thomas were killed that afternoon, shortly after I left. Their workshop was ransacked."

"And you didn't think I'd want to know such details?" Owen asked, his expression incredulous.

"I thought to protect you," Richard replied. "There was nothing you could've done I didn't try."

"I still would've liked to know." Owen dropped onto the bed. "What of the scrolls?"

"Fortunately, they were well hidden, scattered in different locations. Perhaps the murderers have the missing two. It's been almost five years. If thieves had the formula and it was viable, they'd have put it to use."

"Maybe their thievery was interrupted and they had to leave some scrolls behind. Maybe, like you, they couldn't make sense of the contents. Or what if there was a substance they couldn't find?" Owen sat up straight.

"Any of those things could be true. The scrolls are replete with strange symbols and detailed drawings. Mayhap Father wrote in elaborate code only he and Sir Thomas could decipher."

"Who knows which scrolls contain essential information? We have to find out if the formula exists. For the nonce, back to Eleanor. How has she taken all of this?"

"She despises alchemy because of her father and thinks it's the devil's work and. They aren't speaking because Edmund established a new workshop, violating a deathbed promise to her mother. So I haven't shared everything about our father.

"I considered Edmund the primary suspect because he and Father parted so acrimoniously. Not telling Eleanor was wise. Blanche drugged me, so who knows what she or FitzWalter would do to Eleanor if they thought she knew something?" He rubbed his temples to ease the pounding in his head. "Now what? Are all women this much trouble?"

"As with fighting, one learns from experience," Owen

answered. "I've had some feminine predicaments in my day, but none as bad as this. Give me a moment until a solution comes." He closed his eyes. A few seconds passed in silence. "Lo, I have it."

"Already?" Richard sat up, regretting the abrupt movement when lights danced before him. "Well?"

"You must tell Eleanor the whole truth."

Richard snorted. "That's your solution? How does this sound: 'My erstwhile betrothed drugged my wine so I'd reveal the formula for the Philosopher's Stone, which my father is believed to have discovered.' Even if I could forego my concern for Eleanor's safety, how can I expect her to believe that? Or care, when she's so against alchemy?"

"It's called trust, Richard." He shrugged. "You should try it."

Owen's all-knowing tone irked him. "You know better than to expect me to trust a woman."

"Mayhap there is one woman among the masses who'd never betray her man. I can see you care for Eleanor despite your best intentions. What if she wants you, too?"

He couldn't admit the depth of his feelings. "Even if I wanted to, how could I win her trust?"

"You don't win trust, you earn it," Owen said, a smug smile on his face.

"The damned tournament is in four days," Richard grumbled.

"Then, dear brother, you don't have much time."

❦ ❦

Fie on her sister and her practical advice. Eleanor stormed back to her own chamber.

How dare Alyce refuse Eleanor a place in her bed? Alyce wasn't the one who had to deal with a traitorous, albeit temporary, spouse.

She didn't want to face Richard again tonight. All she wanted was some sleep. Maybe the new day would bring a fresh approach to her problems.

She pulled off her headdress and shook her hair free. The

thing made her head ache. Her shoes clacked on the stones, so she slowed as she approached her room. She tiptoed to the door, not wanting to wake Richard. Maybe he wasn't there. What if he'd returned to that cozy nook to finish what he started with Blanche?

No, not that. Never before had she suffered such maddening, strong possessiveness for a man. As long as they were married, Richard was hers. That was that.

Eleanor squeezed the latch. The hinges' high-pitched squeaks made her wince. Richard couldn't have missed that noise. But firelight revealed an empty bed. The ebullient, dancing flames mocked her. Her headdress dropped to the floor. She stood motionless in the too empty, too quiet room, awash with pillow feathers.

Where was her husband?

Her heart ached. Would the pain fade? She was afraid to search within herself for the answer to Alyce's question. Did she love Richard?

God help her if she did.

"You're here."

Eleanor jumped.

Richard had returned. She could breathe again.

"I'm pleased," he said. "I hope you'll give me a chance to explain." He threw another log on the fire, then gestured to the small table and stools in the corner. "Please. Will you join me?"

Nerves on edge, Eleanor sat across from him. She wasn't sure she wanted to hear this. On the other hand, she burned to know that despite what she'd seen, he hadn't wanted to be with Blanche. Her heart, it seemed, had defected from her head. She needed to know Richard wanted her.

"The truth is more than strange, I grant you." He reached out as if to take her hand, then apparently thought better of it and crossed his arms. "But here it is. All of it. Blanche put an aphrodisiac in my wine so I'd lose control of my wits and give her my father's alchemy notes and formula."

Eleanor burst into laughter. She couldn't help herself. His skin was pale, he moved more languidly than usual, but.... "A good tale, but I'm sure you can come up with something I'm more likely to believe. Do try again." She laced her fingers.

"I've never lied to you, but I haven't told you every detail about my past, either. There was no need, given that you don't plan to remain my wife." Richard leaned on his elbows. "Owen says I should trust you."

Relief soothed her. He'd gone to see Owen. Not Blanche.

"He says one earns trust by trusting. So I'll tell you things only my brother knows. My father was one of the few alchemists licensed by Henry VI. When common remedies failed to cure the king's unusual, long-lasting ailment, his physicians and Queen Margaret resorted to all sorts of treatments, no matter how bizarre."

She shuddered. "Back then, I knew so little of my father's alchemy work, not even that our fathers were partners. As I saw the man it turned him into I began to hate it. And understand the ramifications of success."

"Of course I've considered them, as well. Our fathers were appointed to the alchemy commission created to cure the king," Richard said. "And they worked even harder to seek the quintessence, known as the Philosopher's Stone, reputed to be the secret of transmutation.

"Nothing interested me more than my father's work, from setting up the distillation apparatus to the sulfur and mercury we used. That is, until I was old enough to grasp the dangers of succeeding and the precarious position such a scientist would find himself in. Alchemy is science. Not evil in itself, or from the devil."

"I don't agree."

"Have you ever looked at it from the king's point of view....how many people he could help with more gold?"

"No, because the concept is heresy. Not science or medicine, but magic."

"We'll have to agree to disagree on that. I do agree that some science can bring out the worst in some men."

Whether Richard had the discipline to not succumb to alchemy's lure like other men wasn't the most important thing. The pursuit in and of itself was. Could their rift be mended?

"I saw similar things with my father," she said. "Fear of failure, either from offering the king controversial advice, or by ingested stuffs doing more harm than good. Combine that with constant suspicion and fear of anyone who might steal a successful formula and misuse it."

"Exactly. Because of such possibilities, I accepted the Duke of York's invitation to join Edward's household. I began training to be a knight at an older age than most. Shortly thereafter, our fathers had their argument. Mine found a new partner. Several months later, they were murdered."

Eleanor gasped. "I had no idea. I'm sorry to hear that."

She took his hand, trying to focus on their conversation and not how good it felt to be so near him. Alone with him, and away from the distractions of court.

"Father wrote a series of twenty numbered scrolls containing his findings. In several, he hinted that he had discovered the Philosopher's Stone. Scrolls seventeen and eighteen have disappeared, either hidden or destroyed by my father or stolen by his murderer."

A fascinating tale. But why did Richard trust her with his secrets? "You must have suspected my father."

Edmund had kept this, too, from her. Her blood chilled. She added more logs to the fire.

"Yes. Despite an investigation, no proof was found."

"I'm glad of that." Yet Richard must not be convinced, or why would he have seemed so interested in her father's workshop? She faced him, steeling herself to learn more. "Where does Blanche fit in?"

"As I said, she drugged my wine, hoping to make me reveal any secrets I might know."

"Why would she do that?"

"I suspect she's low on funds and owes Lady FitzWalter money."

"What?" Eleanor couldn't conceal her surprise. That bit of gossip hadn't reached her. "No wonder she seemed so eager to participate in the bridal tournament."

"Blanche has no source of income. Her husband died without a groat to his name."

Eleanor collapsed on the bench near the fire. What would she have done in Blanche's place, with no coin and nowhere to live, no family to care for her? She shook off any sympathy.

"Whatever her plight, she drugged you. She lied about her wealth in order to take part in the tournament. Perhaps she has done worse things. Are you telling me being penniless justifies Blanche's actions?" "No, I'm merely suggesting what desperation can do," he said. "How it can change people."

"That's no excuse." But he was right, desperation stole good judgment. Look how her father had broken sacred promises to her mother.

"Like Arthur, FitzWalter's son was attainted by King Edward. My guess is he hopes to earn Edward's favor by offering him the priceless formula. Worse, he may use it to make himself the wealthiest man in all of England."

"As I fear my father would," she confessed. "Alchemy is a practice of the occult, thus heretical. His soul is at stake. I must stop him."

"So that's what you were doing in his workshop the night before we left for Windsor. Trying to hinder his progress."

"I led you right to it. You hoped to find your father's scrolls." Should she tell him of the hiding place behind the stones, help him serve Edward? No. Because then she'd be a contributor, when all she'd wanted to do was remove everything alchemy was and stood for from her life.

Eleanor's head swam. Richard's tale sounded so far-fetched, yet he'd spoken with sincerity. "Do you have your father's alchemy formula?"

"No. Blanche obviously doesn't believe me. I don't know if my father dared commit the details of transmutation to writing, but I can't assume he didn't."

He took her hands. The warmth of his touch reassured her. Again she realized how much she'd missed even such simple contact with him. Just looking at him, talking with him, no matter the subject.

More the fool she.

"I want you to be careful. As a way to get to me, Blanche or FitzWalter might try to harm you," he warned.

She pulled her hands away. "My thanks for your concern. I think it's unfounded, as everyone knows we won't be married much longer. It isn't as though you love me and would be devastated to lose me."

"They know you're mine for now. That's what matters."

Eleanor couldn't restrain a shiver. How closely he mirrored her thoughts of a few moments ago. Was belonging to each other, the commitment to go forward as a team, the key to marital happiness? Was accepting something significant that you despised about your spouse worth the cost of all you enjoyed? Was love as elusive as alchemy?

Here was the crux of the matter. "Knowing what you know, what would you do with the formula if you found it? Destroy it, test it, or give it to the king?"

Richard sighed. "A conundrum, that. Edward wants to fill his coffers and create a symbol of rebirth and hope for the future, which would benefit us all, and England. 'Tis my duty to serve him as best I can, yet blind devotion is not for me."

Silence reigned while Eleanor absorbed Richard's answer that wasn't an answer. She wished she could read his expression. "I believe finding the key to alchemy will lead to disaster, fueled by greed. Whoever succeeds will be ensnared by power and think to rule the world. Or, if he gives his discoveries to the king for sizeable reward, no matter how Edward endeavors to keep them close, someone with nefarious intent will steal them. Evil begets evil."

"Evil does beget evil. But you're jumping to conclusions."

"So are you." Enough of this topic. "We'll never agree. So back to tonight. Why did you go to Blanche?"

"She sent a note, begging me to meet on a private, urgent issue. I'm sorry I agreed, sorrier still you saw what you did." His thumb caressed the back of her hand, relaxing her.

"Blanche told me you once loved her. Perhaps you still do. Perhaps if not for your duty, you'd have wed her instead of me," Eleanor ventured. Her voice cracked. Her heart beat faster as she awaited Richard's reply.

If he spoke true, he hadn't willingly betrayed her. He was still the honorable, desirable man she knew him to be.

"I did love her, to my peril. Now I am married to you," he said.

What kind of answer was that? Perhaps Richard wanted to appease them both. Keep his current wife happy and placate the next one.

She wished she could be sure of him. The pain she'd suffered this night outweighed the joy of the kisses they'd shared and even the intimacy. Waking up with him each morning, the way he'd wooed her.... She couldn't live the rest of her life with a man who could so easily lift her high one moment and bring her so low the next. No man, no person, should have so much control over another.

The alchemy of love.

No. No. She did not love Richard.

"Eleanor, you must cancel, or at least postpone indefinitely, your tournament."

She stood, outraged. "What? How dare you demand this?"

"I don't know what Blanche or FitzWalter will do next. There's no way for me to protect you in a crowd," Richard said.

"You don't need to protect me. Look to save your next bride."

"Until our marriage is officially over, 'tis my duty to keep you from danger. I keep what is mine, whether it be a goat or a wife."

Duty again. Anger sizzled hotter than butter in a cook's pan. He cared nothing for her as a woman, as herself.

"The sooner a new bride is chosen for you, the sooner I'll be safe," she snapped. "Then you can protect her. And the rest of your livestock."

She was a possession and an obligation. Not special or esteemed. To think she'd wanted him to kiss her, hold her. And had almost given him the precious prize of her virginity.

So why did she feel so bad?

This unpleasant night had revealed an even more unpleasant truth. Despite her best efforts to remain aloof, despite his indifference, she didn't know if she could stop caring for Richard.

Even as he withdrew from her.

❦ ❧

The next day, a page in Edward's livery with its large sun in splendour badge on the chest interrupted Eleanor's scrutiny of the final tournament details in the library. She loved the aged smell of shelf after shelf of books, and the peaceful silence.

"The chamberlain of the Royal Household requests a meeting?" Eleanor stared at the note the young boy had handed her. "Why would he want to see me?"

"I cannot say, Lady Glasmere, but he awaits in his office. I shall take you to him." The page bowed low.

Still holding the note, Eleanor followed the boy as he wove through the corridors toward the chamberlain's sizeable, wood-paneled office.

"Please, Lady Glasmere, be seated." William, Lord Hastings, stood behind a wide desk. He dressed to match his elevated position in a long, fur-trimmed robe with puffed shoulders and a tall hat with a rounded top that almost concealed his short, dark hair. He wore a necklace of linked suns and white enamel roses, the king's emblems. Like Richard's.

Lord Hastings waved a hand full of documents toward a carved chair on the other side of his desk. He sat, and began sorting documents onto various piles.

"Since you are newly arrived, I'm not sure how much you know of my duties and offices. I am responsible, amongst many things, for the king's entertainments." Hastings paused, his attention momentarily captured by one of the documents. He put the remaining parchments on the tallest pile. "Of course I have heard of the most unusual event you are planning. I wish to offer my assistance."

That her tournament should be noted by the man many called the king's closest friend was flattering, but the unspoken hint that he wanted to be involved and make changes in her decisions appalled her.

"My thanks, Lord Hastings," she said with a gracious nod instead of a sharp retort, "but all is under control. I wouldn't want to trouble you. I can see how busy you are." She smiled, striving to appear confident and calm.

Hastings smiled back. He steepled his fingers. "Perhaps you misunderstood my intent. Edward wishes to restore jousting to England. I believe your tournament, though far from a joust, could encourage enthusiasm for related events. So I am offering my assistance. I'm certain you know what that means."

Eleanor's stomach sank. She might not have been at court very long, but she knew.

"It means you will graciously accept my aid," he said. He handed her a rolled parchment tied with a pink ribbon. "Within you will find the new plans."

She untied the ribbon with fingers she willed not to shake. He couldn't know how her stomach churned as she prepared to read his proposed changes.

"You may study them later. The primary alteration is that the tournament will now be held at Smithfield."

Eleanor gasped. Smithfield, where royal jousts had been held? A far larger venue than she'd rented. Her stomach roiled again. "But, my lord, I—"

"And I plan to invite the entire court."

She emitted an unladylike gasp. As if it weren't enough the whole court knew of and gossiped about her tournament, now everyone would witness the victory of the woman who would become Richard's new bride.

"I'm glad to see this pleases you," Hastings commented, an unmistakable note of warning in his voice. "I have everything under control. Of course I've mentioned this to the king. You'll be elated to know he has expressed interest in attending."

Eleanor was speechless. No matter where she went, no matter how hard she tried, there was always some man who could overrule her choices and tell her what to do. Was there anywhere in the world a woman could escape a man's control, could make her own decisions and see them enacted?

All she could do now was accept with grace. Act like the lady—the countess—she was. "Since the tournament now is in your skilled hands, my lord, you may wish to know I've just learned that Lady Blanche Latimer, one of the competitors, lied about her wealth to gain entry."

"I see. I'll have that looked into." Hastings continued, "Quite interesting, is it not, Lady Glasmere? The king required you to wed the earl, yet now he supports your generosity in seeking...what do the gossips say...a 'better bride.' I wonder what prompted such a change of heart. I suggest you think on that, and carefully."

He returned to his papers without so much as another look at her.

She rose, fighting the unwelcome wavering of her chin. "My thanks, Lord Hastings, for your munificence."

His head snapped up, likely at the impossible-to-contain sarcasm in her tone.

After bestowing a simpering smile, Eleanor left the chamberlain's office. Though the highest hands in the land were now cooking her pies, there had to be a way to gain some jurisdiction over the ingredients.

CHAPTER 15

"Margaret is dead. My new wife is dead."

Holding his hat in his hand, Arthur stood before Eleanor in Windsor's chapel. He looked haggard as the hat's drooping feather, as if Margaret's sudden death had sapped his energy.

"I'm sorry for your loss," Eleanor said. She frowned. Sorrow was all she felt. Where was hope, where was longing to be with Arthur, now that he was free?

"Margaret came down with a fever as we traveled. We had no physician. No one in our group aided her. She died before we reached the next town." He sat beside her, but she slid down the pew.

"My sympathies for you and her suffering," Eleanor said. "But why tell me? Does Richard know of her death? Or that you've returned to court?"

"Not yet. I wanted to see you first." He turned, as if making sure no one else could hear. "I've lost more than my wife. Since she died without an heir of her body, her lands revert to the king. Edward hasn't accepted me into his good graces. The attainder still keeps—"

"Ah, so you're without coin again." Burning anger replaced sorrow. "That's why you came to me. You want me to plead your case with Richard so he'll help you to another wealthy bride. How many do you think he has to hand?"

Other courtiers gathered nearby. She could almost see their

ears grow larger as they strained to listen. She couldn't wait to be away from court, the never-ending gossip and intrigues, the noisy crowds.

Eleanor lowered her voice. "You could join Richard in my tournament of brides and take home the lady who comes in second. No, wait, you've been attainted and the king hasn't forgiven you. And Richard's brother Owen already has a claim on number two."

"I have another idea—"

"Ask Richard if friendship still holds sway. Or has your well finally run dry? Do you fear Richard has done all he's willing to do, so you seek aid from me?" She couldn't help her disdain. Everyone, from Hastings to Arthur, wanted something from her.

"Eleanor, what has made you so bitter?" He moved closer, too close. She slid away. "How could you forget what we meant to each other? I thought you'd be ecstatic to learn I'm no longer wed. After your tournament, we can finally—"

"Not another word." She held up a hand. "You made it quite clear you wouldn't want me whether you were free or not. Now that you've lost your bride's wealth, here you are. Ha. You want my funds, not me."

"Eleanor, please." The devotion in his gaze made her fear he'd go down on one knee in front of everyone. "It was as you said. Duty bound me to Margaret. I couldn't in good conscience trouble you with my wishes or true feelings. It wouldn't have been fair to either of us, or Margaret or Richard. But I never stopped thinking about you. Missing you. Tell me 'tis not too late for us."

Was he sincere? Her long-held dream could still come true. She searched within for the love she used to feel for Arthur, but found nothing. She didn't know him, if she ever had. He literally paled in comparison to Richard, in more ways than the physical. Why had she taken so long to see it?

"I love you, Eleanor. Can you doubt me?"

At last the words she had so longed to hear. But from the wrong man, at the wrong time.

Suddenly all was as if the sun dispelled thick gray clouds marring her vision. She hadn't known what love really was. How much time had she wasted believing Arthur in his blond perfection represented the man of her ideals? Because the king, her father and even Richard wanted to control her, she'd refused to see the gift she was being offered. Richard, the better groom in all respects.

Alyce had suggested she could have the choice she'd always wanted. She just had to choose Richard. Perhaps that was the true way to happiness: to choose, within your heart, what you were given. To focus on the good as much as possible instead of dwelling on the bad.

"'Tis definitely too late," she said. "There is no 'us.'"

"You're angry," Arthur said. "That's understandable. We'll continue this conversation anon." He bowed and left.

Eleanor watched him without a hint of remorse. What a mess she'd made. Soon Richard would have a better bride. And she'd have nothing. Nothing but her pride.

Unless…. How could she call off the tournament? Her many hours of planning had proved fruitful, though not in the way she'd expected. Working to find Richard another bride served to show her how much she wanted to keep her husband.

Eleanor tracked down her sister, who was strolling through the Upper Ward with her roommates. Though she'd become accustomed to Windsor's grandeur, its vastness still staggered her.

She led Alyce to a stone bench. "Alyce, I need your help. We need to stop the tournament. Even though Lord Hastings has taken over the planning, moved it to Smithfield and invited the king." Her heart sank.

"Oh, Eleanor." Alyce set down her embroidery basket, and took out a wood frame securing a portion of a red velvet chasuble. She threaded the brass needle with silk. "'Tis in two days. Why now?"

Her sister's calm demeanor fueled her impatience. "I've finally made up my mind. I want to stay with Richard. I am the only wife he needs."

"You should listen to me more often," Alyce admonished. "You arranged the tournament only to give yourself time to get to know him."

"That wasn't my goal. Though as it turns out, you're right. I just couldn't sit back and be told what to do. Nor did I want to bind myself to another alchemist."

She made several dainty stitches on the head of a cherub. "Well, it's too late. You're no longer in charge. The brides are eager. Richard too, from what I've seen."

Eleanor clasped her hands and danced a little jig. The sun suddenly seemed brighter, the air fresher. "Alyce, I'm so glad you came to court with me. You're brilliant."

"What did I say?" She frowned.

"It'll be so much better if Richard is the one to call off the tournament. If he doesn't desire a new bride, there's no reason to continue. All I have to do is convince him we should remain together."

"How can you do that?" Alyce asked, disbelief evident in her expression. "You've done naught but endeavor to rid yourself of him."

"By taking matters into my own hands. Men prefer action, not words," Eleanor said. "I shall show him. And remain in charge."

As soon as she returned to their room, she changed into her favorite gown, of indigo silk damask with a draped neckline, fitted sleeves and a short train. Her excitement built as she added a thick gold necklace. Just as she finished brushing her hair, there was a knock at the door.

The news the messenger brought sent her to her knees in despair.

❧ ☙

Richard wanted to destroy the parchment in his hands. Crush, shred, burn. But getting rid of the evidence wouldn't change reality.

His marriage to Eleanor was officially over. She'd gotten her annulment, leaving them both free in the eyes of both Church and state to marry again.

The dangling wax seals clacked as he stormed the halls. Let her see what her foolishness had wrought.

He found her in the new, tiny chamber she'd already been reassigned to, since a man and woman who weren't wed couldn't share a room. She sat with a book in her lap, not reading, but staring at nothing. Her trunks were stacked next to the narrow bed.

Did she have regrets? Why should she, when she was hours away from getting what she'd wanted most since the moment they'd met?

To be rid of him.

"No last-minute details to organize?" he asked in lieu of a greeting.

"Hastings has taken charge of everything." She looked tired and sad as the brown wool gown she wore, as if the life had drained from her. Her skin was ashen, her eyes dull.

Richard wouldn't feel sorry for her. He wouldn't offer to help. She deserved this.

"Here. Congratulations." He handed her the parchment.

Something that seemed oddly like hope flashed in Eleanor's eyes until she glanced at the document. "Yes. I received a copy earlier today." She seemed to sink in on herself. "I'd no idea we'd obtain this so quickly."

"All is as you wanted. King Edward facilitated our annulment because he agrees you should be released and I should be well compensated. Why shouldn't I have a wealthier, superior bride? As you said, Edward needs coin in his coffers more than anything. So a better bride benefits him as well. He needs the wealthiest nobles to support his cause to thwart any remaining challengers loyal to the old king. Until his alchemists succeed."

She said nothing.

"You should be well pleased," he continued. At least one of them should be. He felt sick to his stomach.

"Are *you* pleased?" Eleanor tipped her head up.

"I live to give pleasure to my lady," he said with a sweeping bow. "If she is satisfied, then am I."

"But I'm not your lady anymore." Eleanor stood, the book and parchment falling to the floor. She said no more, but her eyes pleaded with him. For what?

Richard stepped closer until they almost touched. He inhaled her unique, lemony scent for the last time. How he would miss that scent. How he would miss her.

They'd probably never be alone again. If he'd known last night would be their final time sharing a bed, he'd have savored each moment. Tried one last time to convince her to stay with him.

The ache in his heart was worse than when his father had been murdered. "Alack, no, you aren't. And on the morrow I shall have a new lady to please. One who chooses me."

Richard didn't want a new lady. He wanted Eleanor, his beautiful, intelligent, spirited former wife. There was no point telling her now. She hadn't cared enough any of the other times he'd tried to win her. Though at first his goal had been to make her choose him so he could fulfill his duty, he also wanted Eleanor for herself. For her wit, spirit, beauty, and more.

His heart skipped a beat. Did he love her? No. Thanks to Blanche, he couldn't love her or anyone. Feelings that deep were for fools. He cared deeply, desired her, and had hoped to spend the rest of his life with her.

No matter. It was too late. Their legal and religious ties had been severed. Nothing should bind them any longer. His continuing attraction to her combined with her nearness, the bittersweet parting and the intimacy of the small room, made him want things he shouldn't.

They stood as if fearful a single gesture would break the mood holding them enthralled. After a long, long moment Eleanor made the first move.

She kissed him.

🙵 🙷

Eleanor rejoiced when Richard kissed her back. He wanted her still. That was all that mattered.

Without breaking their kiss, he slid an arm behind her knees and picked her up. He closed the door with a swift kick then set her down near the bed.

Her heart lightened by a stone. There'd never be another man for her, but she couldn't bring herself to let him know.

Because all too soon he'd wed another woman because of her foolishness.

They undressed speedily, tugging at laces, ties and ribbons. Pieces of clothing flew in all directions, hitting nearby walls and dropping to the floor. They seemed to share the same state of frenzied need.

Soon she would be in his arms and feel his skin against hers.

She could allow herself this final time with Richard, though he was no longer her husband in the eyes of God or man. Not being wed made him all the more compelling. For they'd finally chosen to be together, no longer ordered by the king or duty-bound by a marriage.

Yet she wouldn't let him inside her, no matter how much she wanted to. Bound by honor and duty as he was, Richard might insist they wed again if he took her maidenhead, whether or not his decision displeased him, the king and lord chamberlain or the other brides. She just couldn't spend the rest of her days knowing she was an obligation.

Eleanor would cherish the sensations Richard aroused and revel in his kisses. She'd have only this too short time to remember him by. To remember what their marriage could have been like if she hadn't been such a stubborn, prideful fool.

A slight frown marred Richard's brow. "Eleanor, please don't tell me you've changed your mind again." As if to prevent her from answering, he drew her into a scorching kiss.

Richard needed her. His words restored her excitement, while his naked body pressed against hers aroused her further. After kissing her thoroughly, when her knees threatened to buckle and liquid desire seeped between her thighs, he released her.

Eleanor drank in the sight of his muscular arms, his broad chest, his flat stomach. His erection enticed her. She met his gaze. The hungry look in his eyes empowered her. Richard could have almost any woman, but he wanted her.

Everything ached when she pulled away. She wanted more than a few stolen kisses. She wanted what she could never have. His love. Unless…. The thrill of hope replaced pain.

She fingered the sapphire ring he'd given her. When had it stopped weighing her down, ceased representing a noose of obligation, and become a comforting reassurance of commitment and promise for their future?

Richard's gaze was hot. "I want you."

She released him to recline on the bed. She opened her arms. "Then come to me."

❦❧

Richard slid into her welcoming embrace. He couldn't think of another place he'd rather be than in this tiny room on this tiny bed with Eleanor.

His ex-wife.

"Can you feel what you do to me?" He rubbed his erection against her.

"I plan to do more," she said.

And though anticipation combined with her beautiful body and deep, soul-wracking kisses had hardened him to the point of no return, his amazing Eleanor had more temptations in store. Slowly she kissed her way down his chest to his stomach, then lower still. His stomach clenched as her tongue trailed downward.

With her hands braced on his thighs, she raised her head, a slight question in her gaze.

"Praise the saints, yes," he murmured.

Eleanor smiled, then leaned over him, her hair falling over her face and tickling his legs. The shimmering curtain of hair exhilarated him because he couldn't see what she was doing yet frustrated him because he wanted to see her perform this most intimate deed.

Then her mouth closed over him. His head fell back against the sheets as her wet heat encompassed him. He could no longer think, only drown in pleasure. A moan escaped him as her tongue licked up and down. As she gently sucked him. He was going to—

"Stop!" He sat up abruptly.

"What's wrong?" He took her in his arms. "Nothing, sweet, all is more than well. Your kisses please me more than I can say. There's only one thing I want right now. You."

She fell back onto the bed and drew him to her. He lavished attention on her breasts, drawing sighs of delight. But he had to taste her. As she had done, he kissed his way to her stomach. Gently he spread her thighs, then touched her woman's flesh. As his arousal pulsed, he stroked her.

Eleanor sighed louder.

He slipped a finger inside her, enthralled by the moisture easing his way. He dipped his head. His tongue stroked in and out as her hips rose and fell beneath him.

The splay of her golden hair on the pillows, the sensual look in her deep purple eyes, her full breasts filled him to near bursting.

Quickly he moved over her. One smooth thrust sent him past her barrier to the place he so longed to be. Inside her. He wanted nothing more than to move, but forced himself to hold still, to allow her time to adjust.

"Richard," she cried. She froze, clenching around him.

He paused. Had he hurt her?

She squeezed him, then tilted her hips, pushing him deeper still.

On the verge of release, but fearing she wasn't ready to join him, he clasped her tight and held his breath. A moment's pause might make the urge subside enough so he could satisfy Eleanor as she satisfied him.

She moved against him, making him slide in and out of her as he longed to do.

That did it. Her sensuous undulations sent him soaring. In the midst of surging bliss, he heard her gasp and felt her shudder beneath him as she called out his name.

His ecstasy was complete.

❧ ❧

Eleanor rested beneath Richard, replete in a way she'd not known possible. The pain of entry had been sharp, but brief. Nothing could've prepared her for the fullness and joy of having him inside her, the rapture making them one.

His warm weight on her was comforting. He toyed with her

hair, then kissed her, softly yet with passion. He showed her he cared without cluttering this special moment with words. She felt protected and cherished. And happier than she had ever been.

What had she done?

She'd done exactly as she wanted. The minute she'd touched his hardness, all thoughts of restraint vanished. She'd wanted to succumb to need, to passion, to everything Richard could share with her.

He raised himself on one elbow. "We must wed. Again. Immediately."

For once Richard reacted as she expected. He hadn't asked her to marry him, but told her she must. Always, always, he acknowledged his duty.

She rolled to her side. The way he looked, with his ruffled hair falling over his cheek, the muscled expanse of his bare chest, brought tears to her eyes. She'd never have the delight of him in her bed again.

"Why? Everyone thinks we did this long ago. Remember your blood on the sheets? No one has to know."

"I know," he said. "I know I just took your virginity."

"You didn't take it. I gave it to you. Besides, should I wed again, my husband would think it most strange if I were still a virgin, knowing I'd been married. And that would reflect poorly on you."

He sat up and glared at her, the indolent lover gone. "So you did this for me? This bedsport was a sacrifice to preserve my reputation?"

"No, not at all," she protested.

"That's what it sounds like. You never cease to amaze me, Eleanor, with your strange reasoning." He pulled on his clothes as quickly as he had shed them.

"Why are you angry? I wanted you, you wanted me. Neither of us is bound to anyone right now."

Eleanor had done exactly as she wanted, and being with him had surpassed her imaginings. Her only regret was they'd only made love once.

"Then why now? Why now?" he demanded. "Why not any of the other nights we've spent together?"

"What difference does it make?"

"It makes all the difference to me."

"Then you should already know. Because this is the first time I could believe you chose me, for me, as a desirable woman. You didn't make love with me because we were legally wed, because the king gave you to me or as part of your duty," she said.

His touch combined with hope to melt the ice the annulment encrusted over her heart.

" We're no longer duty-bound by marriage. At last you chose me. You wanted to be with me. Well, I choose you, too." Eleanor smiled, her first real smile in days. "How can we can cancel the tournament without offending the king?"

Eleanor would do anything for the man she truly loved.

The realization pierced her with a force of a jouster's lance. Why did she have to acknowledge her love for Richard now, to spend mere moments with and send him off to another wife? When she couldn't rejoice in finally feeling what she'd longed for most of her life?

※ ※

Richard wanted to recoil from the lovelorn look in her eyes. Marriage—being bound in the eyes of God, king and man—hadn't been enough for her. She'd only be happy if she ensnared him in the one way certain to defeat him. She sought to trap him with love.

He yearned to escape his feelings for her, which frightened him to the core. If he spent more time in her company, he might surrender to her feminine wiles and intelligence, and fall in love with her. He couldn't allow that. Not even to make Eleanor happy.

Nor could he lie.

"We can't, Eleanor. This is what you wanted. 'Twas you who pined for someone else and refused me. I thought you'd grown up," he said. "But you remain lost in girlish dreams and believe in romantic nonsense. You're a beautiful woman who just threw herself into my arms. Why wouldn't I take what was offered?"

Her face fell. He steeled himself. His harsh words were for the best. But the sting of what he'd just done was sharp as a bee's. And wouldn't fade.

She snatched his ring off her finger and threw it at his chest. It bounced off his tunic and landed on the floor with a dull thud.

He had to take another bride. Whoever she was, she'd be better than Eleanor. Not because she was more beautiful, talented or wealthy.

Because she wouldn't tempt him to love.

❧ ❧

By first light the morning of the tournament, Eleanor was dressed and waiting outside Hastings's office. She had to be the first to talk with him on this all-important day. As she paced the hall, nerves on edge despite deep breaths, she hoped he'd agree to see her, much less grant her wish.

At length he arrived, walking briskly. Not certain of the protocol, Eleanor followed him into his office.

"Countess of Glasmere." He bowed. "Forgive my error," he said with a slight smile. "Lady Eleanor. Have you come to offer encouragement for today's spectacle? If so, I accept your good wishes. If not, I fear you'll have to leave. You are not on my schedule. I must head to the grounds shortly and have quite a lot to accomplish before then." He was already engrossed in a pile of documents, sifting through them, signing a few.

"Lord Hastings, this will take but a moment of your time," she said.

He sighed heavily and pursed his lips, as if to convey how much aggravation she caused. "Very well. You have one minute." He inverted a small hourglass. "Begin."

"I wish to enter the tournament."

Eleanor hadn't told anyone, even Alyce, of her new plan. She'd surprise them all. She wanted Richard enough to risk losing to the others even in the most public of forums. Oddly enough, his cruel words the day before had strengthened her resolve. She'd show him that what they shared meant far more to him than he'd admitted.

Though she'd personally selected women who'd be superior

to her in some way, not one was superior in them all. She stood a good chance at victory, for the Overall aspect carried the most weight. The prize was well worth the attempt.

That got Hastings's attention. He even set down his pen. "You know the rules. No one can enter a tournament the day it is held."

"That rule applies to jousts. This event, as you have said, is different. I hoped you'd make an exception in light of my unique situation." She clasped her hands at her waist to avoid wringing them.

A man in the king's livery hurried in, bowed, and handing Hastings a document. He reviewed and then signed it as the seconds he'd granted her dripped away. The man bowed again and left.

"Typical woman, ever changing her mind. So you want Glasmere back, do you?" He shook his head. "I cannot assist you. 'Tis too late."

Her hopes sank. Typical man, exerting his authority over a woman. That was the way of the world. Men thrived on ruling their domains, whether the man be a peasant in his cottage or a lord in his castle.

"Then I formally request that you cancel the tournament," she said.

He picked up his pen and pointed it at her. "Who do you think you are to suggest such a thing? After the king called stepped in to procure a speedy annulment for you, after twenty-four carpenters spent two days constructing the tournament pavilions at some expense? I think not. The entire court is looking forward to this. Edward, too. There's been nothing like it in ages. Do you really expect me to disappoint the king, and hundreds of others, on your whim?"

"But, Lord Hastings—"

He cut her off with a wave of his hand. "There will be a seat for you near the king. You will be in it."

CHAPTER 16

"I cautioned you to think first," Alyce said as they traversed the corridors on their way to break their fast. "If you'd heeded my advice, none of this would've happened."

The last thing Eleanor needed was a reminder that her sister had been right yet again. Wasn't it bad enough that Richard meant more to her than anything, and she couldn't have him? That soon she'd have to watch other women compete for the opportunity to live with, kiss and touch him?

She shuddered. "How was I to know Lord Hastings would get involved, insist on holding the tournament at Smithfield and invite everyone, even the king?" Shock jolted her anew at the thought of the king attending her tournament.

Could she have anticipated the public spectacle her bride search would become? "For certes I would've found a way to avoid all of this embarrassment. This mêlée. 'Tis awful. I'm the victim of snide comments and insinuations from men and women alike. What can I say when they ask, 'Is not Richard man enough for you?' or 'Think you to look higher than an earl?'" Her voice rose in mockery of her tormentors. She'd thought she was above being hurt by gossip, but obnoxious jokes and laughter at her expense made her stomach churn.

Eleanor didn't appreciate being put on the defensive. She couldn't tell them a combustible mix of pride and hatred of alchemy had led her to this place. Who would understand that her determination to control her life and not be subjected to a man's will induced her to act thusly? The ultimate irony was that control had been snatched from her. Control of the tournament by Hastings, control of her emotions by Richard. The only thing she remained in charge of was maintaining her composure in public. She hoped she could handle the task.

"I envisioned a small affair, with myself, you and Richard, and a few of the brides' relatives as spectators. How was I to know gossip would consume the courtiers as flames burn parched fields?"

Alyce shook her head. "Because you thought of Richard even then, not the ramifications. You didn't even consider that everyone might want to speculate on and be witness to England's first known tournament of brides. Especially with a handsome earl as the prize."

"Would you have predicted the chamberlain would take over the preparations?"

"No. I grant you even I wouldn't have thought of that."

They were close enough to the hall that she could hear the hum of conversation.

"I'm going back to our—my—chamber," Eleanor said. "I'm not hungry."

"This is the first time you've left your tiny room in two days. You're not afraid to show your face, are you? Have you eaten anything? 'Tis not like you to let anxiety restrain your appetite."

Eleanor opened her mouth to retort but a loud, nasal voice coming from around the corner stopped her.

"Who ever heard of a bridal tournament?" a man asked. "I've won rich prizes over the years, from jewels to horses, but cannot recall a tournament where the victor earned someone's hand in marriage."

She grabbed Alyce's arm and pulled her against the tapestry-covered wall.

"And not even a lady's hand, but a man's," said a second man. A shrill giggle followed.

"Eleanor, we must go," Alyce hissed.

"Ssshhh. You see how it is? I have to listen." Curiosity glued her to the spot.

"A man who is already married. How do they plan to get around that? And an earl!" This from a third man.

"Tsk, tsk. You obviously haven't heard the latest. The marriage between the earl and his countess has been annulled."

"Good timing." Another chuckle.

"We're going to watch women engage in a public test of skills. Scandalous."

"More people are looking forward to this than King Edward's coronation a year ago."

The others heartily agreed.

Alyce's face was full of sympathy. Eleanor's fists clenched. Pity from her sister, betrayal from Richard, mockery from her peers. How could she have made such a muddle when all she'd wanted to do was provide herself and Richard with the best spouses?

"I heard the king plans to attend because he may hold a similar event to find himself a bride. After all, he is the most eligible bachelor in all of Europe. Can you imagine, princesses competing...."

Eleanor couldn't take it anymore. She stepped from her hiding place. "Good morning, all."

The horrified expressions on the speakers' faces at being caught almost made the suffering worth it. She whispered a prayer for peace, for guidance, but felt no relief.

No one could help her now. She had failed.

⁂

At Smithfield, long viewing stands draped in rich cloth and filling with excited, talkative spectators lined the field as if this were a tournament described in the book she'd consulted. Nobles and commoners alike had donned their finest garb. Colorful pennons and banners flapped in the strong breeze.

Eleanor could barely sit still as she awaited the proceedings from her prime location in the king's pavilion near his throne, which was covered in cloth of gold. She recognized several members of the council. Close by was Hastings, consulting with various minions and sending them off to obey a multitude of commands.

She couldn't stop her feet from tapping, the only outward display of her roiling emotions. Her heart actually hurt from thudding so hard. She stared straight ahead, forcing herself not to look at Richard, already seated next to the throne. They hadn't spoken since he'd left her room. She'd spent the time in a swirl of wanting to go to him and wishing he'd come to her. But what more was there to say?

Tears filled her eyes. She couldn't help it.

"Eleanor, stop. You're staring at Richard." Alyce said.

"This may be my last chance to see him. Who knows when we'll be in the same castle again? You and I must return home to Middleworth. We'll have no reason to remain at court, and nowhere else to go."

How would she face her father, survive the mortification of being back under his roof? Her only consolation was that she'd be able to return to his alchemy workshop and investigate his hiding place. For now, she had to get through this day.

All Richard needed to make him look like a king was a crown. He was so handsome in a tunic she'd never seen, fur-trimmed with hanging sleeves. Her heart sank to see that his enthusiasm for his new bride was so great he'd purchased elegant new garments. And in her favorite color: purple. The tunic was in the newer style favored by the king, so short it barely covered his bottom.

She couldn't read his expression. His square jaw was set and he clenched his chair's carved arms. His gaze didn't stray from the as yet empty field. Was he happy about the tournament? Who did he want to win?

Eleanor wanted nothing more than to throw herself upon his mercy and implore him to make her his wife again. Like a defeated knight in a joust à outrance might beg the victor to spare his life. She looked at her hands, the only safe view.

More unpredicted than the elaborate display was the anguish entrenched in her chest. When she'd conceived this tournament, her only thought was to escape Richard so she could wed Arthur. How could she have foreseen the changes in her feelings?

Building a true marriage with Richard had become her heart's desire, even though he'd never love her. All he had to do was admit that he wanted her as his wife. Finally she realized that would be more than enough.

Witnessing Richard wed another would surely be the most painful moment in her life. But she'd brought this on herself and had to see it through. When this day was over, she'd endure constant torture of imagining him laughing and smiling with the victor. Of touching his new bride as he had her. Every time she closed her eyes.

At last she sensed his gaze on her. He stared, unmoving. Her besotted mind thought she could hear him plead, "Eleanor, put a stop to this. Only you can. Do it now."

The imagined words rang in her head. What if she were to ask Richard to cry a halt? Most already thought her the fool for wanting to find her husband another bride and arranging a tournament. She'd look even more foolish if she tried to stop the competition now. And Hastings had declined her request mere hours ago. It'd reflect poorly on him if the event was cancelled just before it started.

Despite their unpleasant parting, Richard might take up her challenge. The tournament couldn't go forth if he refused to take part. It was worth a try. Who cared what others thought of her if spending the rest of her life with Richard was the result? She jumped to her feet.

Before she could even draw a breath, the crowd burst into boisterous cheers. The king, resplendent in a short tunic of vibrant orange, strode into the stands. He waved at the spectators, then with a laugh, clasped Richard's shoulder. He settled into his chair and accepted a goblet of wine from an attendant.

Eleanor's heart plummeted as she collapsed into her chair. She'd hesitated too long. As awkward as it would have been to publicly ask Richard to call the event off, neither he nor Hastings would stop now that the king had arrived.

Richard would soon be lost to her forever.

Her life had become the snowball she and Alyce once made. The small, round clump they'd fashioned enlarged apace as they moved down the hill until it grew so unwieldy they could barely handle it. The huge snowball rolled over Alyce, pinning her beneath. She'd managed to wriggle free without injury beyond a couple of scrapes.

Eleanor could see no way to escape the weight pressing on her. The day was fine, but she could barely breathe.

Onto the field strode five trumpeters. One for each potential bride? As the trumpets sounded an elaborate fanfare, Eleanor squelched the urge to shut her eyes. No lives would be lost today as they occasionally were in men's tournaments, yet she felt as if hers was at stake. The joy of knowing love mingled with sorrow and the despair of loss. Her eyes filled again. She could never have Richard now.

The herald cried, "My honored and redoubted lords and ladies, the very high and very powerful, henceforth arrive the brides-to-be, very eager and ready to begin the tourney assigned today!"

The judges' herald replied, "Very high and very powerful king and my very redoubted lords, my lords the judges here present have heard and understood what your herald has said. The brides may enter in God's name when you like."

The quotes from René d'Anjou's treatise were almost as familiar to Eleanor as her daily prayers. Which, unfortunately, had yielded no fruit, either in results or in her heart.

Accompanied by trumpets, the procession began. Despite the king's limited purse, Hastings had spared no expense. Each potential bride entered the field on a horse caparisoned with fabrics fit for royalty, from white cloth of gold to crimson velvet.

What was Blanche doing among them? Why hadn't Hastings eliminated her from the competition?

Each bride was arrayed in new finery. Mary looked like a seraph, her perfect skin and delicate features enhanced a simple light green gown and the tallest, widest veiled headdress Eleanor had ever seen. Blanche's gown of shimmering brocade revealed the most flesh. Eleanor envied her confident ease. Isabel displayed her assets with pride in russet velvet.

Rose must have decided that the woman wearing the most jewels would win the day. Each finger boasted a sparkling ring, and a thick, gem-studded chain circled her neck. The tall Anne dazzled with ermine trimming her wide cuffs, neckline and train.

Their splendor pricked Eleanor's vanity. Though she too had dressed for the occasion, her V-necked velvet gown didn't rival theirs. She'd thought her headdress, cone-shaped with silver tissue, quite elegant until seeing those worn by the brides.

She hoped her brilliant but false smile concealed the agony brought on by the monsters, Jealousy and Envy, who cavorted inside her. The brides were the center of attention, not she. One of them would leave the field with Richard.

She felt just as worthless as the night when she'd been the only woman not asked to join in the dancing. As alone. Even in a crowd. The cheering made her head throb.

Alyce clasped her hand, as though she could read her thoughts. Eleanor's other hand instinctively fingered the cabochon ruby brooch Richard had given her. The brooch she'd worn every day since, but would have to return.

She'd be left with nothing.

The herald cried, "Hear ye, hear ye, hear ye. You who are committed to this do your best. My lords the judges pray and require that none of you tourneyers disabuse the rules of honesty, as you have promised."

She wished the long-awaited bride test would pass in a blur, that she could retreat into a dark crevasse where numbness and feigned calm prevailed. 'Twas not to be. Each moment passed with bitter clarity.

First came the calling of Financial Wealth. The herald handed each woman's list of gold, lands, rents, other assets to the judges, who studied them with great solemnity. They talked amongst themselves, then Owen wrote on a piece of parchment. He glanced at Richard before handing it to the herald.

"The judges have received proof that one of the women lied about her financial resources. Lady Blanche Latimer has been barred from this portion of the competition," the herald cried.

Murmurs buzzed through the throng. Blanche raised her chin. Hastings had found a way to make her pay for her deceit. She'd have to score exceedingly high in the other areas to have a chance of winning.

"Winner of Financial Wealth: Lady Isabel Buntyng."

Eleanor closed her eyes to avoid Isabel's enjoyment of the crowd's hearty response.

Beauty followed. Each woman paraded before the judges and curtseyed low. To prove who had the best cleavage?

"Winner of Beauty: Lady Mary Whyte."

Graciously she acknowledged the cheers while Blanche glared at the judges.

Dare Eleanor steal a glance at Richard? Yes. She knew him well enough to know the cheerful expression on his face masked his true feelings. But she couldn't read the thoughts he hid.

The next task was Embroidery. According to her rules, the spectators would have to watch for a full hour while the women busily embroidered designs of their choice on a square of blue satin. Fabric, stools, thread and needles were carried out on large pillows.

"Begin on my command," said the herald. "Now!"

The ladies began to sew. As time passed, the crowd grew unruly. Her head pounded in rhythm with the spectators' stomping feet.

Mary paused several times to clasp her hands in prayer. Rose ripped out her design and started over, clearly a victim of the pressure. She pricked her finger, staining her cloth vibrant red. The crowd gasped, and she burst into tears.

After viewing the six squares, the judges made their selection. "Embroidery: Lady Isabel Buntyng."

The crowd gasped again and whispers flew. Isabel had won two rounds.

Richard's face revealed nothing.

Time for Music, where each would play and/or sing two songs. Not a note Mary sang matched the tunes she played. To Eleanor's ears, Blanche's mellow alto was by far the best, and her skill on the lute surpassed the others.

"Music: Lady Blanche Latimer."

With waves and a proud smile, she accepted the crowd's mix of cheers and hisses.

Household Management, requiring testimony from three witnesses, was the final event.

"I'm a dried apple," Eleanor whispered.

"What?" Alyce hissed.

"I started the day rosy and ready, fresh as a ripe apple off the tree," Eleanor explained. "But this tournament has sucked the spirit from me as the sun depletes the apple's moisture."

Alyce's sympathetic look plucked at her heartstrings. "Do you regret your choices?"

"Yes," Eleanor whispered, so softly she could barely hear herself over the drone of the crowd. Unexpectedly, her eyes filled with tears.

Who'd want her to wife now? Not that it mattered. She'd lost the only man for her.

"Oh, Eleanor," Alyce moaned. "What have you done?"

On the field, witnesses continued their fulsome praise.

"Lady Mary keeps meticulous household accounts and writes them herself," a man vowed. "You won't find a loaf of bread gone astray."

"My lady cares for the poor. Her alms—"

"Mine oversees her servants with—"

"Enough," the herald cried. "Each to his own turn."

"Maybe it's not too late...no winner has been cried," Alyce said. "What are you waiting for?"

Richard had never felt so numb. Even in the midst of battle, when blood splattered the ground and Death clutched his fellow knights, he'd felt something. Determination, anguish, courage. Today, with his future playing out on the field before him, there was nothing.

Because never before in his life had his best not been good enough. He'd tried to convince Eleanor to care for him and failed. He'd thought the answer was to persist. So he had.

But Eleanor would never be truly his. She'd made that clear by pursuing her tournament. When he'd held her close, when she'd returned his kisses, he'd thought he could win her. He hadn't mistaken her interest, of that he was certain.

Eleanor wouldn't value him as a husband unless he loved her. Love. The one thing he didn't know how to give. Without it, the pure gold he thought they could share transmuted to lead. Alchemy in reverse. Nor could she accept his quest. Given those significant differences, how could he force her to continue their marriage? He'd asked Edward for the annulment, had persuaded the king it was for the best. For Eleanor.

Was this the purest form of love, willingness to do whatever it took to make the other person happy, even if the doing came at a high cost and made you miserable? Or was it mere self-preservation?

He'd accept this "better" bride.

"Household Management: Lady Mary Whyte," the herald shouted. "Lastly, I shall cry Overall." He paused dramatically, until he claimed the attention of every person in the stands. "Are the esteemed Judges ready to pronounce their decision?"

Richard tensed as if a cannonball had been launched directly at him.

He hadn't called the tournament off because he'd been so certain Eleanor would, proving she wanted to stay with him without his love and with his alchemy pursuit as no other action could. If he'd asked Edward to cancel it, nothing would be different between them. Even his need to be with her didn't outweigh his desire to see her happy.

When the rowdy crowd finally quieted to await the judgment, the herald strutted to the center of the field. He turned in a slow circle, clearly savoring the expectant hush.

"The Judges offer a unanimous decision. The winner Overall is Lady Isabel Buntyng."

Some spectators cheered, others booed. Isabel squealed, rather like a stuck pig.

Richard squeezed the arms of his chair, carvings of lion's heads digging into his palms.

He'd failed, but she'd succeeded. She had her annulment, now he'd have a new bride. Her efforts to be rid of him had finally come to fruition.

Should he admit defeat with Eleanor or wage one final attack?

❧❧ ❧❧

Eleanor forced herself to keep her face and body still as Richard rose. Without a glance in her direction, he made his way onto the field.

She had to leave before she suffocated.

Alyce clutched her arm. "Eleanor, stay," her sister ordered. "You can't depart so soon or everyone will think you're upset with the outcome. This is supposed to be what you wanted. Act pleased."

Why did she care what people thought? Only Richard mattered. Eleanor managed a half smile. Alyce held her hand tightly, as if to ensure she remained until the bitter end.

Richard joined Isabel, soon to be Countess of Glasmere, on the field. Eleanor swallowed as he took Isabel's hand, kissed it, then held it high. They basked in the crowd's cheers. His bride to be took a ribbon from her headdress and tied it to his sleeve, as a woman would bestow a favor upon her knight before a joust.

That must have been one of Hastings's ideas.

As trumpets blared, the throng cheered as happily and loudly as if the king's champion had won the day. Coincidentally, Isabel's velvet gown matched Richard's tunic. They made a perfect pair.

Two horses draped in cloth of gold were led out. With knightly courtesy, Richard helped Isabel mount. His smile pierced Eleanor's heart. As they rode off the field, eyes only for each other, golden cloth glinting in the setting sun, jealousy flooded her so forcefully she thought she might actually drown.

She'd never have the chance to win Richard back now. He had his better bride.

CHAPTER 17

"Are you going to take the four remaining women to market?" a man shouted as Eleanor trudged toward her horse with Alyce hurrying by her side. His companions laughed.

"Or are you going to hold a husband tournament next?" called another.

She stopped listening. Each question, comment and snide smile scraped Eleanor's insides. She couldn't wait to leave Smithfield in the dust.

"Are you satisfied?" Edmund caught up with her

"Father, keep your voice down." Alyce took her hand. "Eleanor is tired. Please leave her be."

"Now both daughters disappoint." He shook his head. "Alyce, I take no orders from you. Court life has made you too bold. And Eleanor, you're no longer a countess. Just my spinster daughter, practically penniless if not for my good will. After all you've wrought, how am I to find you another husband?"

More knives to her gut. Because all he'd said was true.

She raised her head. "The tournament went well. Perhaps I will hold more. Men will pay me to find them excellent brides. Rich widows, too."

"You gave away an earl. Now you think to ply a trade?" he demanded. "Why do you live to embarrass me and our lineage? You're under my rule again. You'll live at Middleworth until I decide what to do with you. But for certain I'll keep hold of the keys. All of them."

Eleanor bit her tongue to prevent an argument. She'd go to Middleworth, but only until she could figure out how to get others to pay for her matchmaking services. She'd said it as a jest, but maybe, if she could surmount the challenges, her own business would be her path to freedom. To control.

Keeping busy might be her path to forgetting Richard.

"What would your mother think?" Edmund hammered the final nail into her coffin of catastrophe.

The next day, Eleanor dropped another gown into her open trunk. Her narrow room was a jumble of clothing, veils and the like. With each item packed, she felt as if another part of her disappeared, never to see the light of day again.

Alyce moved with unusual sluggishness as she gathered up several pairs of Eleanor's shoes. "How can you leave?"

"How can I stay? The king will no longer accommodate me. I've no coin to rent a room. You should be happy. You can go to your church now," she said. "Mayhap I'll join you."

No matter how miserable she felt, no matter how worried about her future, never could she cloister herself from the world and spend her days in prayer.

Did every woman need a husband and children to make life complete? Surely some felt fulfilled by responsibilities, work, music and books. But she couldn't be a true chatelaine, as she'd been before her marriage, without her keys. Going to Edmund every time Cook needed something from the storeroom would be too demeaning. And unless she could break the door down, she wouldn't have the satisfaction of undoing her father's work. Not that it would've been enough.

"I don't want to leave court," Alyce whispered. She put a pair of leather boots in a trunk, then sank to her knees. "Or give myself to the Church. I've been right about you, and you were right about me. I like it here. There's so much to do, so many interesting people to meet. I can no longer imagine a life devoted solely to good works, prayer and God."

Her little sister had grown up since leaving home.

"That's a significant decision. Are you sure?" Eleanor folded a veil. The shimmering fabric slipped and slithered out of its tidy packet.

Alyce nodded. "Yes. Like you, I but followed the path I'd agreed to take long before I knew what I really wanted. I believed our parents. Now I know for myself. The life of a nun is not for me."

"Father will stay disappointed with us both, then," she cautioned. "Perhaps there is a way for you to remain here. You could talk to Richard. I'm sure he'd help you to a place. At least one of us could be happy."

"Surely you weren't serious about holding more tournaments. Maybe Richard could find you a place, too. Then we could both stay. Better here than stuck with Father."

Better to endure gossip about her choices or Edmund's censure? Better to see Richard with Isabel? Eleanor dropped the pile of veils and burst into tears.

"Oh, Eleanor." Alyce rushed to her side and enfolded her in a hug. "How can I help?"

"Tell me how I can convince Richard to wed me again instead of his better bride." She'd come to hate the term she'd once thought so clever and apt. She clung to her sister, indulging in this rare opportunity to reveal her feelings and confess her misery.

"I knew it!" Alyce crowed, releasing Eleanor. "You do love him. Have you told him how you feel?"

"I do love him, I do." Saying the words aloud felt strangely comforting. "I should've been brave enough to tell him. Mayhap he needed the words in addition to the— Well, we kissed."

Alyce's face brightened. "You did? And you didn't tell me? There's naught wrong with that, you were wed."

"Not all the times. Our best kiss came after the annulment." And so much more.

"Oh." Alyce frowned, as if not sure what to make of that. "Well, neither of you belonged to another."

Eleanor blew her nose even as more tears fell. "I thought he'd know I couldn't be with a man I didn't love."

"'Be with?' Then you also—"

Eleanor couldn't conceal a smile. "Yes."

"Ah. I wish I knew more about men and their ways," Alyce said. "Tell me how it was."

"Now that you've decided to forego the Church, I will enlighten you," Eleanor began. Memories of the wonderful embraces she and Richard had shared replaced her tears. "I felt so comforted, safe, warm, and things words can't describe. I've learned why girls are kept close to home. For if they knew how wonderful kissing and other things with a man can be, remaining a virgin could be difficult."

Alyce smiled. "Now I know I've made the right decision. I want those feelings, too. Do you think it would be thus with any man?"

"No. I can't imagine it would be that wondrous. I knew I loved Richard when we shared...ourselves, which made it more meaningful," Eleanor said. "To me, at least. He'll always have my heart. Oh, Alyce. How can I ever wed another?"

A knock sounded at the door. Alyce opened it.

"Richard," she announced, surprise evident in her voice.

Eleanor wiped the remaining tears from her face. He looked even more handsome in person than in her thoughts. A short green velvet tunic enhanced his fine form. Anguish washed over her anew. She'd missed his company so very much.

"I suppose I have an urgent errand to attend to," Alyce said. "Though I'd rather stay."

Eleanor stared at Richard, and he at her.

"I'll be back. Soon," Alyce said.

Richard stepped inside and closed the door.

Eleanor savored being alone with him, a state she'd never thought to experience again. Yet the wood paneled walls seemed to close in on her instead of providing intimacy as they had the last time he was here. When they'd made love and she'd been happy.

"What do you want?" Eleanor couldn't keep rancor from her voice. "Have you come to gloat about your upcoming marriage?" And drive the dagger deeper into her chest?

A miniscule sliver of hope gleamed. Was there any chance he missed her, too? Mayhap he wanted to pull her close for a kiss as much as she wanted him to.

"You're leaving." He indicated the piles of clothing. The sound of his voice increased her longing.

"I'm returning to Middleworth." In case he wanted to find her. Would she sit there, pining and waiting like a lovesick lunatic? "Why have you come?"

"To say fare thee well," he replied.

"Ah. Fare thee well, then."

Such banal conversation when they'd once grown close. Eleanor feared she'd throw herself at him if she continued to look at him. She picked up the mass of veils and began to fold one.

"And to retrieve my mother's brooch," he added.

Her hand covered the jewel, which she still wore. More than her wedding ring, the ruby pin represented Richard to her. Touching the smooth, rounded stones brought him near even when they were apart. Gave her hope. She unfastened the brooch and placed it on the bed.

"Here," she said, her voice a mere whisper. "Take this too." She fetched the sapphire band from a small coffer and dropped it beside the pin, then returned to folding.

The finality stunned her. Though their marriage had ended with the annulment, despite the tournament it hadn't felt truly over until this moment. Only pride kept her standing.

"The ring is yours. I bought that for you." Out of the corner of her eye, she saw Richard close his fingers around the brooch. "This is for my wife. Have a safe journey."

She wanted to be close to him more than ever, but watched, taken aback, as he reached for the door. He opened it halfway, then closed it and faced her.

Her heart leapt. Richard couldn't bring himself to leave her.

"I am to wed Isabel in three weeks," he said.

The spark of hope died. He lingered only to speak of his future, which would be spent with someone else.

"When is your wedding?" he asked.

A gauze veil dangled from her fingers. "My wedding?"

"To Arthur. Your dream can finally come true. You're free, he's free. Nothing, no one, stands in your way."

Her heart surged anew. Richard didn't know. He didn't know

she and Arthur no longer meant anything to each other, that she'd loved her vision of Arthur, not the real man.

She'd assumed Arthur would've told him she had no plans to get married at the moment. Maybe their friendship had waned. What if Richard had participated in the tournament only to make her happy, to allow her to follow her oft-expressed dreams?

"There is no wedding. I don't love Arthur."

"What?" Now he was the one to look surprised.

He moved closer, backing her against the bed. His familiar scent washed over her. How she wanted to lean into him, feel his strong arms around her. How she yearned to savor his kisses. One of them should move away, yet each remained, as if rooted to the ground.

She loved him.

The time had come to tell Richard the truth. Even pride, once valued so highly, paled compared to her need for honesty. She had nothing left to lose.

"I doubt I ever truly loved Arthur," she admitted. "I realize I loved the idea of him—an earl's son who seemed a perfect match. I so wanted to choose my husband because most women wed as their parents command. I endured my mother's unhappiness my whole life. It tinged every day, every conversation. I couldn't bear a similar fate."

She had to go further. But the candor she needed didn't flow freely. She'd never had to express such truths before. Her fear of rejection warred with her need to confess all. "My father wants to select another husband for me. You can imagine how I feel about that. Richard, I...."

He watched her with that intent focus she'd come to admire. His head lowered slightly, making her breath catch. For a split second she was sure he was going to kiss her. Then she realized he but nodded in agreement.

"I've seen the effects of such unhappiness," he said. "I too have been betrayed. By Blanche."

Eleanor gasped. Would she at last learn the full story of Richard and Blanche's past? "What happened?"

"It doesn't matter now. Just because I've been hurt doesn't mean I can avoid marriage."

"No. But it does mean you can avoid love, the most important thing. Richard, I—"

"Love?" he scoffed, cutting her off. "Who needs that? Love is for troubadours and fools," he said. "The nobility wed for land, money or politics, whichever duty commands. No other reasons. Most of us accept our lot. I thought by now, after all that's transpired, you would, too."

She drew in a long breath. The wall of pride she'd lowered rebuilt itself in an instant. Thank the Lord she hadn't embarrassed herself by exposing her true feelings. Not only would he think her a fool if she told him she loved him, he wouldn't, couldn't, feel the same. If there'd been no tournament, Richard would have stayed wed to her because he had to. Not because he wanted to.

Would declaring her love for Richard make her feel better? No. It would gain her nothing.

"I suppose some couples can grow to love each other after they wed," he said. "Unfortunately for my future wife, I fear Blanche ruined me. I don't want to love again. The most I could hope for is comfortable compatibility and desire."

She'd vastly prefer love, but comfortable compatibility and desire with Richard didn't sound so terrible anymore. She'd get to enjoy his company and his bed. Share his life. Raise their children and have a family.

"Which, perhaps, is one reason I had trouble accepting your feelings for Arthur," he continued. "I tried to see things your way. I agreed to the tournament because it meant so much to you."

Confusion invaded Eleanor's mind. Did he care for her or not? No man would go to such lengths for a woman for whom he felt nothing.

"I must acknowledge a more selfish reason," he continued, pinning her with his potent gaze. "Though it pains me to say it, you were right all along. Why would I want to live my life with an unwilling wife?

"I commend your persistence. No other woman would have worked so hard nor could have as effectively convinced me she wasn't good enough for me. That I'd be happier with and deserved a better bride." He swept off his hat and bowed. The feather in the brim trailed down her body, setting her atingle. "My thanks, Eleanor."

At that moment she hated him. Though they stood close together, they'd never been farther apart. He mocked her sincere, diligent, albeit somewhat misguided, efforts to make them both happy. He made her feel dim-witted and awkward for ever loving him at all.

Their time together hadn't been significant to him. He didn't view their kisses or lovemaking as extraordinary. Or even special.

"No, Richard," she said, letting her unbound hair hide her face. "'Tis you who were right all along. I now believe your uncaring approach toward marriage yields the greatest results. That way, no one gets hurt."

❧❧ ❧❧

The bitterness in Eleanor's voice took Richard aback. He tipped her chin up until she looked at him. Her hair slid past his hand, the delicate caress of the silken strands enough to weaken his resolve. Faint redness in her eyes proved she'd been crying. Against his will he felt her distress, and yearned to ease her woes.

What had she and Alyce been talking about that upset her so? He clenched the brooch. He'd noticed she wore it every day, even if it didn't complement her attire as well as another bauble might. The pin pricked his palm.

"Have I hurt you, Eleanor?"

Her eyes filled with tears but she refused to blink, staring at him with a strange mixture of defiance, sorrow and indecision. He fought the urge to kiss her tears away, to comfort and reassure her.

He should never have come. No matter how hard he tried to forget Eleanor, he still wanted to see her, talk to her. Seeing her, being near her, made him want stay with her.

What curse was this? The shock of learning she wouldn't marry Arthur and didn't love him anymore continued to flow through him. He hadn't expected his feelings for her would stay so strong.

Ignore the way she makes you feel, he scolded himself. *If Eleanor had wanted to keep you as her husband, she wouldn't have planned the tournament. She would have called it off, or at least told you how she felt.*

Unless she was as uncomfortable acknowledging and expressing her feelings as he was. He hadn't found the words to explain how much spending time with her, making love with her, meant to him. How just holding her brought him more joy than he'd hoped to find in a wife.

What good would dredging that up do? In a few short weeks he'd have a new wife to hold. This wife, he was sure, would keep his life predictable and calm. The new countess wouldn't make him want to kiss her with a mere look, make him jealous if she smiled at another man, or sway his thoughts from his duty. She'd be uncomplicated and safe. And utterly, excruciatingly boring.

"Fie, Richard," Eleanor said with a light tap on his chest and an effort at a smile. "Whatever would make you think I was hurt?"

The glimmer of tears in your eyes. The way you look at me, with sorrow and caring. He clasped her hand and held it fast against his chest, glad for even this small contact. Her pulse beat beneath his fingertips.

Though he'd fought a hard, long battle to avoid it, he'd been hurt, too. He'd tried every way he knew to win her, but even their incredible kisses hadn't been enough to persuade her to stay with him. She'd sat through the tournament and watched him handed to another bride as if he meant nothing to her at all. As if their brief past had never been.

Why had he really come here...in the vain hope she might admit to wanting him? To have one last chance to see her again?

Suddenly he knew why. He loved her.

Shock forced him to step away until his back hit the door with a thud. Eleanor's willful ways, her beauty, her cleverness had undermined his determination to remain aloof.

"Richard, what's the matter? Are you ill?"

Even if he told her, she'd never believe him. Hadn't he just told her he was incapable of love? He'd been right about love being for fools, for he was the most pathetic fool of all. He'd induced himself to participate in her tournament to escape the ache of her rejection, had flirted with the brides to avoid thinking about her. He'd spouted nonsense about not believing in love as a desperate measure to convince himself he hadn't fallen for Eleanor. He'd prayed for strength, though now he wasn't sure if it was to forget her or summon the words to confess.

He, Earl of Glasmere, who commanded vast estates and managed myriad responsibilities and servants, should be able to control his emotions.

"I must go," he said, even as he burned to take her in his arms and divulge all. "Fare thee well, Eleanor."

His heart ached. Who knew if their paths would cross again?

Her chin lifted in that defiant way he treasured. "Fare thee well, my lord."

My lord. They'd come full circle, from strangers to husband and wife to strangers once more.

Richard closed the door and walked away from the woman he loved. It was the most difficult thing he had ever done.

CHAPTER 18

leanor reclined in a cushioned window seat, listless fingers holding needlework. The sun streamed through mullioned windows, its warmth making her sleepy at last. The past three days had been endless. She hadn't seen Richard, the longest time they'd been apart since they met. Nor had she heard a snippet of gossip about him to indulge her insatiable curiosity. She'd hoped to glimpse him, if nothing more, before she left court.

How she missed him. Even when they disagreed, the air around them felt charged. She'd never stop caring for him. Wanting him.

Tomorrow her father's men were scheduled to arrive to escort her and Alyce back to Northumberland and Middleworth Castle. Her failure would be complete.

There was no way to ready herself for the onslaught of her father's dissatisfaction. Who knew when or who her father would want her to marry this time? How could she bear the touch of another man?

Where she went made no difference. She'd be wretched at home under Edmund's watchful eye or with a second husband. What other choices were there for a noblewoman, aside from joining the Church? Could she be one of the very few to ply a trade?

"Will you go fishing with me?"

Eleanor sat up, startled. Owen stood beside her, two willow poles with lines of twisted horsehair in his hand.

"Fishing? My father used to take Alyce and me every summer as he had no sons." She sighed, wishing things were as simple as they'd been then. The pain of her father's deception tarnished the memories.

"I know of a most excellent spot nearby. I thought it might do you good to be away from everyone, if only for a few hours."

By everyone, Owen meant Richard and his new bride-to-be, she was sure.

"I'm not dressed for fishing." She indicated her elegant damask gown.

"The fish will bite no matter what you wear," Owen said. "I've already sent a stable boy to fetch horses. 'Twould be shame if he did so only to return them."

The feigned disappointment on his face was so comical Eleanor had to laugh. His enthusiasm was contagious. It felt good to escape her worries, even for a few seconds. Who knew how a few hours of freedom might lighten her mood?

"Let us be off, then," she agreed. "I certainly wouldn't want to disappoint the stable boy."

After a pleasant ride to the river, Owen spread out a blanket, then unpacked the supplies. They sat on the grassy bank.

Owen handed her a worm. They baited their hooks and cast their lines. Soft plinks as they landed in the calm water and twittering birds were the only sounds. Eleanor took a deep breath, enjoying the sweet air as she relaxed for the first time in weeks. Well, since the day she had married Richard.

Exactly what she needed. Familiar, simple, peaceful activity.

"My thanks, Owen, for thinking of this."

"It's an honor to benefit a lady," he replied. "My brother can be a trial, even on a good day. But when he is forced to deal with matters of the heart—"

Eleanor snapped to attention, jerking her pole. The dark waters rippled as her line swished.

"Be still! You'll scare the fish away," Owen said.

"You were saying?"

"I stopped apurpose. Richard wouldn't appreciate our discussing him. Besides," Owen continued, "what do you care what my brother thinks? 'Tis you who wanted to be rid of him."

He sounded suspiciously like Alyce. Had they conferred about her and Richard? The thought pricked her pride, yet she'd appreciate their concern.

Eleanor hadn't found the strength to confess the truth to Richard. Telling Owen would be easier. Perhaps he'd share their conversation with his brother. Not that anything would come of it, but she wouldn't be there to see, hear and be scarred by, Richard's rejection.

"I did want to be free of him," she said. "At first. But I changed. He made me change. Why didn't he? I mustn't have impressed him enough." That brought on a fresh wave of pain. She took a deep breath and focused on the soothing water. "He acted as though he truly cared for me, and I started to believe it. I thought he wanted to be with me, for myself, not just the woman he had to marry. Fool that I am, I wanted to cancel the tournament. To see him so easily replace me with another proves that holding the tournament was the right choice."

Hearing Richard's cynical views of love had reinforced that view.

"Richard hasn't had the best examples to learn from," Owen admitted.

"What do you mean?" She tried to sound casual. Owen didn't need to know how deep her love for Richard went. Or that she'd do almost anything if she could make him want to marry her again.

Owen paused. "He'd likely run me through for telling you this." He withdrew his line from the water and tossed it farther out. "The women in his life have ruined him."

Eleanor caught her breath. Her hands tightened around her fishing pole. She couldn't wait to hear more. Though it would do her no good to think about Richard, much less his past, she couldn't seem to stop.

He turned to her. "I share this because I can see that you care for him. And I've never seen him look at another woman the way he looks at you. I think he needs you," Owen said, more serious than she'd ever seen him. "Though I can't imagine how you'll get him to admit such a truth before he weds Lady Isabel."

A seedling of hope unfurled inside her and stretched toward

the sun. She had an ally. Eleanor waited, calling on the same patience one needed to fish. Their lines hung motionless in the water.

"Richard and I saw how our mother's affairs hurt our father. And if that wasn't enough, the only woman he ever had the courage to love betrayed him," Owen explained.

Blanche. Jealousy seared Eleanor, hot as if flames roasted her skin, to hear again that Richard had loved another woman. That she knew her, had seen her with him and even asked her to be in the tournament made the pain worse.

"This was years ago, when he was but a knight. The same day Blanche agreed to wed with him, he overheard her agreeing to wed a noble. Richard vowed never to love again."

"You can't expect me to believe he'd keep to a vow made in the throes of anger and pain," she said. "Richard is very smart. He must know happy couples. He must know all women don't betray their men."

"In his head he does, but not in his heart." Owen cast his line again.

What could sway Richard from his vow? Trust. But earning trust took time and persistence. Why had she given up, for the first time in her life, before she got what she wanted?

Something tugged at Owen's line. He lifted his hook from the water. The worm was gone.

"Close. Next time," he said as he stuck more bait on his hook. "Good thing Richard didn't fall in love with you. He'd have been trampled upon again, what with you wanting him to marry someone else. And declaring so before the entire court, including the king who gave him your hand."

Eleanor froze. Had she hurt him, as he'd vowed never to be hurt again? If he cared for her, why had he let her go?

"I arranged the tournament so I could marry the man I thought I loved. And to find Richard a bride better than I," she said. "You saw your brother cavorting with all of the beauties. For certes he looked like he was enjoying himself. He didn't seem upset."

"Richard would never reveal his true feelings in front of others. If you don't know that about him by now, then you know nothing at all." Owen glared at her. "Mayhap he is better off without you."

Eleanor flung her pole aside and jumped to her feet. "Did you bring me out here to make me feel better or torture me?"

"Both, it seems. My pardon."

Her pole rolled into the water. Owen pulled it free and wiped it dry. "Here."

She accepted the pole and sat back down. They fished in strained silence.

Eleanor willed her irritation away. Owen believed Richard cared for her. That was enough.

"How can I get him back?" she asked.

"I can't help you there, for I've never had to woo a woman. I'm fortunate they flock to me. I but choose amongst them."

"You are the most conceited man I've ever met."

"Not conceited, honest," he replied. "What did you do to make Richard want to be with you the first time?"

"Things I have no opportunity to do any longer," Eleanor said. "I disobeyed him and defied him."

Owen laughed, then immediately looked contrite. "Sorry, fish."

Eleanor felt a tug on her line. Her arms tensed against the resistance.

"You've got a bite," Owen said. "May I help?" "No, I can do it."

Eleanor held firm and waited for the right moment. With a sharp tug, she pulled a sizeable trout from the water. The fish dangled from her hook, wet scales gleaming in the late afternoon sun.

"Aha!" she cried. "I've got him!"

Persistence and patience, that's all it took to snare a fish.

If only Richard were this easy to catch.

❧ ☙

"I'd go, but I have to get married." Saying the words made Richard cringe on the chair in Owen's room. "Someone needs to search one more time for clues to Father's missing alchemy scrolls."

Besides, he might see Eleanor again if he stayed. Lady Mary told him she heard from Lady Rose his former wife hadn't gone to Middleworth as planned.

He thought of her too often. Was he obsessed with the woman he could no longer have? How could he, a man who had forsworn caring for women, let one rule his mind?

"But you know better than I what to look for." Owen stuffed several shirts into his bag. "You searched Father's studio right after the murders and found nothing. What makes you think I'll uncover something now?"

"Because you'll look with fresh eyes. 'Tis best to have one of us rather than Blanche or Hugh. Time is short. In the stables, Reginald overheard Hugh's squire asking for their horses to be ready at dawn," Richard explained. "'Tis no coincidence they're leaving court now, after Blanche's attempt to drug me failed and she lost the tournament. They're obviously desperate, and their only hope is to return to the source, even if they'd have to lie or commit a crime to gain access. If you leave tonight, you'll be there ahead of them. You'll be able to look for the missing scrolls and post guards to keep Blanche and Hugh out."

"You go," Owen said. "How better to postpone your wedding than with an urgent journey?"

Owen was right. Richard didn't want to marry Lady Isabel. If he couldn't have Eleanor, he wanted to remain unwed as long as possible. "'Tis my duty."

"That line grows old. And what of your duty to the king?" Owen rolled his eyes. "Eleanor was your duty until you convinced Edward otherwise. Admit it, if only to yourself. You still want her."

"What if I do? She's an attractive, intelligent and interesting woman." He couldn't help but remember her smile, the feel of her against him. *Thinking about Eleanor again.* Most annoying.

Owen moved to his tunics, which hung on pegs. He grabbed a couple and tossed them into the bag. "'Tis more than that. I've seen the way your gaze follows her, the way you set your jaw whenever she talks to another man."

"She was my wife. 'Twas my obligation to protect her."

"What of the duty you owe yourself?" Owen asked with obvious irritation. "Have you no wish to be happy? Must you always worry about others' needs and neglect your own? Sounds a bit like a martyr to me." He shoved some hose in.

"How easy for you, the second son, to prattle on about happiness and avoid responsibility," he said. "I've an obligation to carry on the family name and can't afford to cavort and frolic. Now I'm an earl, so that task is all the more important. Don't you think there are moments when I'd give all to spend my days as you do? Living for pleasure?"

"I'm no stranger to obligation. I've earned my share of scars fighting for Edward," Owen said.

"As have I and many others. That doesn't earn you the right to while away the hours flirting and singing."

"I've seen men, some who were friends, die miserable deaths on the field. Their fate might befall me one day, so I choose to live the life I have to the fullest. Women enjoy my attentions and I enjoy theirs, what of it?"

"'Tis time you acted your age. Your reputation bears on mine," Richard said.

Owen seemed taken aback. "I'm surprised you acknowledge the gossips."

"'Tis a challenge to avoid them, especially as you've been one of their main topics since your arrival. Not only do my new estates and service to the king demand my time, I must deal with the past, which Blanche and Hugh have awakened to haunt us. I can't be in two places at once, and need your help."

"Very well, brother. I'll go," Owen conceded. "Anything to escape your nagging."

Several hours later, Richard was on his way back to his chamber after another feast. Isabel had been seated beside him, in the place he still thought of as Eleanor's. She, reduced in status, sat several tables away. He thought he felt her gaze on him, but every time he looked her way her attention was on her food. Not that she'd eaten much of it.

Now he understood how uncomfortable their wedding and days after must've been for her. She'd had to endure marrying him and sitting beside him while Arthur, the man she thought she loved and believed for years she'd marry, looked on. As he had to accompany Isabel while Eleanor sat nearby.

He couldn't fight it anymore. He loved her. Compassion for her situation, thinking about her, needing her more than he had thought possible...all things he had never wanted to experience.

"Richard," Blanche said, startling him. He'd been so engrossed in thoughts of Eleanor he hadn't heard her approach.

"I'm leaving court and came to say farewell."

What opportune timing. He could learn of her plans.

"I can no longer remain here," she said. "So I go to Pengormel with Hugh and his mother."

"Why tell me?"

Had he been mistaken as to why Hugh wanted their horses? He and his mother could simply be returning home, not plotting to ferret out Father's missing scrolls. Unless Blanche spouted more lies.

"I wanted to congratulate you on your upcoming wedding," she said with a strange smile. "I've come to know Isabel. Her skill in falconry is unmatched, and she—"

He cut her off with a wave. "Blanche, what is this? 'Tis not like you to sing the praises of another. And why are you talking so loud?"

Had he glimpsed a flash of guilt in her eyes? Beneath her cloak she wore a sturdier gown than those she usually favored. She was already dressed for travel. His hackles rose. She was trying to trick him again. Or was he reading too much into everything these days?

"I, um, thought to reassure you I now wish you nothing but happiness."

He heard footsteps. Coming from behind. He whirled to see a tall man wearing a black mask swing a cudgel toward his head.

Richard jumped back, straight into the wall. His heart sped. "Damn you, Blanche. If this is about alchemy, I don't have what you seek."

"I don't believe you," she said. "Hugh knows there are missing scrolls."

The masked man swung, the cudgel slamming into the wall as Richard ducked. Stinging chips of mortar rained down.

"Help! To me!" he yelled. No one came.

He couldn't get close enough to land a punch without getting smacked by the cudgel. Throwing himself to the ground then rolling to the side, he tried to trip his attacker. With a deft leap, the man avoided his kick.

Never trust a woman.

Then all went black.

CHAPTER 19

"Did you have to strike him so hard?"

Heedless of the fact that they could be discovered any moment, Blanche dropped to her knees beside Richard, who lay motionless on the floor. She hadn't wanted to go along with Hugh's plan, but had been too afraid for her own safety not to or to inform the authorities. How could she mitigate Hugh's evil? She could never bring herself to take Richard's life, as he planned to once they found what they sought.

"Aye. He's a strong warrior. I couldn't risk him hitting me back," Hugh grumbled.

"Oh, no, he's bleeding." She held out her fingers, red with Richard's blood. "We must get help."

"Have you lost your wits?" Hugh hissed.

"Have you lost yours? If he dies, what use is he to you?"

"We ride for Pengormel. One of my mother's men will see to him there. Help me," he ordered.

Hugh tossed Blanche a tattered brown cloak with a deep hood. He raised Richard to a sitting position so she could drape it around him.

"I tell you, this is foolish. Let's leave him," Blanche begged. "Whoever finds him will think he fell and hit his head. No one need know we planned to abduct an earl. We'll think of another way to find the scrolls. Without breaking laws and risking our necks." Being underhanded to keep a roof over her head was one thing. Being a criminal was quite another.

"There is no other way." With a loud "oomph," Hugh hoisted Richard over his shoulder. "He's heavier than I thought," he complained as they headed toward the nearest door. A castle guard stood tall on either side. "I thought you were going make sure the way was clear." "I thought you were," Blanche hissed back. Her heart pounded. How had her life come to this? "Why should they care who leaves?"

"What, ho, my lord?" one of the guards asked.

"Nothing to worry about. Just offering aid to a drunken friend," Hugh prevaricated. "An excess of ale, which he'll rue on the morrow."

"I know how that be," laughed the guard. He let them pass.

One hurdle crossed. Who knew how many more lay ahead?

※ ※

"This can't be true!" Eleanor held up the short note she held.

She read it again and again. Why had Richard bothered to send any note after the way they'd parted?

"'I greet you well and send God's blessing. Before you hear it from the gossips, I thought to tell you that Blanche and I have gone away together,'" she read. 'Twas signed only "Richard."

Richard and Blanche? Gone where? And why?

She'd thought her heart already broken, yet felt it crack afresh. He'd never wanted her. Only Blanche.

Unless....

Alyce rushed into the room. "Eleanor, I'm so glad I found you. I've strange news."

"What could be stranger than this?" Eleanor handed her the scrap of parchment. "It looks like Richard's hand. But he wouldn't abandon his duty to Isabel so carelessly. Surely Edward will be displeased if he changes brides yet again."

"What a coincidence. Isabel is my news too. I left her crying," Alyce reported. "Richard clearly affects his women deeply. Isabel, Blanche.... You still care for him."

Eleanor shot Alyce a glare.

"Isabel received a similar letter. She made the mistake of opening hers in public. When she collapsed in tears, it fell to the ground. The nearest person, quite rudely though everyone was dying to hear, picked it up and read it aloud," Alyce said. "I quote, 'Perchance you will forgive me any sorrow this may cause you, but Blanche and I have gone away together.'"

"I can't believe Richard would run off with Blanche."

"You don't want to believe. There's a difference," Alyce warned.

"Alyce, now it's your turn to think. This is most curious. The note is dated yesterday, yet it was just delivered. The hand looks sloppy, as if written in haste. The words don't sound like his. Richard swore he had no feelings for Blanche. And one of the first things he told me was that he's not a liar." Eleanor paused. "Unless that was a lie, too. Let's find Owen, maybe he also received a missive."

Hours later, they hadn't found Owen. No one they asked had seen him or knew where he'd gone. Eleanor's feet ached from searching, and her head pounded. She and Alyce returned to her tiny room and collapsed on the bed, the only place to sit.

She kicked off her shoes. "I've been reviewing every conversation Richard and I had about Blanche. I think I've come up with something."

Alyce sighed. "I hope you're not trying to make something of nothing."

"Be serious. Richard doesn't love Blanche. He and Owen both said he can't love anyone. So why would he leave with her when he's supposed to wed Isabel? He wouldn't, unless he had no choice. Unless he was taken against his will. Richard has been abducted."

"Oh, Eleanor. Richard is a powerful knight and an earl. Who'd dare make off with him? Who could succeed? He could probably fend off half a dozen men." Alyce removed her headdress. "Your imagination is wonderful for lunatic schemes and telling tales to children, but is a hindrance now."

"Blanche already drugged Richard, who knows what else she'd do? He warned me that she and FitzWalter might harm me to force him to give them alchemy formulas. What if he was caught unawares? That has to be it!" Energy restored, Eleanor jumped off the bed. "Help me change."

"Drugged him, whatever for?"

"No time to explain. I must go to him."

"You? If Richard *is* in trouble, it's too dangerous. Do you even know where he is? Besides, a lone woman can't rescue a knight and shouldn't travel alone in any case."

"I'll have some of his men accompany me." She pulled on one of her plainest gowns of darkest blue wool. The gown she'd worn the night Richard came upon her in her father's workshop. She tried to breathe slowly as she braided her hair. "Hand me my boots. If anything has happened to him...."

Alyce clutched the boots to her chest. "Eleanor, Richard isn't yours to cry over anymore. He's not yours to save. You saw to that, yet now you dash off on a crazed journey to who knows where assuming you can rescue him from who knows what? Think, Eleanor, think!"

"Alyce. Give me those boots," Eleanor demanded. "I have to help him, if I can't find anyone else who will. I can't rest knowing he's in danger. You were right once again. I love him."

✖✖ ✖✖

Eleanor urged Saffron into the night toward Hugh's and his mother's castle. Her heart raced as fast as her mount's hooves. Scenery flew by, blurred in moonlight muted by clouds. Cool night air whipped off her cloak's hood and ruffled her braid.

Unfortunately, she'd wasted precious time seeking aid. And only Richard's squire, Reginald, accompanied her.

Richard's men had been too well trained to laugh at her, but they clearly thought she'd gone mad. They said they acted on Richard's orders alone. But what if he wasn't able to send orders? Who at court could do so in his stead, save the king? Even she wasn't so foolhardy to approach the most powerful man in England when she lacked convincing proof.

Reginald had refused at first because she was no longer Richard's wife and lacked authority to command his squire. In the end, fears for his lord's safety and hers persuaded him to join her.

Those same fears kept Eleanor on edge. Mayhap she was

mad as Alyce had said. She couldn't stand still, doing nothing, waiting for Owen to turn up. And if Richard's men wouldn't help her, who would?

She tried to ignore the pain nipping at her after hours in the saddle. She tried not to worry about everything that could go wrong, yet dire thoughts paraded through her mind as determinedly as soldiers on patrol. If they got lost, if brigands prowled this road and chose to attack, if they were too late, if Hugh's men captured her, too....

At last the round towers of Pengormel rose in the distance. The rising sun illuminated signs of disrepair: gaps in the walls, missing stones.

"Lady Eleanor, the gate's closed. I don't see a guard," Reginald's voice wavered, revealing his fear.

Eleanor stared at the weathered wood barrier. How could they gain entry? What if she'd been wrong, and Hugh and Richard weren't even there?

Suddenly the gate swung open, revealing a cluster of bedraggled men brandishing daggers and rusted swords. She and Reginald exchanged a nervous glance.

"Maybe we should leave," he said.

Surely facing a group of armed men with only a squire was the most foolish thing she'd ever done. What if she led Reginald into certain death? But doing nothing would have been even more foolish.

She swallowed rising panic. "Look, they invite us in."

"How do we know it's not a trap?"

"We have faith." Her hands shook on the reins as they rode forward, but she held her head high. She may not be a countess any longer, but she was still a lady, far above this pack of ruffians.

"I'm Lady Eleanor de la Tour. Take me to Sir Hugh," she commanded in the most imperious tone she could muster.

"This way," a heavily-bearded man grunted.

The inside of Pengormel looked no better than the outside. Small buildings sagged, some reduced to piles of rotting wood. Meandering sheep were filthy and emaciated. Only the main keep directly ahead seemed in good repair, a square limestone stronghold.

A scraggly, greasy-haired man reached for her reins. She fought her reluctance to hand Saffron over. Not only was the mare her only means of escape, Eleanor didn't want her maltreated.

Another man escorted them into the great hall, such as it was. A small fire burned in the huge fireplace. No tapestries or banners graced the smoke-stained, unpainted walls or the timbered ceiling. Reginald followed close behind her.

Sir Hugh, seated with several men at a rickety table, didn't rise. His lean face registered surprise, quickly veiled. Where was his mother?

"Countess? I mean, Lady Eleanor."

How she wished people would stop doing that.

A fat man in ragged clothes made a lewd gesture. The others laughed.

"Enough." Hugh raised his cup in a salute. "What brings you here?"

Richard and Blanche were nowhere to be seen.

"Lady Latimer invited me," she lied. "I'd grown weary of court, and wasn't ready to return home."

Hugh frowned. Did he believe her? "Lady Latimer is...indisposed."

So Blanche was there. Could Richard be, too? "Perhaps I can be of assistance if she's unwell. I have some skill in healing," she offered. Thankfully her skirts hid her unsteady legs. Thankfully Reginald stayed close by her side.

"That won't be necessary," Hugh said.

"I'm parched from my journey. Might I have something to drink?"

Hugh nodded. One of the men brought and set down a pitcher and a cup with reddish crust on the rim. Good thing Eleanor didn't plan to indulge.

Not surprising that she'd have to serve herself, but in this case doing so served her purpose, too. As she picked up the pitcher, Hugh waved to his men. They moved away from the table and conferred. Devising a strategy about what to do with their unexpected guests?

She turned her back and held the pitcher away from their line of sight. In her other hand was a small vial she'd fetched from the apothecary before leaving the castle, which contained a drug guaranteed to put any drinkers to sleep. Her heart pounded as she poured the contents into the wine, then refilled each man's cup.

This has to work. It has to.

After filling hers, she mustered good cheer and a hearty tone. "Come, let us drink."

With wary glances, the men returned to their seats. They drank deep while she toyed with her cup. Eleanor released a breath she hadn't realized she was holding.

"You've come at an opportune time," Hugh said with obviously false politeness. "I have need of you."

One of the men snickered.

"I need information. I tried asking nicely, but the Earl of Glasmere just wouldn't share."

She forced herself to remain still and keep her face blank. She had guessed correctly. Richard was here.

"Then I asked, shall we say, less nicely. That selfish earl still kept quiet."

Eleanor felt herself pale. Her mouth went dry. "What do you think I can do?"

"When he sees you, maybe he'll be more helpful. 'Tis a shame Blanche was unconscious before I thought to use her. But you'll do. Would you accompany me to the dungeon?"

Eleanor tensed, prepared to flee. How could she escape and free Richard?

Then one of the men fell forward. His head plopped into his bowl, splattering gravy onto the table. Another tumbled off the bench.

"What the—? You drugged us! I'll make you pay." Hugh staggered toward her.

Reginald stepped in front, but Hugh swept him aside as he would a fly. He slapped her so hard her head snapped back. Pain flared. He toppled forward, knocking her down and pinning her to the garbage-strewn floor, so heavy she could barely breathe. She tried to shove him off.

Reginald headed for her, aghast. "Lady Eleanor!"

"Behind you." She couldn't draw in enough air to scream.

A fat man hit Reginald on the head. He collapsed in a heap.

The drug claimed the men one by one as Eleanor pushed to dislodge Hugh. At last she slid free, then tugged her gown from beneath his legs. A large ring of keys hung from his waist.

Her throbbing face and swelling eye were the least of her worries. She snatched the keys and hurried to Reginald, who had a nasty lump on his head but was breathing. She grabbed a torch and lit it in the fire.

Now to find Richard.

Eleanor hurried down the only staircase and through the corridors, stopping at every door. Storage room after storage room, mostly empty. The last door was locked. She held up the ring of keys. Which was large enough to fit? Aha. She opened the heavy door and burst into the dungeon.

As she ran across the stone floor, she took in the dimly lit, large room. A pervasive, dank stench made it difficult to breathe.

Thank the Lord, she'd found him.

Richard was chained to large metal rings high on the wall. Blanche and Lady Elizabeth were chained to the opposite wall. Worse and worse. Hugh had chained his own mother. Both women's heads drooped onto their chests. Lank hair draggled over torn gowns. Asleep, unconscious, or dead.

She hurried toward the man she loved. Tears rushed to her eyes.

"Richard," she whispered.

Both eyes were swollen, bruised purple-black slits. Dried blood lingered on his split lower lip. His hair was matted, his clothes shredded and streaked with grime. Through a tear in his tunic, a red welt marred his chest.

"By the rood, Eleanor. What are you doing here? Get out!" His voice was scratchy and hoarse.

"I'm glad to see you, too. I don't see any of your fellow Knights of the Garter rushing to your rescue. You should be on your knees thanking me. Oh, forgive me, you're chained to the wall." How did he manage to raise her ire with only a few words, and in such a dire setting? "We're safe for the nonce," she reassured him.

"I meant, get out of here before they do this to you," he rasped.

"That's better."

"Who hit you?"

Lightly she ran her fingers over her cheek. "Sir Hugh. 'Tis nothing. I copied Blanche's idea and drugged their wine. He figured out what I'd done just before the drug took effect." If only she knew how long they'd stay asleep. "I've got the keys. Can you walk?"

His injuries made her wince, but she was so relieved to see him her legs felt weak.

"I think so. How did you find me? Why did you come?"

"First let's set you free. How are Blanche and Hugh's mother?" The chill air made her shiver, numbed her fingers.

"Don't know. Neither have moved for a while," he answered. "I've lost track of time. Are you alone?"

"No. Yes. I couldn't find Owen. Reginald is here, but Hugh's men hit him on the head."

She fumbled with the ring of keys. The first didn't fit Richard's heavy manacles. His skin was rubbed raw around the metal, so she tried to be gentle even in her haste. Any pain she caused was sure to be minor compared to what he'd already suffered.

"Reginald? Of course. I sent Owen away," he said. "How many drank your wine?"

"Seven."

"Damn. There must be more men in this castle."

"I didn't dare search for others."

The next key didn't work either.

His head dropped against the wall. He licked his dry, chapped lips.

Neither did the next key or the next. Panic swept through her. Her hands shook, making the keys rattle.

None fit.

"So hot," he whispered.

Richard was hot and she was freezing? Eleanor felt his forehead and swallowed a scream. He burned with fever. Oh, no. She hadn't counted on this. Her plan was falling apart.

What was she going to do? With two women unconscious, Richard very ill, no way to free them....

"There must be another set of keys," she said. "Don't go away, I'll be right back."

She needed a bit of humor to lighten the oppressive tension. He didn't respond.

Eleanor ran, holding up her skirts. She retraced her path down the long corridor and up the stairs, panting hard.

Reginald hadn't moved. Seven men remained slumped over the table.

Quickly she searched each, leaning back as best she could to avoid their various disgusting odors. She couldn't identify some of the things she felt in their pockets, but there were no keys. She dropped to her hands and knees, ignoring the filthy floor. No luck there, either. Her heart pounded as she wiped her hands on a rag.

Richard must be right, there were more men in this castle. Awake men.

And one of them must have the keys.

CHAPTER 20

Richard opened his eyes. The cold, damp dungeon wall barely appeased his heated flesh. Fever devoured him. Whether brought on by festering cuts on his wrists and ankles from the chains or drinking putrid water, he didn't know. How long had he been ill...days, weeks? How often was he lucid? He wouldn't last much longer.

Because delirium had set in. He was seeing things.

But what he had seen! An angel in the form of a disheveled Eleanor, coming to rescue him. He laughed, a hacking sound more like a cough. The rational remnants of his mind knew no woman would try to save a man or could invade a castle without significant aid.

Yet he thought he remembered hearing her voice and the jangling of keys. Hadn't he felt her soft, cool hand on his forehead and the soft caress of her hair on his neck? Hadn't he smelled her lemony scent, so out of place in this chamber of despair? More likely he'd only imagined her. Desperation born from isolation, injury and misery brought the person he most wanted to see to life.

If he had to die, at least his final thoughts would be pleasant ones. Thoughts of Eleanor.

The woman he loved.

Another harsh laugh escaped him. He must be going mad. Not only to admit he loved at all, but to realize it when chained in a dungeon....

He'd never have the chance to tell her.

His eyes drifted shut again.

ॐ ॐ

Keys, keys. Where were the keys?

Eleanor raced through Pengormel, searching room after room. Time and luck were running out. The slumberers could awaken at any moment. Or she could encounter men who hadn't drunk her wine. Then she, Richard, Reginald, Blanche and Elizabeth would be doomed.

Eleanor moved on to the dilapidated structures outside. Fetid air and cloudy skies made everything dreary. Avoiding clucking, scrawny chickens and sheep, she rushed to the small gatehouse.

Her heart skipped a beat. There, on the wall opposite the door, dangled a ring of keys. But to get them, she'd have to reach over the burly man dozing beneath. She'd hadn't seen him before, so he couldn't have partaken of the wine, yet he slept tipped back on his stool with his scruffy, gray-streaked head inches beneath the keys. Her heart thundered as she sneaked closer.

Closer still. Her fingers itched to get those keys. Keeping an eye on him, she rose on her tiptoes and cautiously reached over his head. His ale-washed breath made her gag.

Her hand touched the key ring. Though she wanted to grab it and flee, hasty actions and jangling keys might startle him awake. Eleanor forced herself to move with care.

Ever so slowly her fingers closed around the metal circle. Ridges of rust scraped her fingertips. Bit by bit she lifted the ring off its nail and over the guard's head. A rumbly snore froze her, stretched out over in his face. He slept on.

She had the keys.

Suddenly the stool fell from beneath the guard. He crashed to the floor. His eyes widened.

"Where do you think you're doing, you pretty baggage?" he roared, grabbing her skirts in his meaty hands.

She ripped them free. And ran.

"Wait 'til I get my hands on you. I'll show you what's what," the guard called. "To arms, to arms!"

Her feet flew over the dirt yard. Harsh breathing told her he was close behind. She swerved around a bleating sheep and almost tripped over a slow-moving goat. Sweat pooled between her breasts.

"I'll get you, wench," he shouted. "Don't think I won't."

As she reached the castle door, she glanced over her shoulder. The guard was doubled over, wheezing. Faster, faster she dashed to the dungeon, past still slumbering men, down the stairs.

Richard's chin rested on his chest. His eyes were closed.

Her chest heaved as she caught her breath. She pressed her hand against a cramp in her side. "I've—got—more—keys."

He didn't move.

"Richard, wake up. Please, wake up."

First key, no. Second key, no. Third key, yes!

She unlatched his manacles. No longer held up by chains, Richard collapsed to the stone floor.

She dropped to her knees beside him. "Oh, dear Lord. I'm so sorry."

"What?" he mumbled, face down.

"You're awake. We have to leave. There's a guard after me. Who knows when the others will awaken." There was so much more she wanted to say. No time.

"Too hot. Tired."

"Please, Richard. You must stand. I need your help to get us out of here."

Why hadn't she considered that he might be incapacitated? She would have come for him no matter the odds she faced.

He braced his hands on the stones and pushed himself to his knees. "Dizzy."

"You can be dizzy later."

With all her might she tugged, helping him to his feet. He swayed, then balanced himself against the wall. She clutched him, offering her support.

"I can walk," he said, his voice scratchy and low. "Let's go."

"What about Blanche? Elizabeth?"

"We'll have to come back for them."

They held hands as they made their way down the corridor, Richard gaining strength with each step. He used the wall for support as they climbed the stairs.

"My thanks, Eleanor," he said. "I've never known a woman so brave. Or so foolish."

She smiled. Richard must be feeling better.

"What awaits us upstairs?"

"Seven drugged men, an unconscious Reginald, one awake guard who's furious and huge, but slow," she answered.

"I want you to stay out of danger. Can you promise me that?"

"No." Eleanor shot him a glare.

Richard stopped short. He caressed her good cheek and leaned in. "I can't be worrying about you. I must focus on the enemy."

She placed her hand over his. God willing, they'd survive this so she could tell him the truth. Even if he threw it back in her face, she had to share her love. "I promise to be careful."

They hurried into the great hall as the guard entered the main door, sword in hand. Richard grabbed a sword from a sleeping man's scabbard.

Eleanor froze. She didn't want to watch the upcoming fight, yet felt compelled to.

Richard looked as though a breath might topple him. Despite his admonition, she had to help. She couldn't wield a sword, but perhaps she could find a weapon in a poker or pan. Wary of the sleeping men, she backed toward the hearth.

"Get up, sluggards," the guard yelled to the insensible men. He slapped one on the back as he stormed toward Richard.

Reginald struggled to his feet and clutched his head.

Richard's sword clanged against the guard's. He stood tall, as if energy flowed into him from a hidden source. He slashed and swung, muscles bulging. The guard was no match for Richard, even injured and ill. A powerful lunge sent Richard's sword through the guard's gut. He fell to the floor with a resounding thud.

She'd never seen this side of Richard, the fierce knight. His fortitude amazed her.

"Let's get out of here. The three of us can't carry two women.

We'll send for help." Richard pulled the sword free, then wiped it clean on the dead man's shirt.

Richard's skin was pasty, but Eleanor kept her concerns to herself. Sweat, whether from exertion or fever, dripped from his brow.

Eleanor didn't feel guilty taking one of FitzWalter's horses. Slowly, with a grimace, Richard mounted.

Soon they'd be safe. Soon Richard would receive the care he sorely needed.

Relief rushed through Eleanor. And a hint of sinful pride. She'd done it. She had rescued the man she loved.

Richard sagged on his horse. Fighting had drained what little remained of his strength, but he had to lead them all to safety.

"I know this area," he said, as much to keep himself awake as to reassure Reginald and Eleanor. The landscape had no defining features, just rolling hills and trees, but he had been here before. "The nearest castle is Wiggenfield, only a few miles. Lord Upton lives there, should help us."

"What happened?" Eleanor asked.

"Blanche and Hugh kidnapped me. She drew me away from a meal to bid me farewell. Stupidly, I followed. I didn't even have my eating knife. Not sure I believe her, but Blanche said she had no idea Hugh would take things so far. He's desperate to learn about our fathers' alchemy work. She tried to refuse her role in my abduction. But had nowhere else to live."

He was too tired, too sore to say another word. Later, later he'd tell Eleanor that he loved her. His head hammered so he could barely think.

He couldn't keep his eyes open. If only he could rest for a minute.

He collapsed on his horse's neck and knew no more.

Richard slept in his huge bed at Glasmere Castle, ashen and

still as death. If not for the painfully shallow rise and fall of his chest, Eleanor wouldn't know he lived.

Owen rushed into the room. "Is he...."

"Dead? No, thank God. But the physician and I fear he is closer to death than to recovery." Eleanor spared Owen only a fleeting look. If she focused all of her energy on Richard, her strength of will, the power of her love, might help him live. That was why she hadn't moved from his side since they reached his Northumberland home two days ago.

If he woke, she'd find the courage to tell him how she felt. To express her love.

Owen brought a stool and sat beside her. "I came as soon as I got your note," he said. "He looks awful."

"The swelling has gone down a bit, and the bruises will soon fade."

"You don't look well, either," Owen commented.

Vanity had no place while Richard hovered near death. She wore the same gown she'd worn during the rescue. So what if the blue wool was smudged with dirt and blood? What did it matter if her hair tumbled in riotous tangles down her back, if one eye was black and blue?

"Have you gotten any rest? Have you eaten?" he asked.

"Richard's housekeeper has kept me well supplied with foodstuffs." She indicated a table laden with cheeses, bread and dried fruit.

"Which do you no good on the platter. Here." He handed her a slice of bread with a hunk of cheese. "Eat. You have to keep your strength up. Who knows how long he'll be like this?"

Tears of gratitude stung Eleanor's eyes. She was exhausted, but wouldn't have a good night's sleep until she knew Richard was on the mend. She accepted the bread and cheese and took a bite. "Thank you, Owen. For understanding that I need to be here, even though I have no place in his life."

"My views on that issue haven't changed since we went fishing. Besides, you were the one who found him. You saved him, you belong by his side."

Eleanor shook her head. "I don't want his gratitude. I just," her voice cracked, "I just want him to get well."

"You want more than that," Owen said softly.

"Yes. I want him to be content."

"I'll let that go for now. Are you up to telling me what happened? Your missive was short on details," Owen said.

Eleanor related their adventures.

"That's quite a tale. What happened to the others?"

"They've been arrested and sent to prison. Blanche, too."

"Good. All while I was away on Richard's fool errand. I found nothing. There may never be an answer to the mystery of what my father thought he discovered." Owen sighed.

That was a relief. "No sense worrying about the past." She'd look only toward the future. The one she prayed she'd have with Richard.

"Where is he? Take me to him this instant," a familiar shrill voice cried.

Oh, no. Eleanor and Owen shared a glance.

"Isabel," they said in unison.

"Why wasn't I notified immediately? How dare you keep this from me, his soon—"

She stormed into the room like a captain leading a charge, but stopped short when she caught sight of Eleanor. Richard's steward, Henry Watson, almost rammed into her.

"Eleanor. What are you doing here? Get out. I'm the woman he's going to wed." Isabel strode to the bed, the skirts of her burgundy wool traveling gown brushing against Eleanor. "I will hear the whole story. Then I demand that you leave."

Owen stood. "Who sent for you?"

"No one, more's the pity," Isabel screeched. She glared at Henry, a tall, balding man, and Owen in turn. "Can you think how embarrassing it was for me to hear about Richard's injuries from someone at court? Me, soon to be the earl's wife?"

Eleanor bit her lip to keep from snapping. Had she made a mistake in choosing Isabel as a potential bride? She'd focused on the prospects' outward qualities and talents. There hadn't been much time to spend worrying about their personalities.

Clearly Isabel's concern for appearances and possessiveness outweighed her concern for Richard's well-being. She wasn't good enough for him.

Isabel turned to Eleanor. "You look quite a sight. Have you no other gowns? And who allowed you to sit by my soon-to-be husband's side?"

"I did," Owen said. "She rescued him. And Richard isn't yours yet. You aren't even officially betrothed."

Eleanor looked up in surprise.

"Richard has been busy." Owen answered her unspoken question with a shrug.

She couldn't resist a smug smile. Without a betrothal to bind them, Isabel had no more right to be here than Eleanor did.

But which of them would Richard want to see when he awoke? Eleanor steeled herself against the pain that would undo her should he ask for Isabel.

"It's just a matter of time until we are bound to each other. I'm staying, too. Steward, fetch me a chair." Isabel snapped her fingers.

The portly man rushed to do her bidding.

The vigil continued.

❧ ☙

All Richard knew was that every muscle ached and his eyes were stuck together. He wanted to speak, but his mouth was gritty and dry as desert sand.

It took all of his strength to force his eyes open. At least his mind worked. He hadn't gone mad as he'd feared. He remembered being chained in Pengormel, and Eleanor rescuing him. He knew he was at Glasmere Castle, in his own bed, though he had no recollection of how he'd come to be here.

He turned his head, sending streaks of pain resonating through him. Owen and Isabel dozed in their chairs, mouths open. A third chair was empty. Eleanor's, he couldn't help but hope. A long, narrow table held platters of food, while jars, small pots and piles of cloths cluttered a smaller table.

"Owen." He couldn't even manage a whisper. He swallowed, then tried again. "Owen."

His brother's eyes flew open and a smile creased his face. "Richard, at last. Our prayers have been answered."

"Water."

Owen filled a cup. He slipped one hand behind Richard's back to help him drink.

"Ow," Richard grunted as Owen lifted him high enough to sip. Water had never tasted or felt so good. "Enough." Slowly Owen lowered him to the pillows. He moistened his dry lips with his tongue. "How long have I been like this?"

"Almost a week. We thought—"

"Richard!" The shriek pierced the quiet. "My love. You're awake."

Isabel appeared in his line of vision. "I've been so worried. I haven't left your side since I arrived." She clasped his hands. "Now our betrothal and wedding can go forth as planned."

Richard grimaced. He couldn't think of getting out of bed at the moment much less marrying this woman. Her strident tone grated on his nerves. "I appreciate your devotion, Isabel," he said. "I'm sure you could use some rest. I need to speak with Owen."

"Very well." She sat.

"Alone," he said.

"I'll be back soon." She left with obvious reluctance.

"Eleanor? Is she here?" Richard had to know.

"Yes."

He smiled. He felt better already.

"Hugh? Blanche? Elizabeth?"

"All in prison," Owen said. "I think Isabel remained by your side only because Eleanor wouldn't leave," Owen said. "She's in the kitchen making another batch of her special poultice for your chest. I'll get her."

"Help me sit first. Then take me to the garderobe."

"You need to rest. I'll get you a pot."

What he needed was to see Eleanor. "No, I've been lying here too long. I need to work out the stiffness and get my strength back."

With great care, Owen eased him into a sitting position. Richard closed his eyes against the pain, then slowly stretched his arms.

"Everything seems to function," he said. "Let's go."

⁂

Down in the kitchen, Eleanor stirred a cauldron hanging over the fire. With the back of her hand, she wiped sweat from her forehead. The kitchen staff smiled encouragement every so often as they bustled about, but otherwise left her alone.

The physician's warning a few hours ago frightened her. If Richard didn't awaken soon, he might never recover. That wouldn't stop her from doing everything in her power to help him.

Isabel swooped in, a smile on her face. "Richard's awake!"

Relief overwhelmed her.

Isabel blocked her exit. "And he was so glad to see me," she crowed. "He doesn't need you, his former wife. You gave him away. He has me. His wife to be. I'll take the poultice to him. I'll be the one to care for him now. And forever."

Eleanor let loose an unladylike snort. "You haven't lifted a finger to help him all week."

What Isabel had done was laze about in her chair and bark orders at Eleanor, Owen and Richard's servants as if she were the queen. She'd almost driven them mad with her criticisms and complaints. Isabel was two different women: a happy, if a bit simpering, one at court and a shrew elsewhere.

"Let me pass," Eleanor said.

"He didn't ask for you. He doesn't want you."

Eleanor wouldn't let Isabel's jabs hurt her. "I'll see for myself what Richard wants. Move aside."

"No. He's mine," Isabel declared.

"Owen and Richard's steward agreed I should remain. They had authority until Richard awoke. If the only way you can have him is by forcibly keeping other women from his side, then he isn't really yours, is he?" Eleanor asked, her voice low.

Isabel's mouth gaped. "What difference will a few more minutes make? He'll make the right choice."

"I'm sure he will."

Eleanor squeezed past her and ran to Richard's room. Isabel followed close behind.

CHAPTER 21

Richard smiled as Eleanor raced into his room, her face alight with joy. She wore a plain, stained gown. Her cheek and one eye were swollen and black and blue. Strands of hair tumbled from her simple braid, but she'd never looked more beautiful to him. Not even on their wedding day, garbed in finery and jewels. Because on that day, she'd looked on him with disdain and denial. Now she looked at him with love.

And how he loved her. He'd been a fool not to accept it sooner, but his past wouldn't let him admit the truth until Death stared him down. He'd spend the rest of his days cherishing her if she'd let him.

The time had come to disclose the depth of his feelings.

Before he could welcome her and take her hand, Isabel ran in. The two women caught their breath, clearly waiting to see which one he preferred. They glared at each other with such aggression he thought they might break into a fistfight.

Isabel stepped forward. "Richard, your future wife is here."

Eleanor moved past her. "Your color has returned. Is there anything you need?"

"I told you I'd see to him now." Isabel shoved her out of the way.

Owen, Watson, and his housekeeper Agnes crowded into the room, all talking at once.

"Your Grace, 'tis glad to see you up, I am!"

"I've brought some nice hot pottage." Agnes held up a steaming bowl.

"Richard, do you—"

"Silence!" Richard shouted, pleased to find he sounded like himself and not a weakling invalid.

Five faces turned toward him.

He didn't want to hurt Isabel, but he couldn't pretend she meant anything to him. He wouldn't marry her, but would help her to a better groom.

The only person he wanted to talk to, to be with, was Eleanor. "Eleanor, you stay. Everyone else, out!"

Isabel's face fell. "I'll be waiting. You put her in her place."

"That's exactly what I plan to do," Richard agreed. Eleanor's place was beside him, always.

Silence reigned after the others left, but it felt strained, not comfortable. Eleanor hadn't moved. Only he could make things right between them, but articulating his feelings for her would be one of the hardest things he'd ever done.

"How can I ever thank you for rescuing me?" he began. "You saved my life."

"I put two and two together," she replied. "You did the rescuing in the end."

"I don't remember."

"The fever was upon you. Despite that and your injuries, you fought like a madman to free us."

"We did it together, then," he said.

More silence stretched as he gathered courage to speak. How had he faced enemies on the battlefield with greater confidence than he had this woman?

"Eleanor, I had many hours to think in that dungeon. Mostly I thought of you," he said. "I want to ask you something. Will you marry me again?"

For a brief second joy flashed across her face, but deep disappointment replaced her happiness. "So my reward for helping free you is your hand in marriage?"

"No, 'tis because I love you," he confessed. "I need you with me."

"What?" She looked confused, as if he'd spoken in a foreign tongue.

Perhaps he had. He hadn't said "I love you" in years and had told her he never would, much less feel and accept the emotion behind the words.

"Never were truer words spoken. I love you," he repeated. "I know now that I have for some time, but couldn't admit it to myself, much less to you. No matter how much it hurt when we parted." He pushed back the covers and slowly swung his legs over the edge of the bed. "At last I understand the power of love. When love is real, the joy and contentment it brings defeats all doubts."

Eleanor took a step closer, eyeing him warily, as if he'd gone mad. "Another quote?" she asked, reminding him of the poem he'd once recited.

"No, but I'll shower you with them should they please you," he said. "I've known I loved you since the day you were packing to leave court. I wanted to stay married to you from the beginning, but I refused to believe my attraction and interest meant anything more than that. I wanted, and want, you and no other as my wife. Never for one minute did I truly consider any of the other brides. I was afraid to let myself love again.

"I can see now the ways you tried to show me how you cared for me. Your stubbornness is greater than mine, for you didn't give up. 'Twas I who gave up on you."

For once Eleanor seemed speechless. He'd have to dredge up more to convince her.

"Making love with you should've persuaded me you were the only one I'd ever want. Even then I refused to acknowledge what we shared. What we still could have. If you're willing."

She stood frozen, as if moving would break the spell his words had woven.

"Your unselfishness wiped away any remaining doubts that true love can exist," he continued. "You risked your life for me. I'm so sorry it had to come to that end to make me accept my love for you."

He couldn't read her expression.

"Do you have any feelings for me? Can you find it in your heart to care?" He didn't dare hope she loved him in return. If she were willing to marry and live with him, that would be enough. For now. He'd spend every day showing her how much she meant to him. "Will you be my wife? Again?"

Radiance suffused her as the morning sun brightened the night sky. "Yes, Richard. Oh, yes. I love you, too."

"Kiss me." He held out his arms.

Eleanor bent forward, then stopped. "Your injuries...."

"I won't break," he said. "Kiss me."

She did. The instant their mouths met, desire blazed within him. He slid his fingers into her hair. Without breaking the kiss he lay back on the bed. She followed, nestling close by his side. He'd never been happier.

"Kiss me again," she said.

Richard had one last confession to make. With great effort he sat up straighter. "I want everything out in the open first."

"Have you been keeping a secret?" Concern flared in her gaze.

"Not exactly." He stroked her good cheek to reassure her. "'Tis just that as you planned your tournament, I had a plan of my own. To keep you as my wife. Though it didn't work as well as I'd hoped."

"You've known all along you'd never let me go?"

"Yes. At first, I admit, only because the king wished us to wed. Your hard work and persistence, your devotion to your cause, made me love you," he acknowledged. "I was touched that you'd go to such great lengths to find me a better bride so I'd have more than I bargained for. Most women would have looked only to themselves, but you thought of my needs. I realized that instead of watching you laboring so hard to be free of me, I wanted you to put all your efforts into keeping me."

"Then how could you watch me pine over Arthur and arrange the tournament?" Her chin went up. "Were you laughing at me?"

"Of course not. Not telling you my plan was the hardest part." He paused, trying to think of the best way to explain. "I knew two things. First, if I forbade you to hold the tournament or if I asked Edward to put a stop to it, you'd feel as ensnared as you had on our wedding day. You'd continue to think Arthur the perfect spouse and never accept me.

"Second, we could only be happy if you realized on your own that you wanted to be with me. You've always said you wanted to choose your own husband and you wanted to love him."

"You seem to know me well. I'm glad my stubbornness paid off for once," she said.

He stroked her cheek. "I didn't want to love my wife. I can admit why I feared such a thing. To love means to trust. But trusting a woman opens a man up for the agony of betrayal. You convinced me we could have more. That trusting a woman can even be rewarding."

"I'm honored to have your trust. You've revealed all, now 'tis my turn to be completely honest." She sat up and held his hands. "I do love you. I'm not certain that's enough anymore. Because I don't think I can endure watching you search for your father's scrolls. This must end, one way or the other. So I'll tell you that my father hides his alchemy writings in his workshop. Perhaps your father's missing scrolls are there, too. I want us to live a life free of alchemy. I want to destroy whatever we find."

"Thank you for telling me. I'd best hie to Middleworth."

"You know I'm going with you. Else how will you know where exactly to look?"

A chill ran over him. A remnant of the fever or a premonition?

He hadn't agreed to destroy whatever they unearthed in that hiding place, nor had he agreed to cease his pursuit. Would that lack shred their newly found trust? If they found the scrolls or any information of value and he delivered it to Edward, she'd never forgive him. Could he destroy his father's life's work? For love, or his own reasons?

❧ ☙

Two of the happiest weeks of her life later—because she'd spent them with Richard as he healed—they crept toward her father's workshop in the wee hours of a moonless night. Eleanor had managed to make a pressing of the key and have a new one made. As before, they waited for Edmund to finish his labors and return to the castle. Anger glowed like embers of his dying fire as they entered. If anything the space was more crowded owing to the addition of another array of glass vessels.

"He's been busy," Richard said.

"Unfortunately." Trepidation made her fingers shake as she pointed to the secret spot above the hearth. She'd waited so long for this moment. What would they find? "Here. You need to remove these four stones."

"Being here brings back so many memories of my father." Richard was tall enough to reach them without the aid of a bench. He ran his fingers over the wall. "Amazing. Even this close I can't tell if they'll come loose."

He left the stones and took her hands. "Are you sure you want to do this?"

"Absolutely. But let's take care to leave everything the way it was when we arrived. I don't want him to suspect that anyone has been here. Especially me." She wouldn't feel guilty. He had betrayed her mother. She did this for her memory, and because it was the right thing to do. No matter what the king wanted. But he was God's anointed....

Eleanor lit a candle and set it on the floor so the flame couldn't be seen through the window.

Richard grabbed the first stone, which came free with a high-pitched scraping sound. He handed the stone to Eleanor, who put it on the floor as she'd seen her father do. Perhaps the order and position of the stones was essential. She'd face them the same way so they could be replaced easily. The next three followed suit.

Richard reached into the hole. "Nothing."

"All this for nothing?" Anger mixed with relief. "Maybe that's for the best. Can we leave, and give up this quest?"

"I haven't hit the back wall yet." He pulled the bench into place, stood on it, and stretched. His eyes widened. He pulled out a stack of vellum and gave it to Eleanor.

She wanted to know what the pages contained, and she didn't. What if alchemy was real? What would that mean to her, and to England?

"Well?" he asked.

She appreciated his making her a partner in this endeavor. Her chest tightened as she examined the pages. "'Tis my father's writing. Seems to be a step-by-step journal of his endeavors followed by his thoughts. 'I was positive this was the solution,'" she read. "'Alas, no. Do I lack a substance, and if so, what? Am I mixing the wrong amounts, for the wrong amount of time at the wrong temperature? The combinations of ingredients and measurements are infinite. Why, why, doesn't it work? What more can I do?'" The desperation made her sad and frightened for Edmund. "Here, take a look. Do you think there's anything of import?"

He bent to the candlelight. After glancing through the writings, he shook his head. "From what I can tell, Edmund isn't close to the formula for transmutation. Most of his underlying assumptions are incorrect. I can safely say his work is years behind my father's."

"That's a huge relief," Eleanor said. "I'll burn a few pages, just in case he's closer than you think."

She selected three random pages and brought them to the hearth, confident she was doing the right thing. Slowly the embers caught, turning the edges of the sheets bright red. Relief burned hot as the flames.

"I think I felt something else in the hiding place, way in the back," Richard said. "I can't quite grasp it."

He climbed on the bench again, then reached as far as he could.

And retrieved three thick scrolls.

Slowly Richard stepped down. His wounds had almost healed, but his left leg was still stiff. For a moment he simply looked at them.

"Three?" they asked together.

He sat, untied the thinnest one and spread it across his lap as Eleanor peered over his shoulder. "Well. Not exactly what we came for."

"Some rolled-up receipts, for chemicals, glassware.... Look. This one shows my father purchased two scrolls from yours."

"That's good news. At least we can be fairly sure your father didn't kill mine."

"I'm sad that I'm glad Edmund is merely an anxious alchemist."

"The other two resemble the scrolls I gave to the king. I'd never have found them without your help." He closed his eyes. "After all this time, I'm not sure I want to know what they contain. I'm not sure if I'm relieved or wish they'd never been found."

"I wish they hadn't been found here," Eleanor said. "Let's throw them in the fire and be done with this."

"After all this, we need to know what's inside. You take one, I'll take the other."

Reluctantly she accepted a scroll. They untied the red ribbons.

"At last," Richard said, his voice low and ragged. "Scroll Eighteen."

"This one is labeled 'Seventeen.'" The joy of discovery mingled with fear. She held Satan's work in her hands. But her husband didn't agree.

As Richard examined Scroll Eighteen, she couldn't help but admire the elaborate drawings and carefully laid out charts filled with unfamiliar symbols. Such skill and so many hours of work devoted to the cause. He opened the other scroll and scanned it.

Tension rolled off Richard like clouds in the sky before a storm. He stood and pounded his fist on the table. The glass vessels rattled.

"Nothing. There's nothing different from the other scrolls. Most are in code, so the casual reader wouldn't ascribe any meaning to the words. But I know the key. There's nothing of use. No formula I can ascertain. Unless after years of study, I still don't know enough about what works and what doesn't. No one does."

She wished she knew how to ease his disappointment. But she wouldn't hide her relief that they'd found nothing worth bringing to the king. Now they could destroy the scrolls, as she'd asked. And if she could convince him not to help the king's pursuit of the formula in other ways....

"Even so, maybe the king's alchemists could make some sense of these," he said. "Perhaps some of the charts or explanations will be useful when combined with their resources. I should turn them over to him."

She could see him struggling with the decision. Eleanor couldn't breathe. She didn't know if their love could surmount his interest in alchemy.

"I know how you'd feel if I did. And you'd wonder, would this be the end?"

Who would give?

"On the other hand," he continued. "We've seen the lengths people will go to get their hands on the secrets of alchemy. I don't know if I could give the formula to the king had I found it. How could I be sure the Philosopher's Stone would be used to benefit others, when I see how even the potential for wealth and power corrupts? My duty is to serve the king, not blindly, but for his good and the good of England. I no longer know if this would. Maybe you're right, and all of this effort could be put toward work that would yield results."

Her heart soared. "I'm so glad to hear that. Let's move on, and think happier thoughts." As she helped him roll up the scrolls, she added, "We've another wedding to arrange. Ours."

After carefully replacing the papers and stones and locking up the workshop, they strolled hand in hand toward Middleworth Castle.

"Richard, there's one thing more I need to know. If you planned for us to stay married, why did you fawn over the potential brides?" Eleanor asked. "You seemed like you were having a most wonderful time."

"I had to convince you to choose me, and hoped seeing me with other women would make you jealous," he answered. "Also, I admit, I wanted you to feel the pain I felt when I saw you mooning over Arthur. Of course I was mad at myself for being jealous, which didn't help matters any."

"Your plan worked," she said with a smile. "I was horrified when I thought you might actually care for Isabel. I feared I'd lost you. And the whole thing was my fault. My pride wouldn't let me tell you how I felt, for I wasn't sure you felt the same. I was finally going to confess before I left court, but then you told me how foolish you thought love was."

"Ah, Eleanor. Even if another woman might be a bit

wealthier, a finer musician or more docile, I could never find one with the wonderful combination of characteristics that make me as content as you do. For me, no woman could be a better bride." He snuggled her close and kissed her. "Because I already have the best bride. You."

EPILOGUE

The day of Eleanor and Richard's second wedding dawned clear and bright. Just like their future, Eleanor thought as she dressed in the room they'd share tonight. Excitement filled her veins.

'Twould be a small wedding, and so much more meaningful than the first. For this time she and Richard were in love. Her dreams of loving her husband, choosing him and being free of alchemy had come true.

"Eleanor."

Richard stood in the doorway, especially handsome in a deep red brocade tunic that matched her new gown. He took off his beaver hat and joined her by the window. She welcomed him with a kiss.

He pulled her close. "Ah, Eleanor. A most excellent way to begin the day." He kissed her again. "I came to give you this." He handed her his mother's cabochon ruby brooch. "Will you wear it?"

She smiled. "Of course. Always. I'm so glad to have it back. This time I have something for you, too. Here."

He took a small pouch from her and pulled out a brooch designed to match hers, but with a single cabochon.

"An ideal gift," he said with a smile as he pinned it to the brim of his hat.

Eleanor turned her brooch over to release the clasp. Sunlight set the gold aglow. "Richard, what's this?"

"What?"

She showed him the back. "This tiny crease. I don't know why I never noticed it before. Is there a secret compartment?"

"I never knew of one." He pressed the crease several times. "It doesn't open."

She stuck her fingernail in the crack. The back popped open, revealing a folded scrap of parchment.

"Look." Eleanor gasped. She plucked out the parchment and gave it to Richard. "I assumed the brooch was so thick to support the stones."

He held the parchment. "My father gave this brooch to my mother when I was born. She wore it almost every day until she died." He unfolded the small note. "'Tis my father's hand. It says, 'Eureka! But secrets cannot be written, 'tis clear. From learned master to apprentice hear.'"

They stood in silence, absorbing the message.

At length Richard said, "I can't help but wonder what he found. We'll probably never know. I was right about one thing. The scrolls don't contain his best ideas. They must've died with him. Perhaps, by leaving to become a knight, I denied him the chance to tell me of his discoveries. I don't think he hired another apprentice while I was away."

"Clearly my father never knew," Eleanor mused. "What if that was the source of their dispute? Could your father have made a discovery he refused to share, leaving mine to salvage what he could and start anew?"

"It's possible. Mayhap he sensed your father's lust for power."

"Perhaps your father's second partner, Sir Thomas, knew. Did he have an apprentice?"

"Not that I know of."

"Despite my aversion to alchemy, I feel sad for your father, to labor so long and hard without being able to share his successes," Eleanor said.

"His work meant more to him than anything, so I'm sure he found satisfaction in the doing of it."

Eleanor folded the parchment and put it back in the compartment before pinning the brooch to her gown. "All of your and Owen's searching, all of FitzWalter's and Blanche's machinations were for naught."

"Not quite," he said, enfolding her in his arms. "In a strange way, my father, Blanche and FitzWalter brought us together. If not for them, we might not have accepted how we feel about each other. I love you, Eleanor."

"And I you."

They sealed their vows with another kiss. Arm in arm, they descended the stairs to enjoy their wedding and life as man and wife.

AUTHOR'S NOTE

Dear Reader,

Thank you for reading *The Bride Tournament*, which I summarize as the *Gone with the Wind* love triangle meets *The Bachelor* in late medieval England. I hope you enjoyed reading Eleanor and Richard's story as much I as enjoyed writing it. I had so much fun researching the tournament that I gathered many more details than I could use. Perhaps I'll compile them into an article for my website in case anyone else is interested.

I'd appreciate feedback on what you liked and even what you didn't. You can contact me at RuthKaufmanBooks@yahoo.com and if you're interested, you can learn more about me and my writing at www.ruthkaufman.com. To be notified about future books and important news, please sign up for my newsletter on my home page at www.ruthkaufman.com. If you'd like to follow me, I'm on Facebook at Ruth Kaufman Author & Actress and Twitter: @RuthKaufman.

If you're so inclined, I'd really appreciate a review of *The Bride Tournament*. My Amazon author page is www.amazon.com/author/ruthkaufman, and my Goodreads page is www.goodreads.com/ruth_kaufman.

ABOUT THE AUTHOR

Ruth Kaufman is an Amazon bestselling author, on-camera and voiceover talent and freelance editor and speaker with a J.D. and a Master's in Radio/TV who loves living in Chicago, peanut butter and chocolate milkshakes and going to the theatre.

Writing accolades include Romance Writers of America® 2011 Golden Heart® winner and runner up in *RT Book Reviews'* national American Title II contest.

She's appeared in indie features, short films, web series and national and local TV commercials, and has voiced hundreds of explainer videos, e-learning courses, commercials and assorted characters.

Learn more about her at www.ruthkaufman.com and www.ruthtalks.com. Follow her on Twitter: @RuthKaufman or Facebook: Ruth Kaufman Author & Actress.

www.ingramcontent.com/pod-product-compliance
Lightning Source LLC
Chambersburg PA
CBHW021232130626
46554CB00004B/1448